MANIFEST

MANIFEST

Yuki Song

Knots Publishing

This is a work of fiction. Names, characters, places, and incidents either are the product of the author's imagination or are used fictitiously. Any resemblance to actual persons, living or dead, locales, businesses, companies, or events is entirely coincidental.

To my family – Papi, Gabe & Lizzy

You lift me up unconditionally

Loving you forever and always

TAKE A PICTURE, the note said.

I raised the Polaroid to my face and snapped a selfie. The camera vibrated, making a clicking sound. A picture appeared in black and white. The image set transfers light into shades of black ink.

She glared at me in disapproval, the young woman in the picture. Asian eyes with winged lashes, the nose of her European ancestry, and the lips of a fairy tale princess.

I looked at the mirror in front of me. A head of silver curls and wrinkled skin. Kindly eyes with hardened lips.

The woman in the mirror frowned. I stared at her, staring back. My head hung heavy on my shoulders.

That was not my face.

—||—

Alice

1

KANSAS
April 2008

No one saw me lying in the back seat of his red car. At six years old, it was easy to be snatched away from a playground surrounded by trees. I was playing with an older girl with gold-pleated hair. She saw him first — the man who took me while she ran the opposite way.

Each time our car passed another car, I tried to shout, choking on my gag. I tried to wave, but my arms were tied, and my little head could barely reach the window. Still, I pushed up, straining my breath, and then dropped. Again and again, I struggled as my childish brain fixated on getting out.

He laughed at my tantrums. The sounds of him were terrifying, like claws scratching over metal.

A switch flipped. My bravado was spent as fear clung to my skin. My arms and legs became anchors, and the further we traveled, my heart sank, drowning with the flame of hope that I would get out of this alive.

Storm clouds crowded the sky and chased our car. From a distance were streaks of stardust. It was a gazillion years before we finally stopped in front of a red barn.

"I'm taking it out." He pointed to the sock in my mouth. "Scream, and you die, China doll."

I nodded, tears welling up, and the man grinned with his eyes. He pushed me through the barn doors, and I fell, scraping my knees. He loomed above me, a large blot of darkness against the light.

I screamed.

I was startled by the engine's roar, and then he was gone. The storm rose with high winds and whistles in its place.

Rain pelted the metal roof like bullets, dripping down into inky puddles on the damp floor. The scent of stale hay, manure, and dirt clogged my nose. From a window above, lightning zapped across the darkening sky, mirroring the emotions in my small chest.

Each time it struck, thunder followed fast, shaking the earth. With every boom, I skittered and dove deeper into the hay — my tangled brown hair clinging to my neck as the nylon rope bit into my wrists like a plastic knife cutting through colored clay. The smell of my blood permeated my nostrils, adding to my pounding heart.

I wanted Daddy. I wanted to go home.

Suddenly, from the depths of the barn, a low, hollow moaning, followed by the sounds of chains, appeared. Ghosts, zombies, and every scary thing sneaked into my head. I screamed, clamoring to the barn doors — banging, shaking them with my scraped fingers, begging for help.

Lightning flashed, illuminating the floor. I turned slowly to the source of the sounds.

An older boy was lying spread out on a blanket across the room at the other end of the dirt barn. He was shirtless and in his underwear. Scrawny and white like a well-fed skeleton. Thick blonde hair matted with blood covered his face, and a silver collar strangled his neck. He raised his head up and then dropped it back down again, groaning. The chain attached to his collar slithered on the ground as he moved.

Relieved, I scampered over with my shoes, squishing muddy hay. The moment he saw me, his arm darted out and grabbed my leg.

"Who are you?" His voice was an angry whisper.

I shuddered but didn't pull away. Being here with him was better than being scared alone. His face and body were peppered with bruises.

"Alice," I tilted my head to the side. "What's your name?"

His anxious blue eyes pinned my teary brown gaze. "Peter."

"Is he coming back?" I squeaked when the thunder boomed.

The boy looked up as the lightning flashed again; like a lighthouse, it lit a circular wooden clock hanging on a stretch of timber.

"Not yet..." He grabbed my wrists and tried to untie the rope binds. His chewed-up fingernails buried in the flesh were bloody and raw.

It was useless. The rope was too tight to unravel.

He glanced at the clock again and dropped his hands from my binds. Scowling, he pushed himself up and grabbed my arm.

"Come!" He dragged me to the haystack.

His chain rattled, stretching across the barn till it couldn't go any further. The tiny lock on his collar swayed as he forced another step. He gripped his strained neck, coughing as he pointed to the bale of hay I was sitting on earlier.

"There's a hole behind that." His voice cracked. "G..get out...." His lungs were wrecked with more coughs. "Cut through the... cornfield." He paused. "Keep...going till you see the road!"

When I didn't answer, he opened his eyes. Angry daggers pierced through me. "Got it?"

I reached for his hand, and he backed away. "Got it?"

I nodded and cried.

"Call for help...." His voice trembled, and I nodded again. "You can, Alice."

There was a loud screech of tires. We turned to the barn doors, our hearts in our throats. "Go!" He pushed me forward.

I stumbled and mustered my strength to push the hay aside.

The barn doors flung open, and the man stood silhouetted against the storm. Behind him, lightning cracked the sky, angry that it had lost its prey. Rain and winds came hurling in. Against him, we were ants. His giant boots stomped in, and when he caught sight of us, he laughed.

I scurried back to the boy and hid behind him.

"Where do you think you're going?" His haunting voice was an echo of nightmares. His teeth were sharp, and his eyes, lit by his torchlight, were fire.

He pulled out a knife, and I screamed, an endless cry across time and space.

"What are you seeing?" a voice asked suddenly from somewhere above.

I looked up at the barn ceiling and then back at the frozen man and boy. The sounds of the storm died instantly.

"Who...who are you?" I spun around with my fists raised.

"It's me...Dr. Bailey," the voice said. "Alice, you're under hypnosis."

"Hypnosis...?" I repeated. My mind drew a blank. Slowly, reality sank in amidst my dream state, and memories flickered from the time before this.

I saw him. Dr. Bailey was sitting in the shadows with his legs crossed and a clipboard on his lap.

"What do you hear?" he asked.

"My heart —" I placed my hands over my chest. "Beating."

"Good. Now I want you to count to ten beats out loud. Then, I'm going to snap my fingers."

"...eight, nine, ten."

He snapped his fingers. "You are tied to a bungee cord. There is something at the bottom of a flowing river. Your rope is secure, and the equipment won't fail you. Rest assured, I'll keep you safe."

"Okay..."

"Good. Now jump!"

I imagined myself falling — the wind blowing at my face — the rush of adrenaline. Despite diving down, I was not afraid. I was promised. Whatever happened, I am going to make it back alive.

I plunged headfirst into the dark waters of the river. My subconscious was revealing the secrets it held like a vise. Then, my mind snapped, and I was brought back to the present while reliving my childhood past. It felt strange to be both awake and asleep — to be fifteen years old and also six — unsettling — trusting this doctor to keep me safe, both here and in my head.

"What do you see?" Dr. Bailey asked.

I chewed my dry lips. "Lightning, thunder, and red...everything is red. The barn, his hair, his shirt, the knife, and he is looking down at...."

Blood dripped from his knife, forming a congealed pool by his muddy black boots.

I swallowed hard. Tears were brimming under my closed eyes. "At what?"

"Peter!" I gasped when I saw the ghost-white body of the boy. Multiple grisly gashes sprinkled across the boy's skinny chest — blood gurgling from the poor boy's lips. "He's been stabbed!"

Anger surged through my body as a humming buzzed in my ear, and I raised my arm and struck hard. Inhuman screams pierced through my head. Lightning slammed onto the barn. Flames raced through the dry parts and abandoned trash, surrounding the boy, myself, and the man in an inferno. "Fire! The barn is on fire!" I grabbed the boy's shoulders.

He didn't resist.

"Wake up!" I shook him.

His yellow hair flopped back, and his eyes rolled. He struggled weakly against my grip. "Go!" He pushed my small hands off. "Run!"

"Is the boy dead?" Dr. Bailey asked.

I shook my head. The burning flames licked with hunger as I heaved, moving my hands to lift him, choking in the thick smoke.

"Where's the man?" Dr. Bailey asked.

Smoke ballooned in a cloud of grey. A gust of wind blew in from outside, clearing the smog. I spotted the man pinned with a rebar sticking through his pelvis, anchoring him to the ground. His once menacing eyes were vacant and lifeless.

"He is dead," I said, surprisingly calm. I peered at his corpse in my memory.

"How did he die?" Dr. Bailey asked.

Thunder boomed, shaking the barn. A pyre of flames rose to the ceiling. The beams swayed and groaned as debris fell in chunks of splintered wood and ash.

"He...help!" I choked. Imaginary soot scorched through my esophagus, rupturing my stomach with excruciating pain. "Help..." I raised my flailing arms.

Fingers snapped. The barn, the man, and the boy vanished. The bungee cord bounced, and I was lifted to safety.

It took seconds for my heart not to burst, and then, I squinted as my irises adjusted to the bright artificial light. Wisps of the smoky barn lingered in my thoughts. I was confused as to what I was seeing.

I uncovered my mouth and took in the fresh office air. The droning of the air-conditioner anchored my reality. Slowly, my brain receptors accepted the sight — a room with its earth-toned walls and white waistcoating, an oakwood table with a paper desk lantern, and where I sat was a medium grey plush couch.

I blinked.

Dr. Bailey, in his blue cashmere sweater, was waiting in his armchair. His leg remained crossed over the other as he wrote on the clipboard on his lap.

He looked up. There was a gentle manner about him. No mean eyes or cruel lips, unlike the red-haired abductor who appeared in my head. The instant I recalled his glassy eyes, my fear shot up. My lungs squeezed, and I slapped my ears as a high-pitched ringing bounced inside.

She was coming.

"I'm coming." She echoed. Her fingers wrapped around my mind, testing my boundaries as I heaved and sobbed.

Dr. Bailey dropped his clipboard and leaned forward.

"Blow into your hands. Like this —" He cupped his hands in front of his mouth.

I looked up.

"Slow and steady, and then do this." He squared his shoulders, rubbed his stomach, and repeated those actions.

I mimicked him, again and again.

My heartbeat lessened. The ringing stopped, and the dark fog vanished.

"How are you feeling?"

I stared at his face.

"Alice? How are you feeling?"

I looked at him and watched eagerness grow in his gaze.

"Is it you?" I heard his anticipation. "Or are you..."

I scowled. "It's me."

He remained bent for a few seconds and then leaned back into his chair.

I pressed my hand over my chest. "I'm better."

"Good. That's good." He smiled warmly, although I already saw his regret when I answered him earlier.

"Do you want to talk about what you saw at the end?"

"There were three of us— me, that man, and a boy."

He wrote on his notepad and then looked up. "The police said there was only one body — an adult male."

"No!" I slapped my thighs. "Peter was there! He helped me escape!" My shouting didn't rattle Dr. Bailey. Cool as ice, he waited for my temper to dissolve.

No one believed me.

The police found me lying by the road next to a cornfield that day. I didn't remember how I got there. For a week, the police combed the area and sent out flyers.

No one saw the boy called Peter. They ruled him out as a figment of my imagination.

The panic attacks came and went, rendering me breathless,

or worse, blacking out. Nothing stopped my attacks and my fear of the color red. Bouncing from therapist to therapist, Dr. Bailey, with his hypnotherapy, became my last hope.

"I believe you. I think Peter is real, too."

Hot tears drenched my cheeks.

He offered a bottle of water. I took a few sips and breathed out loud.

"Was she there too?" Dr. Bailey asked.

"Who?" I pretended, knowing what he wanted.

"Her. Isn't that when she first came to you?" he asked.

"Huh?" I replied.

He wrote something in his notepad. "How about next time? Can I talk to them?"

"Isn't this session about me?" I snapped.

He held his breath—silence stretch. The sound of white noise from his CD player in the room filled my ears.

I imagined rolling waves rushing onto a golden, sandy beach, taking a stroll into the sunset, hand in hand with the person I loved. And then, after a couple of waves crashing, I heard Dr. Bailey sigh.

"Yes," he replied.

I smiled into my bottle of water, scanned the books on his bookcase, and then at a small wooden clock on the shelf.

He closed his leather folder over his clipboard and dropped his pen on it.

I looked at him. "We have ten more minutes. What's next?"

Much as I didn't like his questioning, I didn't want to leave, knowing who was waiting outside.

"About what I said the other day..." his voice dropped.

I shot up in my seat. "Can we rewrite it?"

Bailey pushed up his glasses. "I can try."

"Do it. I want you to do it." My voice shook.

Their ghostly faces were pale and terrifying. My guilt. Their manifestations. Every single day. I braced myself for war, rewatching them die, snapping from an accidental brush of a person's touch, and panicking whenever I saw the color red.

Broken — that was what I was — shards of a cracked mirror with no face of my own — melded together by constant professional help, a never-ending patchwork of me.

I should remember that boy. His sacrifice.

I should not forget that day. I wanted to forget.

I should have died. I am glad I survived.

"First, take this." Dr. Bailey handed over a purple pill.

My hand shook as I rolled the pill in my hand. Then, I popped it in my mouth and gulped down some water.

He lifted his hand to my eyes. "On my count to three, I'm going to snap my fingers."

I took a deep breath.

"It wasn't you. He took her — the girl with gold pleated hair. The kidnapping wasn't your fault. You were a child, and he was too big to stop."

He paused and breathed in deeply. "What was lost is lost. It is time to move on. Let the guilt go, Alice. This is goodbye."

My heart beat fast. A feeling of unease grew.

I should say something. I should stop him. A surge of anger exploded from inside me, and she erupted, forcing my mouth open.

"One, two, three —" Dr. Bailey snapped his fingers.

And I forgot what I wanted to say.

2

The April drizzle didn't stop the moon from casting its ethereal glow. A halo surrounded the edges of its smooth, pale surface, etching out its sides in perfect clarity, making it pop like a sticker stuck on a blanket of dark blue sky.

I was never like that — the thing to behold. I wasn't meant to shine bright and bring joy to others. My existence was to drag people down into the pit — to highlight their worst sides and give them reasons to be cruel.

I smirked. Maybe I shouldn't admire the moon. It was a piece of rock with no power, unlike the sun, the real star with its heart of flames. For billions of years, a star burned till it finally exploded into a cloud of light. Yet in death, we still see it, brilliantly shining in our night sky when it was long gone.

Would that be me? I wished I were. Watching others basking in their happiness and success, I wanted to make my mark too. I deserved a chance. I deserved to be remembered. And, if I knew how much time I had left, I would know how much longer I had to bear.

With my eyes wide open, I let the rain sting my irises. My mother was late again. This time, she was a lot later than usual.

"You're still here?" I heard footsteps coming down the concrete stairs. I turned around to the three-story brick building behind me.

Dr. Bailey smiled, stepping forward with his umbrella to cover my wet head. Unlike me, his smile reached his eyes. There was warmth in them that I could trust. As a child psychiatrist, I guessed it was a prerequisite to have this skill. Empathy was crucial in his profession, and as a pioneer in hypnotherapy in Kansas City, it was essential that he made his patients feel at ease.

I sighed. "She was supposed to be here two hours ago."

Dr. Bailey pulled out his phone. "Did you call your father?"

"Don't!" I snatched his phone. "He's busy…" I tossed his phone back and stepped out, letting the rain wash away my anger.

Dr. Bailey's fingers twitched. I could tell he wanted to jot down my reaction. The therapists before him sensed my resentment against my parents. None dared confront my father, Dr. Harris, and my mother, whom my father protected with a cloak of steel. Instead, they blamed the situation — the trauma I suffered when I was six, which, after what Dr. Bailey did, I couldn't remember what it was. Only that I was glad, it was over and swept into the tiniest box and locked in the deepest crevice of my mind.

Dr. Bailey lucked out when he met me. I was an excellent case study to showcase his abilities. An experiment, a real Mary Shelley's baby Frankenstein, who could jump-start his career. That was why he offered twice the sessions for half the price. The condition was that he could tape my sessions and interview me.

My mother agreed to anything to save money and get me out of her face for a few more hours. She didn't tell my father about the filming because he wouldn't like it, and I didn't mind being in Kansas City more, so I kept it a secret.

"I need a ride home." I knew it would take an hour to drive

home from the city. Our house was in a small farming community chosen for my mother's research. She was an agronomist from Japan who specialized in super seeds.

Dr. Bailey crossed his arms, dangling his leather briefcase in his hand. I watched his bag sway, getting more nervous each second and trying not to show it.

"You can talk to me in the car," I suggested.

His brows perked up. "Can I ask about the others?"

I frowned. I hated talking about the others. I didn't talk about them to my parents, and so far, I had been putting my foot down, arguing that the sessions were for fixing my attacks and phobias.

I looked up at Dr. Bailey with his early silvered hair and a wrinkled face. He saw through my charade. In this negotiation, I had the weaker hand. It was frustrating to be powerless. Being dependent on the adults was annoying, and I couldn't wait to grow up.

I chewed on my lip and reached out my hand. The rain was getting heavier, and calling my father at work to pick me up was worse than talking about them.

"If you send me home after every session, you can ask about the others in the car."

I sensed his hesitation. This deal wasn't great, but it would save time from the long ride home with my mother.

"And...you can interview her —" I pointed my finger up. "Once".

A gleam burned in his gaze. He stretched his hand out, and I took it.

———

We arrived just in time before the questions became too difficult to answer. Partway through the journey home, I wondered if I had made the wrong choice. Talking about them and her increased my anxieties. I dreaded waking up after my blackouts, not knowing what troubles they caused, and having to lie and pretend to save myself. Worst of all, I hated how they, especially she, made me feel dirty, oily, and not myself.

It was pitch dark when Dr. Bailey's car pulled into our long driveway. The city's cloudy drizzle gave way to a stretch of cloudless sky with the sparkling constellation Orion overhead.

Our farmhouse had acres of land, both in front and flanking on both sides. Behind us was our neighbor, the Johnsons — an old couple with three grown-up sons. Their youngest was a senior in college, and their two older sons worked in Kansas City.

My mother was out front digging in a patch of dirt close to her precious seedlings. A small camping light on the ground lit her feet and the bottom half of her body in a circle of light.

"Okaasan, I'm back," I called out as Dr. Bailey and I walked to her. Her back was facing us.

"Okaasan?" I said in case she didn't hear me. "Okaasan... I'm home."

She continued digging. Her elbow moved in a robotic motion, not once pausing.

I clenched my hands. "You forgot to pick me up."

She reached down with her gloved hand to pick up an object and dropped it into the hole.

"Mom!" I raised my voice, and Dr. Bailey placed his hand on my shoulder and held me firmly.

"It's okay, Alice." He patted my shoulder. "I'll talk to her."

He pushed me back and stepped forward. With a smile

plastered on his face, he said, "Good evening, Mrs. Harris. Sorry to intrude."

My mother, Junko Harris, looked up. Her gaze fixed on his face. "Dr. Bailey. What brings you here?"

"We had a session today. I brought your daughter home."

"Oh really?" She stood up, pulled off her gloves, and patted the dirt from her pants.

I slid over to his side. "Okaasan, I'm hungry. What's for supper?"

She pinned Dr. Bailey with her empty eyes. The silence stretched as we stood frozen in time.

Dr. Bailey cleared his throat. "Mrs. Harris, do you have a few minutes to chat?"

A grim line stretched across her lips. "Please leave. I'm alone, and my husband won't be home till later. Next time, you should call first before coming down."

She picked up her spade and strode to the house, not looking back.

Dr. Bailey and I exchanged looks. "I told you. It's getting worse," I said.

He nodded. "I'll call your father. Let me suggest a few sessions with her."

I sighed and turned to pick up the camping light by the hole and gasped.

"Teacup..." Ice washed through my veins. My hands trembled, and tears welled in my eyes.

Dr. Bailey followed my gaze and stiffened.

A surge of panic came rushing up. In desperation, I held my breath. My gaze glued onto the wet, broken body of my little white and blue lovebird pet. His orange beak and chest stained with blood, and his neck bent at an awkward angle. I imagined his terror in the hands of my mother and his misplaced trust in us, his family.

"I shouldn't have brought him home." I stepped back.

«Alice…" Dr. Bailey placed his arm over my shoulder.

I bit my lip hard until I felt the imprint of my teeth and the iron taste of blood.

"I'm sorry," he said. "If you want to let it out, I'm here."

I turned around. This was her revenge. She wanted to break me like she was hurt. I had to hold it in. I had to believe I was strong enough.

I strode to my house, up the stairs, and straight for my bedroom. I didn't care if Dr. Bailey followed. Holding onto the memory of Teacup chirping happily in my head as I violently pushed aside any thoughts of his mangled corpse. Back in my room, I methodically locked the three locks on my door, one of which held a key from my secret hiding spot, and then I pushed my dresser under the knob quickly.

The piercing shrill attacked my ears, and then the floodgates opened. I dropped to my knees, fighting to breathe, drowning as they surged, crowding my mind, clamoring to get in first. Darkness came, and in a snap, I was lost.

Merle

3

Merle got up from the hardwood floor and scowled into the mirror hanging on the wall. Her waist-length inky hair was a mess, and its beautiful shine was dull. There were shadows under her coffee-colored, almond-shaped eyes, and her nose was pink and sore from crying. She cursed under her breath when she spotted her cheeks. The grooves between the uneven flooring left two long marks across her right cheek, which would be hard to hide even with makeup. Her clothes were dusty, and muddy footprints were visible in the room. It wasn't like her twin to be this dirty. Something bad must have happened to Alice before she woke up.

Her phone said it was Friday, eight p.m. Jamie was probably hanging out with his pals.

She grinned. There was enough time to get drunk and make out with Jamie before heading back by midnight. Peeling off her dirty sweater, jeans, underwear, and shoes, she hopped into a hot shower and cleaned herself thoroughly. Instead of tossing those clothes in the laundry basket, she threw them in the trash. Alice needed a wardrobe makeover. It was high time Alice took care of her blooming body. She pulled out a new set of bra and panties from the bag of clothes after a shopping spree with Daddy's credit card. Alice would thank her for this later, after they switched.

She checked her phone. Maybe another hour more was fine. Mom wouldn't notice her coming home late. Daddy might be home earlier since it was the weekend.

Whatever. In her favorite silver sequin tank top and low-cut jeans, she was ready to have a blast. After turning fifteen last Summer, she plumped up in all the right places and caught the high school boys' hungry attention. If it weren't for Daddy keeping her a year behind starting Kindergarten, she would be in high school now. Alice dreaded graduating and going to high school. She, on the other hand, couldn't wait. New friends, new hot boys, new mayhem. Fun, fun, fun. What's not to love?

She giggled and pushed the dresser aside, picked up Alice's key from under the mattress and another key from the underside of the drawer with their underwear, and unlocked the latched door.

The hallway was dark, with soft white light at the end of the tunnel. The sounds of a TV turned on made her stop to listen. Who was it? The aroma of freshly ground coffee whetted her mouth when a man walked out of the kitchen with a mug.

"Daddy!" She hugged him tightly from behind. "It's you!"

Dr. Michael Harris's icy gaze rested on her hair and then softened as he smiled. "You're awake."

"Yes!" she chirped. "Did you miss me?"

He stroked her head. "Of course, my Sweetie."

Her stomach growled, and she led him to the breakfast table.

"I'm starving!" She rummaged through the pantry. Alice could whip up a meal with the produce in the fridge; she, on the other hand, was a terrible cook. She grabbed two cups of spicy instant noodles.

"How about ramen?" She shook the cups and glanced at her father, who was watching her like a hawk.

"I already ate. Sweetie, those are bad for you." He pointed to the cups of dried noodles and stood up. "I'll cook some ham and eggs."

She waved at him. "Nah, this is fine. I love MSG!" She poured the hot water from the kettle her father used and peered at the doorway. "By the way, where's Mom?"

He gulped his coffee. "Okaasan left with Dr. Bailey."

"What happened?"

He put the mug down and sighed. "Teacup is dead."

"Teacup?" Merle stirred the soaked noodles with her chopsticks. Bits of noodles clung to the thin wooden sticks like a lifeline. "She loved that bird." She dropped her shoulders. Frankly, she couldn't care less about the bird dying. It just pissed her off that Mom made Alice cry again. Only she was allowed to do that. After chewing and swallowing her meal, she picked up her empty ramen cups and tossed them in the bin. "Let's buy her another one. Alice won't know the difference."

Daddy looked up from checking his phone. "Your sister is weak."

"Yeah, for sure." She scrunched her face and then rummaged the pantry again, pulling out a tray of chocolate chip cookies. "Want some?" She offered him.

Daddy shook his head. "No." He took another swig of coffee. Knowing him, it probably wasn't only coffee in that mug.

After more chewing and eating half the tray, she looked up. "How long is Mom going to stay in the city?"

"We'll be back this weekend. I'll be going up in a few hours."

"So what happened? Why did she relapse?" she asked while trying to keep a straight face.

"She ran out of her pills and forgot to tell us. I should have paid more attention," replied her father.

"Oh…" She dropped the almost empty tray of cookies back in the pantry and hid her smile.

A few months ago, she switched Mom's pills for vitamins, which looked the same. Dr. Bailey's hypnotism worked too well on Alice. His efforts made it hard for her to appear, but she knew she could count on Mom to break Alice down. Without Alice's blackouts, she could never come out.

"Maybe we should leave the farm. Seeing us makes Mom worse. How about we move to the city and stay with you?" She let her words sink in.

Daddy waved his hand. "No, we can't leave your mother here by herself."

"Can't you hire a nurse? Or ask Mrs. Johnson to check on her. She likes that old couple. They listen to her well." She dug her heels. "We'll stay with you during the week and go to high school in the city, and we'll come home together during the weekends."

"Okaasan can't be alone here." He frowned.

"No one's going to dare touch Dr. Harris's wife." Merle pouted.

He patted her head. "I know."

"Mom never talks to me…she probably doesn't think I'm real." She scrunched her nose.

"Sweetie… that's not true." He held her hand.

"Who do you love the most?"

"You. You're my princess."

"Liar!"

"I love you both." He leaned back in his chair.

She pouted. Daddy's obsession with Mom was too much. She

was younger and prettier than her. Mom grew old fast and was no longer that mysterious Asian beauty Daddy stole from Japan.

He squeezed her hand. "Sweetie, of course, you're my blood."

Her heart swelled. No matter what Alice believed, Daddy was the best. Dr. Michael Harris was renowned, highly respected, and handsome. Everyone admired him, and most of all, he was her god.

"Come on." He stood up. "How about a movie? When was the last time we saw one together?"

She let her frustrations go and looked up. "What do you want to watch?"

"Anything you like." He smiled.

She could see him glazed over. Not sure if it was the drink or Mom.

"Do you want the Exorcist or the Wizard of Oz?" He flipped through their DVD collection.

Dorothy? Dorothy was dumb, just like Alice.

"Exorcist!" She smiled.

"Okay," he replied.

She beamed happily. "I'll pop the popcorn, and you set up."

The movie was about to start. She sat beside her Daddy with a massive bowl of buttered popcorn and two cans of Coke, ready for a great time.

Alice

4

The mascara she wore left streaks of black stains on my newly washed comforter. Her sequin mini dress and hi-top red boots from last night were scattered over my floor, and my dresser was a mess with her makeup. I wiped the gunk off my face, picked up my phone, and switched the phone covers from hers, a diamond rose gold, to mine, a simple pale green. After a good shower and scrub, I put on my forest-green plain T and jeans and surveyed the path of her destruction to the open door. She was smarter than the others. Despite my attempts to hide the keys well, she knew just where to find them.

I made a mental note to buy a pin-code lock. Dad never questioned when I decided to install a latch on my bedroom door a few years ago. He didn't ask why when I requested to change the handle and lock on my door three times. Between us, if we spoke more than twenty words in one weekend, it was a feat.

I avoided the empty white birdcage hanging by the window as I tiptoed down the stairs.

The wood floors creaked. The thudding of my heart was in sync with my ragged breath. Sweat trickled down my temples and under my armpits. Being alone in a dark space always terrified me. Even living with my mother was better than having no one around.

In my hand was a wooden sword. The bokken weighing down on my wrist belonged to my father, and when I was alone, I practiced with his heavy blade in the sanctuary of my backyard with its willows, maples, and Japanese fir trees and shrubs artfully placed behind an enormous pit of sand and boulders. Beside the desert, Dad had his Koi pond, and surrounding the water was a secluded arbor under which were Wisteria flowers and my mother's hideout.

Bubble glass bells hung on beams, singing light musical notes when a flirty breeze danced. My place was under the eaves by the rain chimes. There were a few good days when the three of us would sit in quiet solitude, each in our nook as we got lost in our thoughts.

From the deck, I heard a stranger's voice. I jumped with my sword raised.

A man stepped from behind a pillar and blocked my blow. Our eyes met, and I dropped my sword. "You're home."

He eyed his sword in my hand. Instead of his usual temper, his lips lifted into a soft smile. "Good stance," he whispered and then lifted his phone to his lips.

"Ravi —" The man who was talking on the speaker stopped. "We'll talk more when I'm back," Dad said and pressed the phone off.

I picked up a cushion, dropped it to the edge of the raised deck, and sat down, swinging my legs against the side of the deck, letting the wind evaporate the sweat from my body.

He sat down shortly after, without bothering to use a cushion.

Dead air hung over us as we stared at the ocean of sand. The circles my mother carved using her rake were equal and proportional in distance from each other. The further the ripples, the greater the inches, like gravity pulling an object in constant motion, forever apart.

"Why aren't you at work?"

"I came to let you know…" he said to the rocks.

"Why? You could just call."

"Okaasan will be staying with me. We won't be coming back till this weekend."

"Is she okay?"

He nodded slowly. "I thought about what you asked."

"About what?" My mind was blank.

"You can go to high school in the city —" He turned to me. "I won't be home much. You'll have to fend for yourself."

I held my breath. I was planning to bring this up next month after getting my results. I had the benefits listed in my head on how the city schooling would advance and challenge my mental growth, meeting new people, going to therapy on my own, etc.

"Do you want to?" he asked.

«Sure…I mean, yes!" Happiness bloomed in my heart for in that moment, I felt recognized. Then, a gnawing sensation crippled my breath. He wouldn't have done it for me.

„Dad…"

His clear-sky blue eyes caught my gaze. This must have been one of the reasons why my mother fell in love with him.

I searched his face. All my life, my mother came first, then her, and then the others. I was so far down the totem pole that I wondered if I was his family. I was long past understanding.

"What, Alice?"

"It wasn't me. She was the one who told you she wanted to move to the city, didn't she?"

He let my question hang till the breaths between us ran out.

"What does it matter?" He met my gaze hotly.

"If I had asked first, would you have said, 'no'?"

He turned to the sand. "I'll submit the paperwork today. Pearson has an excellent program in the bio-science field. You'll still have to test in."

"And what about Okaasan?"

"She'll stay here, and we'll see her during the weekends."

"You sure she'll agree?" I frowned. It's funny how I was happy to be leaving seconds ago, and now, because it wasn't my idea, I wanted to stay.

"I'll get your mother a helper." His voice was resolute.

"I'm not leaving till I graduate," I said, ready to fight back.

"Okay, finish Norton Middle and then leave," he surprisingly complied.

Our eyes met — his crystal blues and mine, the color of dirt with a sprinkling of leaves. Did I see them soften? I held my breath.

He stood up and dusted his pants. "I'll pick you up next Friday after Dr. Bailey's. You'll use the guest room. Paint it, buy some furniture, change the locks, whatever you want."

"Okay," I said, feeling the wind leaving my sails. On reflex, I almost thanked him. But he was my father. This was his job. I was his family, too. He should have done this earlier, separating my mother from me.

I didn't need to thank him.

—||—

5

"Did you bring your journal?" Dr. Bailey asked, peering from his glasses after reading the notes on his clipboard.

I dropped my journal on the table, settled on his grey couch, and placed my feet on the armrest, my hands on my stomach.

"I was the bubble, and the bubble was me," I muttered.

When I moved from the farm to live with my father in the city, Bailey stopped giving me lifts home. Somehow, he finagled an agreement to teach me his hypnotism techniques if I shared more.

I watched him from the corner of my eye as he flipped through my journal. The pages were neatly scripted with my notes of what I could remember, or clues my personalities left behind, or did after my blackout.

"You switched once this week. You're making progress."

He stopped, studying my Polaroid for this week. The photographs were usually taken in the same way. Faced front, my eyes unblinking with either my bed in the background or my bathroom with the shower to the back. In the Polaroid, my face was the same — a sixteen-year-old mixed Asian girl with long brown hair and eyes. However, in the mirror that reflected me, I was seeing someone else. This week, it was a teenage boy with spiky blonde hair and piercing blue eyes — Peter.

My D.I.D. was different from anyone with this disorder. Bailey did not know this. To him, I looked the same when I switched, except for my personality. He didn't know of the crimes they committed, and the secrets we kept. Therapy was a facade to keep the adults happy.

"What about Merle?" he asked.

"What about her?" I chewed on my lip. She was the worst — the hardest to control. Merle loved watching me suffer. She tested my boundaries and did everything she could to spoil my good image. The kids at school think I'm crazy. I waffled between being the best student and the one most sent to the principal's office.

"You like sneaking into the ER," he said.

Bailey, in his thirties, had his hair receding and crow's feet at the corners of his eyes. He cured me of my phobias of the color red, and my nightmares and hallucinations were less frequent.

I wanted to trust him, but Merle hated him the most.

"What happens at the ER?" he asked.

I peeled my chipped nail and sought out another. A cold shawl wrapped over my shoulder because Peter was grumbling about needing heat. It was hard pretending I didn't hear my two major personalities.

"It gives me peace." I finally spoke.

"Peace? In the emergency room?" Bailey raised a brow. "Kansas City Hospital is one of the busiest."

"The more they rush, the calmer I get."

"And you like that feeling?"

"I like watching them." My lips lifted despite myself.

"The doctors and nurses? Is that why you want to go into medicine? Or was it your father…"

"No." I cut him off and picked up my mug for another drink. "Watching the patients dying."

"Dying?" Bailey straightened his back and pinned his owl eyes onto me.

A smile stretched across my face. The mask I was wearing was cracking. I covered it with my hand and closed my eyes to hide my excitement.

Death was thrilling. Death came at their last breath. Peter and Merle think it is hilarious that I pretend to be the angel. To me, this was what made me different from them.

"Who is talking?" He asked.

Seconds passed, and then I breathed.

"Nobody wants to die," I said.

Bailey wrote something on his pad.

"They deserved a second chance," I said, and he looked up.

"Really?" Bailey bent forward eagerly.

I was his lab rat. I knew that, and so did my mother. We went into this with open eyes, without my father knowing.

Although I hated being filmed, knowing my father would hate it more made me do it. I was Michael Harris's only heir. God made him infertile after me as a sick joke.

"If I can become them for a day and help them with their last wish. Maybe I'd get more merits?" I grinned.

"Merits?" Bailey frowned. "Does that make you less guilty?"

"Sure," I said.

"Sure, what? A penance for her?"

"Who?" I pretended. Bailey was now so close that I could feel his breath on my arm. I smelled his excitement. This was the reason why we met a second time on Fridays.

"What's Merle been up to?"

I scooted away and threw my journal at him. "Check it yourself."

Bailey sat back and flipped through my book, stopping at the torn-up pages and a large cartoon drawing of Bailey crucified with a spear through his body and flames all around. "Who did this?" He asked.

I breathed out heavily. "Who else?"

The clock in his room beeped. He glanced at it and then sighed. "What about Peter?" Bailey ran his fingers over the charcoal art of us kissing. "What's this?"

"That's never going to happen," I said.

"His obsession with you is an obsession with yourself." Bailey let the other words linger in the air. "How did Peter look this time? Has he grown?" Bailey asked.

"About the same."

"When can I meet him?" He asked.

I kept quiet. It was goddamn annoying. Bailey was persistent, but he was the only doctor willing to play.

Peter

6

Seven years ago

Peter sat on the edge of the dock, skimming his feet over the water in the lake. The sun's autumn rays cut through the forest of fall leaves, dappling the wooden deck and setting the tips of his pale blonde hair on fire with hues of red and gold.

He hummed softly, one hand absently patting the head of Alice's dog, Pitty, and in the other, his fingers rolled a burnt-out sparkler. Beside him, there were five empty boxes, and in the water, hundreds of used sticks floated like broken shafts of a boat.

Luck was on his side earlier when he found a bag of these little fireworks in a cabinet under the sink. A tremor caused his fingers to tap the wood. He itched to light another one and felt the heat of its flame on his skin.

He scratched the dog harder, and Pitty groaned with delight. The air was quiet, except for the occasional sounds of a contented dog and the gentle chirping of birds high in the trees.

No one lived in these woods. The cabin was the only one for miles around.

Alice's mother was taking a nap, and her father left in the car. It was a good thing seven-year-old Alice was exhausted. Her blackout timed perfectly with this trip, and it was a treat to be outside roaming free.

Little Alice's nanny was shocked when he first appeared months ago. Peter was quick to pretend that he was a neighbor and got away. He hid in their farm's barn on the days he appeared, preferring to sleep in the bales of hay and absorbing the heat of the Summer's day.

After stuffing himself with leftovers in the kitchen and a box of animal cookies in the pantry, he explored the woods and was content to spend the rest of the afternoon lazing here.

"This is private property."

The boy heard the sound of heavy footsteps approaching him across the deck. Stuck between the lake and the man, he had no choice but to turn around. Both boy and dog looked up guiltily at Alice's father.

"Who are you?" Alice's father took a long, good look at him, taking in the boy's crumpled grey T-shirt and jeans. His fourteen-year-old body was five feet four inches long and bone-thin compared to Alice's stout, small-kid size.

Peter chewed his lip.

"So, boy?" Her father stepped closer. "How did you get here?" Her father scanned the lake and forest. "The closest cabin is a good thirty miles away."

Should he say he was camping with his family and lost his way, or maybe he's a wild child living in the woods?

This wasn't the first time Alice's father caught him. Months ago, he found the boy locked in Alice's closet, forgotten by her mother for days. His nails chipped, his fists were bloody from banging, and his stomach was eating itself. Her father didn't say a word after Peter fell out of the closet. Instead, the man went to get the first aid box. After he returned, Alice switched back.

"Peter?" the man tried his name. Bailey must have told the doctor about him. Her father took a step forward, and Pitty growled at the man.

Peter held on to the dog's collar.

"Peter, right?" The man asked.

The boy kicked the water and watched it ripple.

"Where's Alice?"

Peter tapped his heart. "She's sleeping."

Her father sat down on the deck beside him and stared at the blue waters with him.

The sun bathed their heads, and the water lapped on them, running in between their toes and sandals with its cool touch. Eons passed before the man spoke again. "Since Alice is my daughter..." He paused for a breath. "Can I call you son? If you like, you can call me Dad."

He gawked at her father. Peter never had parents. He couldn't remember anything about his past except for the burning barn.

Peter tried on a smile, and the man smiled back. His heart warmed with rays stretching across the horizon. He couldn't stop grinning, "Yes, Dad."

"Are you hungry?" Dad asked.

Peter nodded. "I'm always hungry."

He patted Peter's head. "Good. You're a growing boy. How about I whip you some bacon and eggs?"

Peter made a sound and licked his lips.

Dad laughed and got up. He put out his hand to Peter. "Come, let's go, son."

For ten seconds, Peter's eyes riveted on his new father's large hand. Then, he took it and stood up. The smile on the boy's face could light the world.

Behind them, wet shoe prints of the adult male and a little girl's size eight marked their path, evaporating fast in the hot summer air.

———————

KANSAS
July 2008, Present

The fire exploded in reds and oranges against the chilly spring night. Sizzling as it snaked across the dusty soil towards the brightly polished blue pick-up truck six feet away. The sky was jet-black, except for the twinkling of stars, with the Big Dipper leaning downward, pouring its inky darkness into the blooming flames.

Peter clamped his mouth to stop laughing. He watched his newest creation with glee as it sped in circles, minutes from lighting up the canned propellants surrounding Jamie and the stupid fifty-thousand-dollar truck that his father gave him for his birthday.

Groaning and lying on the wheel was Jamie, with his head bleeding from the stone Peter threw. This time, Peter could watch that asshole go down. There was no one to stop Peter here.

In the past, all Peter could do was watch, crouching on rooftops or in shadows. It became his mission to stalk Merle's boyfriends and stop them before they went too far. He didn't care about Merle. Peter and Merle were acidic and alkaline, and Peter wished he could kill Merle for hurting Alice. But Merle wore Alice's body, as did Peter, making it an impossible dilemma. Everything was fucking unfair, especially seeing Alice grow while he stayed the same.

Peter loved Alice. He would do anything to keep her safe. His only wish was to hold her in his arms, but he couldn't. This was their ill fate.

Jamie Langston — the rich, popular high schooler who was once a contestant on America's Voice- was Merle's new fling. He was a narcissist who basked in crushes of stupid girls because he could sing a little. If Peter could put on more weight and build his muscles, he definitely would catch eyes too. Lucky for Jamie, Alice despised him as much as Peter did. Perhaps it was because Merle and Alice alternated between hot and cold, which kept this idol brat coming back for more. Whatever it was, tonight Jamie lost his chance. Peter caught that traitor hooking up with some cheerleader in the boys' shower room and heard her calling his Alice half-breed fugu. Jamie and that bitch laughed. Their racist jokes were enough to warrant them to burn in hell.

When Jamie sauntered off, Peter dropped a rock from the roof. But killing a person was harder than Peter thought. Jamie didn't die, so Peter had to pull the five-foot-ten jerk across the school's parking lot into his truck and take him away.

The scent of smoke and Peter's concoction of flammable chemicals was perfume in his nostrils. Jamie was waking up and slamming his body against the window, trying to get out. Their eyes met, and Peter's mouth stretched wide. His teeth glinted white in the rearview mirror as smoke engulfed the truck and firecracker cans lit the ground with blues, greens, and purples.

Just as Peter was about to dance, he heard the buzzing of bees. "No! Alice!" Peter clenched his fists. "That bastard fucked up! He screwed you and made you cry!" He felt her smooth hands wrapping around his mind, and in a snap, he was gone.

Alice

7

The fire lapped its dirty tongue. Heat was his rage as he rose taller like a genie watching an ant fight back. The ground littered with rocky teeth. My shoes crunched as I tore off Peter's undershirt, wrapped it around my neck, and covered my nose and mouth. Picking up the sharpest rock, I sprinted for the burning truck, kicked the spray cans aside, and threw sand on the fire.

At another time, I'd be terrified, drowned by the past. But the call to action blinded the voices. My heart numbed, and instinct raw. A life was at stake, and I lunged forward.

The fire hissed, throwing smoke and blurring my eyes with my tears. The back of Jamie's pick-up was burning with newspaper and trash. With that rock, I smashed the window on the passenger side, again and again, till the glass gave way with a shattering whiz. I didn't feel my bleeding hands. My eyes were on him, struggling in his binds. Tears and sweat ran down his once-perfect face. For once, he was happy to see me, Alice, not Merle.

He coughed.

"Don't move!" I shouted amidst the popping cans.

I slashed the rope tied on Jamie's wrist to the wheel, and together, we clambered out of the truck, stumbling as far from it as we could.

The explosion threw us forward with Jamie cradling me in his arms. The shards hit his back, and I cried for him.

The voices were wrong about him. They were wrong about people. No one was black and white. The world was filled with grey.

Everyone deserved a second chance, and it wasn't up to Peter or Merle to decide who should die.

8

SEOUL

June 2010, Two years later

The summer sun shone warmly on my back. The sky filled with clouds, and the scent of being somewhere new was thrilling. The last four days in Seoul alone were a dream. Ancient palaces, temples, the sights, sounds, and smells told me I wasn't in Kansas anymore. Lost in a sea of black-haired people with faces similar to my own. No one to judge or know who I was. Everyone was busy and had places to go.

Living with Dad was like a never-ending winter. Our conversations were brief, and our meals were quiet and somber. Dad had new patients to meet in Seoul, and my mother made plans to visit her family in Kyushu. A year ago, I wouldn't have imagined this possible. It took months of practice with Dr. Bailey and the voices protesting. After Dr. Bailey's persuasion, my parents relented.

Gwangjang Market was flanked by tall buildings and alleys stacked with hundreds of little shops selling mountains of noodles, dumplings, metal bowls of vegetables, and *tteokbokki*, sweet and spicy rice cakes. Steaming waves of delicious smells melded with colorful flags of every country overhead, dipping to everyone's heads as we passed.

I eyed the garlic-soy-glazed grilled meat on sticks and the crispy honey pancakes filled with peanuts and cinnamon brown sugar. My hands were full with a deep-fried mochi hotdog, and I had shopping to do, so those would have to wait.

Pop-up stores, phone accessories, and souvenirs. Billboards of neon colors in Korean lettering, banners, and more restaurant menus standing like sails on a pirate ship. The grey streets were sweltering outside, bathed in the heat of the summer sun, and I soaked in the vibe of the crowds of tourists laughing and taking pictures. By one p.m., the food alleys were packed with people. Having tasted freedom, I didn't want to go back.

"Eolmana manh-i?" I asked in my limited Korean and lifted a pretty crystal-crusted blue hair clip to the shop owner.

The middle-aged woman said something back in Korean, and I waved my hand. "Sorry, I don't understand."

She shook her head and wrote five thousand won, gestured with three fingers, and then pointed to my hair clip with one finger and wrote three thousand won.

I chose two more clips and reached for my wallet in my bag.

"Where is it?" I muttered to myself as my heart raced, the deeper I dug into my tote bag. My passport, two shirts, makeup, lotions, *gimbap,* and my phone. Only the wallet was gone.

Then it dawned. Five hundred US dollars in Korean won, all my event tickets, and the K-pop concert tonight were in that wallet.

The shopkeeper frowned.

The sounds hit fast. My mind spun as I looked around. Anyone passing by was a suspect. I studied each face, hoping to remember if any of them looked familiar. But I didn't know when I lost it or who had taken it.

"I...I...erm... I'm sorry." I handed the shopkeeper the hair clips and waved my hand, "No..." Tears welled in my eyes, and I brushed them quickly. "My wallet is taken." My voice was whiny and young. I stuffed my things into my bag. The weight of my embarrassment and her angry words hung on my back as I turned.

My lungs constricted. My world was collapsing. Winds grew in g-force as I was pushed forward and bounced around in an ocean of locals and tourists, struggling like a small fish swimming against the tide.

Then, the ringing came, softly at first and then crescendoing. I gasped for breath as I fought them. For so long, I kept them away. I was proud of my achievements. I believed I was stronger and could live a normal life. Now, because of my carelessness, they were coming back — locusts swarming and swallowing up the sun.

"No!" I shouted inwardly. They were rejoicing after being locked away for so long. Merle crept up from deep within, determined and furious. Her nails clawed at the sides of my consciousness as she pushed herself forward into my reality. "No! Stay back!" I cried out, crashing into a group of people.

Strong hands caught me as I fell. People gasped, sounding worried as they spoke in their alien languages all at once. The words meant nothing. They were all background noise to the shrills in my head. He, who held me up, slowly led me to a bench to sit.

"It's okay," he said in English when I didn't respond earlier to Korean.

My vision cleared.

They peered at me, including my savior. Three guys and a

girl. Looking slightly older than I, with their backpacks and street clothes. Carrying the air with confidence, college students have their future filled with hope.

The girl offered me her handkerchief, saying something in Korean.

I shook my head.

"Are you okay?" The guy holding me up asked.

"Yes," I replied, breathing in deeply.

"Do you need a doctor?" he asked.

I waved my hand lightly. "No, I'm fine."

Our gaze locked, and I caught his concern in his deep brown eyes, and then turned to his hand on my shoulder, where my scar buzzed happily like a bee.

He dropped his hand quickly, a blush forming as his friends laughed and teased.

"Where are you from?" One of the other male friends with glasses asked in thick English.

"USA," I said, suddenly curious. In my small town, I was the only one there. Part-Asian, a minority among three hundred other than my mother. Coming to Seoul was initially a culture shock. I was no longer alone, yet I still was a stranger because I didn't understand their language.

"Where in the US?" the girl asked.

"Kansas," I said.

"Kansas?" Smiled the one with glasses.

"Oh! Dorothy!" The shortest guy in the group grinned.

"No, no…" I waved. "I'm Alice," I blushed.

"You don't look like Alice." The guy with glasses peered down at me. Laughing, he turned and spoke rapidly to his other friends in Korean. The girl in his group giggled.

My shoulders caved in. It was like those days in middle school all over again.

The young man who saved me gestured to his friends and spoke harshly in Korean. His friends backed off, sulking, and then walked away.

He turned to me. "Are you lost?"

"Someone took my wallet...I had it an hour ago..." I opened my bag and pointed at the empty spot.

He frowned. "This doesn't usually happen in Korea. I'm sorry. Come," He said, standing up and grabbing my arm.

"Where are we going?" I asked.

"To the police."

"The police...?" My words trailed as I let him pull me with him.

He was a head and a half taller, about six feet. Dark brown hair and bright eyes. Pale skin and strong with broad shoulders compared to his friends, and as handsome as one of those K-pop idols. From my experience with Merle's boys, the hot ones were the worst. She loved them all, and they flocked to us like bees.

I dug my feet and pulled back. "No. Let's not. I don't want to go there."

He turned around. "How much did you have in your wallet?"

"Five hundred and forty thousand Korean won and some concert tickets."

He whistled, and he took my hand and dragged me on. "You must tell the police. We have CCTVs."

I saw a flash of Dad's face. His brow twitched when he was mad. "No. I won't go." I clenched his fingers hard.

He flinched.

"I'm sorry...I don't want the police involved." I could see

him trying to process my words. Maybe he was thinking I was a runaway.

I pulled his hand off mine. "I'll go to my hotel and tell them what happened. My father is busy. He doesn't have time for this."

He pinned me with his gaze. Heat crept up my cheeks and burned my eyes. "I'm okay…Really. I'm good," I muttered and turned.

"Wait…" He caught my arm. "Is your hotel close?"

"Yes, I can walk or take a cab."

He pulled out his wallet. "Here." He placed fifty thousand won, which was about fifty dollars, into my hand.

"That's too much," I said.

"No, no." He held my hands from giving back. "It's okay. Make sure you tell the hotel to find your wallet."

"I will." I smiled.

"You sure don't want to go to the police?" He bent till his face was inches close. His hand was a warm blanket. His touch sent strange feelings racing through my body. We both stared at our hands together, and he dropped his first.

"Yes…" I swallowed. "Do you have a phone number? I will return the money later."

His cheeks were blushing now. "No. Don't worry about it." He waved off. "You keep it." His friends were calling him from an ice cream stand.

I grabbed his sleeve. "Wait. What's your name?"

«*Park Ji Woon*." He smiled like a thousand suns.

«*Ji Woon*…," I said to myself, and he rubbed his head in embarrassment. I smiled. "Thanks, *Ji Woon*."

His eyes pinned mine for the last time. The world seemed still for a moment as our hearts beat loudly. "Ermm…well…okay…well, take care, Alice. Goodbye." He said and ran off to join his friends.

I watched his friends pat his shoulders and tease him, turning their heads to me.

I watched as his back grew fainter and fainter as they left, jealous of the smiles they shared. I wished I had a friend like that. Maybe, if I did, I wouldn't be so twisted.

9

The restaurant was in the Gangnam district, inside a shopping mall with high-end brands. Through the thick wood double doors and into the inner courtyard, we stepped into Korea's Joseon royal past.

Willow trees bent over a burbling artificial stream, an array of potted flowers and fauna, and bamboo rock gardens hugged tables of four and two-seaters. The waiters were dressed in hanbok, traditional Korean attire, and there were individual pavilions scattered around the courtyard's perimeter, each with colorful, wood-carved eaves.

Dad insisted on coming along to dinner. Last night, when he heard I lost five hundred US dollars and K-pop concert and musical tickets, I was grounded. That didn't stop me from contacting the Jekyll and Hyde musical producer to buy new tickets. I had memories to make, and I wasn't going to give up my dreams.

Our hotel concierge, who referred me to the producer, called my father an hour before my meeting. Surprisingly, Dad canceled his last meeting and came to pick me up.

"Please leave your shoes here," the hostess gestured to small cubbies by a private pavilion for our footwear and gave us soft slippers instead.

We followed her up the steps and entered a room with a long, low table and six upright seats on a pinewood floor. The table had a spread of twenty little side dishes of many colors and textures, like pickled kimchee, bits of preserved seafood, thin slices of brown fishcake tofu, bite-sized stewed meats, dried anchovies, and glass noodles.

"Miss *Shima Miyako* called. She apologized for running late," said the hostess. "She said to start first, so Sir, can we begin service?"

The sides came, and I spent the time tasting them while Dad worked on his phone.

Ten minutes in, there was a knock on the sliding door. We looked up as a beautiful woman with a curtain of black hair stepped in. She knelt to our eye level and smiled.

"I'm sorry I'm late. There was an accident on my way here," she spoke in English and extended her hand out to my father. "I'm *Shima Miyako*, executive producer of Jekyll and Hyde."

Dad clasped her hand. "Dr. Michael Harris." He glanced over to me."

I waved at her from across the table. "I'm Alice. We spoke on the phone earlier."

"You're Alice! Wow, you look younger than I thought." She smiled.

I grinned and checked the doorway. "Where's your friend?"

"Oh! I'm sorry, he couldn't come. He had a family emergency."

"I see…" I chewed my lip. "What's his idol name? Maybe I might know him."

"Idol? Oh no, he's not an idol. What made you think that?" She pretended to look confused.

I frowned. That woman lied. One of the reasons I wanted to meet was because she promised to bring an idol. I could have asked the concierge to get the tickets for me.

Dad saw our exchange and glared at her.

Miyako slid into a spot directly in front of my father and pulled out her business card, and my father did the same.

He took a cursory look at it and back up at Miyako. "I'm disappointed with our concierge services. Inviting a sixteen-year-old to dinner without parental supervision isn't something we allow in our country."

She bent her head. "Please accept my sincere apologies again for not asking to speak to you first. I connect with many of your hotel's guests to provide a unique experience in our musical industry. I didn't know your daughter was still a child."

I squirmed in my seat. "Compared to our children at school, she sounded mature and independent on the phone."

"Alice said you have three VIP tickets with backstage passes for June fourteenth."

"Yes, and if any of your party wants a photograph with the actors, I can arrange it too. Would you like other tickets? I have the MIX2 summer concert and RoyalPink's fan meeting concert."

"Aren't those sold out?" I asked eagerly.

Miyako grinned. "They are, but I have my connections."

"How much are the VIP tickets and the two concert tickets?" Dad asked.

The food came right at that moment. Hot plates of sizzling meat, a spicy seafood soup, and *Bimbibap*, a mixed rice in a cast-iron pot.

Miyako gestured to the food. "Why don't we eat first?"

Throughout the meal, Miyako led the conversation and shared

her experience as a producer. We heard her insider views on the business, and my father peppered her with questions about the musical industry's growth.

After the meal, dessert came in individual bowls of milk-shaved ice with red Azuki beans.

Dad snatched the bowl from me. He must have remembered what happened when I was eight years old. I could still recall.

The bowl of red beans flipped from the table and rained down on my small head. My screams broke the air. I covered my tiny hands over my face and screamed. Each bean burned a hole in my skin. Blood spurted out from each hit, and my lungs compressed, causing me to gasp for air. For twenty-four hours, I was touch-and-go, stuck to a ventilator.

The illness was in my head, the doctors said. It was then that my father realized the severity of my trauma.

I stopped his hand. "It's okay, Dad." I saw worry flicker when he looked at me for the first time tonight.

"Seriously, I'm fine." I insisted. He dropped his hand, and I took the bowl of blood-red beans back, scooped a big mouthful of *Bingsoo* and beans, and ate it.

He was shocked, but he didn't say a word.

The panic attack didn't come, and I wasn't scared. My heart swelled with joy. I made a mental note to thank Dr. Bailey.

Miyako watched our exchange without saying a word. After we were done, she gave a sly look. "Did you like the beans?"

"Yes. Just the right sweetness." I smiled back coolly.

Dad slammed his spoon on the table.

"What do you want? I'm sure you're just as busy as I am."

Miyako straightened her shoulders. "You're right, Dr. Harris. I'm here to make a deal."

"Deal? I don't make deals." My father crossed his arms.

"My friend, who was supposed to be here today, has a benign brain tumor. His doctor advises removing it as soon as possible. His family wants you to be his surgeon because you're the best. But, they were put on a wait list and told to call back next year." She inhaled. "Can you help him? They will pay you whatever you want to do the surgery this year."

Dad clasped his fingers together. "You said it's benign?"

"Yes."

"My schedule is full the rest of this year and —"

She cut him off. "I heard you value connections." She leaned in eagerly. "We have that too."

The clouds drew in. I was instantly uncomfortable. I glanced over to my father. His growing was twitching. It seemed he felt the same. The food in my stomach churned. I could foresee bad things to come.

"My friend's family has connections with the Blue House," she persisted.

Dad frowned.

Blue House? Like in the White House, but blue? I thought.

He crossed his arms. "What's his family name?"

"Park Entertainment Group," said Miyako.

He frowned. "Don't know them."

"His family can pay you to triple your usual fee or more. They can have the surgery anytime and anywhere. I'll throw in the VIP tickets and the two concert tickets for free." Miyako countered.

Dad tossed his napkin on the table. "I'm not switching out my patients."

"What if we ask our connections in the Blue House for a favor?" Miyako suggested.

Lightning shot through his face. Dad stood up angrily. His knee struck the table, and the plates went clattering. "The answer is still no." He rammed open the sliding door and strode out of the room.

I got up sheepishly and blushed when the hostess rushed over. Glancing over to Miyako, I dropped my head.

"Er...well...sorry about that. Let's forget about those tickets, and thanks for dinner." I said and hurried out.

Miyako didn't know how much trouble she caused. Dad had that frightening glint in his eyes. She insulted him by pulling rank to force his hand, and my father, who believed few people in this world could rank him, was pissed.

There would be consequences. I prayed that giving him time and some space would cool him down. The last thing I wanted was to be his punching bag. He would not hit me, but the feeling would be just the same.

10

It was almost midnight when the screen on my phone went dark. My charger was in my father's room, where I had left it before heading out for dinner. I wasn't waiting for a special someone to call, and the few superficial ones who asked for updates hung around in Pearson High School because I was Dr. Harris's daughter.

Dr. Bailey might call. I was reporting my progress to him from Seoul after we had become close over the past six months.

The hallway on my floor was empty when I made my way to the elevator. Hopefully, Dad was calm now. During the ride back to our hotel, his jaw was clenched so tightly that it formed a sharp angle that could cut through flesh.

Dad's Executive Suite room was on the twenty-ninth floor, while mine was on the fourth, unlucky floor. There were ten doors on the suite floor, and only those with a card key could enter.

The velvet carpet was soft under my shoes. White marble sculptures, pottery, and artwork lined the hall. The lighting was warm, and it smelled fresh, like a cool morning mist, unlike the stale air and cigarettes in mine.

Dad's room was two doors down from the fire exit. The light at his door flickered ominously as I stood outside, suddenly nervous to knock.

I placed my ear on it and listened, hoping to hear his snores so I could sneak in, grab the phone charger, and leave. There was a sound of constant thumping, loud smacking of flesh against flesh.

My face heated up.

A scuffle. Somebody is falling onto the ground. Sounds of fist meeting body. Muffled groans and cries of a woman begging, then followed by stumbling feet as she ran to the door.

Her hands grappled and twisted the knob as I stood paralyzed on the other side.

The door flung open. Heavy footsteps came charging behind.

A glimpse of a naked woman's breast, half the face of the woman I met at dinner, and then the door slammed shut.

Someone's head slammed against a wall, followed by the squeaks of a body sliding to the ground.

My foot slipped. I staggered back. The lamps along the walls flickered in fear. I backed as fast as I could to the exit.

Then the door flung open again, and I met with my father's angry gaze. My eyes dropped to his bare chest as he hurriedly put in pants.

"Alice?" His eyes were bloodshot. A monster in human form.

I spun around and sprinted for the fire exit, my heart about to explode.

"Alice!" He called out in an urgent whisper.

I slammed the exit door behind me.

He wrestled the handle, and I held onto it on the other side, using my body's weight and placing my foot against the wall to latch onto the frame.

"Alice, open!" He hollered.

I wanted to hold on. I didn't want to see him. I wanted all those bad thoughts to go away. Tears and sweat rolled down my face. The horror seemed unreal. Stuck in a dark stairway, air short and breaths long. Fighting to live through this, to forget this, wishing this never happened. And then, an invisible bomb dropped its weight on my shoulders. My sweaty fingers slid off the handle, and I let go.

Dad fell with a thud, and I raced down the dimly lit stairs. Above, the door flung open. The giant kept chasing. The worst wasn't over yet.

"Stop!" Dad shouted down. "Alice! Stop!"

I kept running, skipping over the steps down. I was going to get back to my room, no matter what.

I saw her bloody, puffed-up face. The snotty producer. Before the door swung shut.

I really wish I didn't. I wished I didn't need the phone charger or that I'd just gone to bed.

At a young age, I learned that Dad's anger was terrifying if he felt justified.

Miyako shouldn't have come back to the hotel and messed with him. Even kids knew never to play with fire.

I didn't see those steps.

My foot touched air, and I dropped. With my heart in my throat, I screamed and crashed. The next thing I knew, the lights went out.

Merle

11

Merle woke up with a grin on her face. Peering down at her was her favorite person in the world.

"Merle?" he asked.

"Daddy!" She reached up to hug him tight.

"Sweetie…" He pulled back and studied her closely. A smile lifted his lips, and he patted his favorite daughter's head. "You're back."

"Daddy, what's going on? Where's your shirt?" She laughed, pointing to his bare chest with a fine dusting of golden hair and solid lines of abs. Then, she glanced up at the tower of grey stairs and back down at an identical set below.

"And where are we?"

Daddy stood up and sighed. "We're in Seoul."

"Seoul? I knew it! And why here?"

"Alice tried to run and fell." He gestured to the stairs.

"Help me up." She raised her arm.

He lifted her to her feet. One of the flip-flops Alice wore broke and was five steps down. Her foot was bruised. Although she had pants, pain sliced through her scraped knees when she moved. But Merle wasn't worried. Her body healed fast.

"Can you walk up?" Daddy pointed to the stairs. "There's a camera in the elevator. We can't get caught."

"Sure." She looked up the flights of stairs. It wasn't the first time he needed her.

Gritting her teeth, she took a step up. Her leg stung, but she kept on going, plastering a smile on her face. Daddy hated tears. Soon, the pain receded, and the bruise and scraped flesh vanished.

Merle grinned and put her weight back on her foot. "Come, I'll race you to the top!"

———————

A woman with long black hair was slumped outside the bathroom behind the front door of Daddy's suite, unconscious. The dried-up blood on her lips and bruises on her face and body that her hair didn't cover were purpling up.

Daddy threw a towel over the naked woman. He didn't have to explain. People who didn't respect him got what they deserved.

Merle surveyed the large suite, starting from the left, with a bathroom, followed by a living room, and then a bedroom to the right. There were two wine glasses on the coffee table, and their clothes were scattered on the carpet.

"She'll go to the cops." Merle frowned.

Daddy pulled out a broken camera from under the pile of clothes. "She drugged and stripped me." He pulled out a memory card from the camera. "She threatened to post them."

Merle strode over and jerked the woman up by her hair. Bitch…"

He touched Merle's arm. "Let go, Sweetie. You're leaving evidence."

"Did you punish her well?"

He nodded, and she grinned. A thought came to her, and she smiled. "I've got an idea."

"What is it?" he asked.

She picked up a new set of gloves from his kit.

"Help me bring her to the tub," she said.

Together, they dumped the woman in the bathtub. "Where's your syringe?" she asked.

Daddy injected the woman with his signature sleep drug.

"Go take a shower. I'll clean her up," Merle turned on the water spray and began her job of covering her Daddy's crimes.

Alice

12

Morning came when the police were knocking on my door. I wanted to believe last night wasn't real. However, the sight of my pants torn up at the helm from running down the stairs broke that hope. Although my knees and feet healed, my body shook, and my fingers trembled when I tried to comb my hair. Also, the hospital chemicals and soap clung to my overly washed skin, another reminder of what they had done.

Father got up from the armchair by the window and walked to the door.

"Remember. You had stomach flu, and I stayed with you the whole night," he instructed.

I stared at him blankly. His brow raised in question.

"Yes," I finally replied. My mind was muddled. I vaguely recalled our earlier conversations when I woke at four a.m.

'I was drugged and stripped. That woman took pictures," he explained earlier.

"You could report her for blackmail...." I argued. "You didn't have to fight her…"

It wasn't self-defense. I remembered the sounds I heard behind the door and the flashes of her bruised naked body before my mind blanked. Besides, who could fight the giant Dr. Harris?

Excuses. Justifications. Lies.

My gut retched.

I didn't want to remember more — the violence, the look of terror on her face.

Why? How could he?

I had no part in this. He was my father. I shared his DNA. I arranged to meet with Miyako. This was my fault.

"Where is she? Is she in your room?" I had to know if she was safe.

"Yes. She's sleeping," he said.

My fingers felt powdery, like I had worn surgical gloves.

Merle liked to play with his gloves. Growing up, she pretended she was a surgeon like our father and experimented on backyard rodents and our neighbor, Mrs. Johnson's embalmed cat.

Our neighbors never found poor Kitty. That cat became one of Merle's prized possessions in her shed of horrors until Mrs. Johnson took it back.

"Dad? Did Merle come out?" I asked, my heart racing.

His smug look said it all. Worry mounted. "What...what did you do to Miyako?"

"It's all taken care of." Dad got off his bed.

"What do you mean?" I gripped my covers.

"Keep to my story. You came up to see me at midnight because you felt sick. You had stomach flu and a high fever. We went to your room at twelve-thirty, and I stayed with you the rest of the night."

"No one will believe that," I said.

"They will." Dad looked too smug. "Stick to it if you want to go home. If I get arrested, "Okaasan's in charge."

Putting me under my mother's care was a death sentence.

That was when he stabbed me with the syringe -- a drug Dr. Bailey prescribed to be used in an emergency when my panic attacks made my voices come out. The medicine helped calm my nerves, increase my oxygen intake, and put my mind in a state of complete rest.

I blinked back my tears. If this were Kansas, there were places I could hide, but here in Seoul, I didn't know where to go or anyone who could help.

Two Korean men were standing under the arch of my door. Both wore lanyard badges with Korean characters, which probably read 'Detective,' with names printed in the English alphabet and Korean below them. The partners could easily pass as twins with their similar haircuts and tanned faces. To add to the confusion, both had the last name Lee.

"Dr. Michael Harris?" The taller Lee stepped forward, speaking in English. "You're under arrest for assaulting Miss Shima Miyako."

His partner pulled out a pair of cuffs and grabbed my father's wrist.

"What're you talking about?" Dad resisted the Detective who held on.

"You have the right to remain silent and the right to an attorney," said the tall Detective.

My father turned to me. "Get my phone."

I grabbed his phone from the console table by the TV. The other Detective, who cuffed my father, stepped back.

I shuffled uneasily as the detectives surveyed my room. Was there evidence? I sat down on my bed and clutched the sides of my sheets tightly. Sweat trickled down my temples. I gave a worried side glance and met the shorter Detective's gaze. His stare pierced through my thinly veiled mask and saw through my rotten core.

My heart shrank. He got me. That Detective knew what happened. I am as good as dead.

"Hello? Mr. Kim?" Dad spoke to his phone, and both detectives turned to him.

I looked out the window, gnawing my bottom lip till it bled. The sleep drug's side effects kept my emotional spikes down, bringing lethargy to my body.

"Yes, I'm well. Seoul's been okay...." Dad glanced at me and then at the cops. "Look, Mr. Kim, I've been accused of assault. No. The police are here in my hotel room." He looked over to the two detectives who stood straight as nails and frowned. "Where are you taking me?" he asked them.

"Gangnam police station," said the tall one.

"Gangnam," Dad told his lawyer. "Okay. I'll see you there." He ended his call and handed the phone to me. "My lawyer said you can't handcuff me till there is clear evidence."

"Miss Shima Miyako said you assaulted her. A hotel cleaning lady found her in your bathtub," argued the tall Detective.

"What?" Dad gave them an incredulous look. "Why the hell would I hurt her and leave her there?" He stared down at the detectives. Dad was six feet two with broad shoulders. If he wanted to, he could be an imposing foreigner. "Have you talked to hotel security?" Dad snapped.

"Not yet," said the tall Detective who refused to be intimidated.

"I reported a disturbance last night around eleven. Miss Shima was drunk and banging at my door. She wouldn't leave."

The detectives looked at each other.

"I don't know how she entered my room, but I wasn't there."

Dad pointed at me. "Alice came by. She had stomach flu and a high fever. I was with her all night."

The three men turned to me. I squirmed under their scrutiny.

This was it. My father wanted me to vouch. After what he said and what I thought I had witnessed, I wasn't sure what to believe. The sleeping drug he gave me earlier fogged my mind.

Silence stretched as precious seconds flew by. They were waiting, and so I went with what I memorized. "I ate something bad at dinner. My father gave me medicine."

"What time were you with him?" asked the tall Detective.

I closed my eyes. "I went upstairs around midnight."

"Did you see anyone in the hallway or your father's room?"

I tasted the blood on my lip. "No."

The tall Detective spoke to his partner in Korean and then turned to us.

"Both of you need to come with us," he said.

Dad raised his handcuffed hands. "Take these off."

Grudgingly, the shorter Detective compiled. My father rubbed his wrists, and I grabbed his arm in panic. "Dad... I'm scared...."

He placed his arm across my back. "Everything's going to be fine."

It was fortunate that my mother wasn't here. Things could only get a lot worse if she were involved.

———————

In a dim restaurant at lunchtime, Dad and I sat across from each other with our steaming bowls of udon. Never had I ever been so glad to be with him. It turned out that Lawyer Kim was a famous attorney from the largest and most prestigious law firm in Seoul.

He informed us of our rights and what to say, as well as what not to reveal.

The police kept us apart and tried to find ways to break me down. I was the sole eyewitness and my father's alibi. The security cameras in the elevator corroborated our stories, and the one located near the elevator on my floor, in the lobby, captured us at the right times. The detectives collaborated with hotel security and found Dad's complaint logged in at eleven-fifteen last night. A security guard met Shima Miyako outside Dad's room and escorted her out of the hotel.

Something happened between 11:00 and midnight. My father told the police he was sleeping till I came by. That was a lie.

I kept to my story. Telling them Dad followed me back to my room after. When asked again if he was alone when I visited his room, I said, 'Yes.' The detectives informed me that Miss Shima Miyako had seen me. It took every ounce of courage to stay calm.

Lawyer Kim said it was my word against hers. They were painting Miyako as a drunk, opportunistic woman. I didn't have to be afraid. Lawyer Kim would protect us.

Stuck in the interrogation room, I was suddenly reminded of the sounds of sex. Miyako's bruised face and parts of her naked body flashed in my fogged, drugged thoughts. Then there were the parting glimpses of Merle's thoughts before I woke up — Merle in Dad's shower with a body in a tub. Merle is on Dad's bed with her legs crossed over a man's bare back — an Asian guy, grunting and thrusting into our body.

I felt sick. I didn't want to know what she did while I was sleeping. The months with Dr. Bailey's intern, Ryan, were terrifying and strange. He was hot. He was Merle's first. I felt guilty knowing what she did. Excited? Maybe. To be honest, I was jealous they liked her. Those hot boys fled when I woke. I was the weird one, the fake, and the uncool.

Merle always boasted she was Daddy's right hand. She hinted she dealt with his messes.

Could I have stopped Dad? Warn Miyako of the danger she was putting herself into? Did I care enough? Maybe, not. Thinking back, this wasn't his first assault. The clues were there. Foggy memories of their faces. Glimpses of Merle's thoughts. The women were East Asian, and every one of them had that same look — a type he liked: — beautiful, fragile, yet strong-willed, difficult to deal with and a challenge to break, just like my mother.

Why would he leave Miyako knocked out and raped in his bathtub? Lawyer Kim argued that someone else did it. Dr. Harris wasn't stupid. He was framed. The police needed to find the third person instead of blaming Dad, who was an easy target. The more my father and Lawyer Kim talked, the more their reasons made sense.

The forensic test results arrived. The fingerprints found on Miyako's body didn't match those of Dr. Harris or mine. The police needed more time to investigate and rushed the semen DNA from Miyako's rape kit for screening.

In two days, we will know the results. Two days were going to feel like forever.

My father picked up his chopsticks and slurped his hot noodles. I followed him and burned the roof of my mouth.

"So, what's after this?" I gulped down my cold water, no longer hungry.

"We'll have to stay till the DNA test clears." He slammed his chopsticks down and looked annoyed. "I had to send an apology to my patients. And my schedule is a mess."

Dr. Michael Harris hated to apologize. He never apologized.

"Okaasan is flying in tonight."

I choked. My mother wasn't supposed to be here till the day after, in time for my birthday. I was more afraid of her reaction than the hours I spent with the police.

He frowned. "I won't be home for Thanksgiving. I'll be operating on Lawyer Kim's mother-in-law this November."

Thanksgiving without Dad meant my mother and I would have it with our neighbor, the Johnsons, who would be uncomfortable with their sons and families coming home.

My eyes grew wet. I didn't want to cry. I hated being weak in front of him. It made Dad angry and reminded him of everything I wasn't. I slipped my finger to the corner of my eye.

My father was quick to catch on to it. "Are you crying?"

My heart shriveled. I was ten when I pretended to be Merle. Just once, I wanted to hear Dad say he loved me. My heart ached when he hugged me and ruffled my hair. When he learned I was Alice, he was furious.

"I'm sorry... I'm sorry...." I kept repeating. My mind was locked in a never-ending loop. I drowned in self-pity and hated myself even more.

"Alice...just stop it." I watched him clench his hands into fists. His knuckles were white as bleached skeletons. "People are watching."

I couldn't stop. I was pushing him to the edge.

An old Korean couple sitting in the corner was staring at us. They shook their heads in disapproval. I didn't understand what they were saying, but their condemning looks spoke volumes.

Dad stood up and left.

The elders continued to stare.

I was sick of Seoul, my mother's farm, and my father's apartment. I was tired of Merle's manipulations and the others who didn't care about what they had done to my life.

I wished Dad had never raped Miyako.

I wish I had never come to Seoul.

13

June 14, 2010
My birthday

Heat melted my skin, burning through my flesh. The smell of iron was strong, and my knees were covered in Miyako's blood. It oozed out fast, spilling across the wet floor and turning the swimming pool a shade of crimson.

Everyone reacted at once. I watched in slow motion and listened to the screams intensify as the scene unfolded in a panoramic rendering. Padded feet slapping over wet tiles echoed in the heated indoor space, people dashing out with grotesque expressions on their faces.

Her bright red blood contrasted sharply against her snow-white skin, exposing an impossibly large gaping hole in her abdomen with pale guts pouring out.

It was an accident. Yet, one could curse fate for its cruelty. In that one blink, she hung seconds from death. Miyako slipped on the wet floor and fell on her nine-inch dagger while chasing after my father, and now, her eyes were glazing over, and her breath came in short bursts as spasms took control.

Their voices snickered, mean and callous as they commented in my head. They were the buzzing of bees and witches cackling with laughter at her. They saw what I witnessed, and my sister, Merle, was most happy. Miyako got what she deserved, she said. The voices, which I wished would go away, went strangely silent when I rushed forward. My father, the brilliant doctor, swam up to the other end of the pool and snuck out the other exit, abandoning me to the aftermath. Life lapping as the shadow of death walked in.

"Get more towels!" I shouted to Park Ji Woon. Fate was such that he showed up. Ji Woon, the college boy from the market, the good Samaritan, came rushing into the pool after Miyako slipped and gutted herself.

Miyako heaved and gasped as pain tore through her. Tears wet her cheeks, and her voice was a gurgle of sounds.

Ji Woon's hands shook as the new towels he brought soaked up more blood.

I grabbed the rest of his clean towels. "Keep her eyes open!"

His scared gaze flickered between Miyako and me. He was as pale as Miyako. Being a surgeon's daughter, I spent too much time hanging about in my father's hospital. My favorite place was the ER, where I witnessed my share of casualties. Death by knife was painful but usually fast.

«*Noona!*» He squeezed her hand as she struggled to breathe. "You mustn't sleep! *Noona!*" He choked. "Open your eyes! I'm here. Look at me. Please."

Miyako shuddered. Her head drooped.

It wasn't easy putting her guts back. The emergency department in my father's hospital was my playground. Every summer, I sat in a corner and watched as writhing bodies of the injured came wheeling in, and the doctors and nurses sprinted to save them.

I covered the clean towels over her wound. Infections would come later. First, we needed to try to stop her from going into cardiac arrest.

"Help's coming," I said calmly, although my heart was tearing through my chest.

It felt like there were two parts of me staring at this dying woman —my mind in one and my emotions in the other. The clean towels on her abdomen were completely soaked.

The adults abandoned us. The hotel staff stood at the side, wringing their hands and holding walkie-talkies to their mouths. No one wanted to step in. Everyone was afraid to be held responsible.

I couldn't bring myself to tell Ji Woon that Miyako wasn't going to make it.

The medics were on their way up, the hotel staff said, who then gave us more towels.

Miyako's heart was slowing down, and her skin was growing colder than ice. The signs were clear. She was slipping fast.

Ji Woon was sobbing. The more he cried, the colder I got. Regrets would come later, along with the other emotions I had compartmentalized and pushed aside. Having witnessed the throes of death in my father's hospital, I often thought of the guilt of those who lived, not having the chance to voice out their last thoughts to the ones they lost.

Regrets festered. They could turn into something dark and nasty. I might not know Miyako's regrets, but I knew mine.

Lies. They were all lies. I caused this. I lied, and this was my penance.

Guilt hung like a noose above my head. My foot is on a box, ready for my next step.

Miyako faltered beneath my hands. Anger burned in my chest

as I recalled the calm, unaffected manner of Dr. Michael Harris as he left. This should be his calling, and saving Miyako was his redemption. A small pathway towards asking for her forgiveness. Instead, he chose himself.

Ji Woon and I turned to the running footsteps of the EMT medics coming close, and my hate for my father grew.

There was no excuse. Dad could have saved Miyako, but he chose not to.

14

The cab caught up to the ambulance, which turned into the hospital's parking lot. Ji Woon and I jumped out and sprinted to the ER.

Waiting at the doors of the emergency operating theaters was a man in his fifties, dressed in a plaid shirt, and a petite elderly woman in a blue-and-white kimono. Their faces were painted with worry. The man, from his looks, must be Miyako's father.

When the old woman, who must be Miyako's grandmother, saw us, she shouted, "You!" in Japanese and charged at us. She pulled Ji Woon's bathrobe and dragged him forward, forcing him to kneel.

"You killed her!" She hammered her fists on his head and against his chest, but Ji Woon didn't fight back. "She wanted to save you!"

"I'm sorry…" he cried in Japanese. "I didn't know my sister was going to —"

"Your family is rich! You can get another doctor!" The grandma shook Ji Woon. Her weathered cheeks were wet with tears.

"I'm sorry… I'm so sorry…." Ji Woon bent his head.

She wobbled, and Miyako's father held her up as she glowered at Ji Woon in pure hatred. "I told Nana not to keep you! Bastard child!" She gripped Ji Woon's hair and jerked his head up. "Bastard! Your mother should have aborted you! Why take your sister, too? Miyako is ours! She's our precious child, not the Parks!" she cried.

The double doors to the operating theater swung open, and a surgeon in green garb appeared, speaking in Korean and mentioning the name Shima Miyako.

Miyako's father rushed forward, and the rest of us followed.

It was two p.m. The doctor repeated the name Shima Miyako, and the faces of everyone fell.

The old woman clung to the doctor's shirt. "No...no! Why are you lying? Miyako's alive! Where is she? Where's my little firecracker?"

The surgeon wrenched her hands from his clothes, and Miyako's father attacked next, jabbing his finger into that doctor's chest. "We know powerful people! You, save my daughter!"

The grandma wobbled, wailing with her arms in the air. "God, give her back! You can't take her! Give her back!" She fell sideways, and then Ji Woon caught her. "Miyako! My beautiful child! Miyako-chan!" she wailed.

Miyako's father punched Ji Woon in the face, and he fell back. He kicked Ji Woon hard in his ribs. "It's all your fault!"

Two hospital guards caught the older man before he kicked again.

"Devil spawn!" Her father shouted, foaming at the mouth. His eyes were crazy with murder. "Bastard!"

I took my chance and grabbed dazed Ji Woon, dragging him to the entrance. That man's swear words rained down on our backs, but we kept going.

"Come, come." I kept saying as I struggled. "Almost there." When we got through the automatic doors, Ji Woon rushed to the nearest bush and puked. Two officers in uniform — a woman and a man were standing outside and watching us. They strode over as I patted Ji Woon's back.

"Excuse me?" The woman officer asked in accented English. They were the same pair who arrived with the hotel's emergency medical staff. "Please come with us. We need to take your witness statements."

Ji Woon, who was slumped over my shoulder, didn't respond. "Where are we going?" I asked.

"Gangnam Police Station."

"Hey...Ji Woon." I tapped him lightly. "Can you stand?"

"Yes." He lifted his arm off my shoulder, slowly straightening up.

I caught him as he stumbled back. My muscles screamed under his weight.

"I'm okay…." He waved me off. With sea legs, he tried to find his footing again.

I flexed my aching shoulders and arms. "Can you walk to the car?" I pointed to the police car in the parking lot. The officers were already waiting beside it.

He stumbled again when he tried.

I caught him in my arms and almost fell. His hair covered my eyes, and I couldn't see. He sobbed on my shoulders as I stroked his head.

"It's okay. It doesn't feel like it now, but it will be at some point." I pushed him up to stand. "You can do this. Just hold it in a little longer till we're done with them." I gestured to the police with my chin.

He tilted his head to the side to study the two officers in uniform.

I breathed in deeply and out, and he mimicked my actions. After a couple more times, he pulled himself up, squaring his shoulders. "I'll walk." His voice shook, but this time, his legs were steady.

It was difficult to watch him grieve. However, I knew he wouldn't want me to intervene.

He wanted to be punished.

Miyako's family had the right to be angry. Ji Woon was the friend Miyako had mentioned, the one who didn't show up for dinner. Anyone would point fingers. He needed my father's favor, whether he asked for the surgery himself or not.

Ji Woon clasped my hand tightly, and together we climbed into the backseat. Then, he surprised me by threading his fingers with mine and leaning on my shoulder like I was the only thing that stood between him and the edge of madness.

He stared out the window while I sent a message to my mother with my other hand. Ji Woon didn't use his phone once.

The police car sped through the streets, passing office buildings, little market alleys, temples, and a park filled with pink floral trees.

The scent of blood was strong. Even in the clean blue hotel guest robes, I snatched for Ji Woon and me before we ran out after the medics; they couldn't hide the obvious. Death hung over us. Miyako was still here in blood.

As our police car pulled into the station, it suddenly occurred to me — today was my birthday. Today, I turned seventeen.

Shima Miyako. Fate made her death my birth, so I would remember. My lies, my weakness, and my cowardice were the cause of this. If there was a lesson to be learned, it was that people around me always died. For Ji Woon's sake, I shouldn't be here. He had every reason to hate me if he knew, but today was my birthday, and I deserved the right to be selfish.

It was my wish to share his sorrow. Just for today, I wanted to be with him, and to do that, I'd lie a little more.

15

The police station was a hallway of rooms. A bullpen for investigators, followed by numerous rooms for interrogations. Grey, white walls, and bright lights. Illuminating the secrets and lies convicts told to keep themselves safe.

Could I do the same? In the week I'd been here, I'd visited this place twice. I never want to be back here again. And here I was.

They split us up. Ji Woon headed to the Detective's desk, and I went to a room for someone to take my statement in English.

I didn't want to go. I was scared of what they might ask and what I might accidentally reveal. The lies from the other day crushed my esteem. Without Lawyer Kim, I was a bomb ready to explode.

Ji Woon didn't know this. He didn't know anything. Before he left, he placed his hand on my head and gave me a small smile. "Don't worry. Everything will be alright." Now he's the calm one, and I was the weak one. This role reversal sat strangely on my chest. I was losing this battle. His encouragement made me feel even guiltier. I was the bad one, and this feeling of being evil was worse, like any moment, Merle was going to reveal herself and tell him the truth.

My legs refused to take another step. The thought of being interrogated again hampered my ability to speak.

"Give me your phone," Ji Woon instructed. I watched him type his number on mine, and his phone rang in response.

"Can't we go together?" I begged, clutching his arm. "Your English is good. You can translate for me with the Detective."

He shook his head. "If you want to get out fast, we need to follow their rules. Fighting them won't stop the pain." He squeezed my hand. "I'll see you outside when you're done. Over there." He pointed to a row of benches in front of the police station.

My lungs strained. My head felt light. They all left me — my parents and now, Ji Woon. The familiar sounds of buzzing grew. Inside Merle, and the others rejoiced. Bright red sparks lit my sight. The whole world was burning.

"You'll be fine. Tell them what you did. You tried your best." He gave a shaky smile. I could hear his grief coming back. His Adam's apple wobbled, and he blinked back his tears.

"Okay," I replied to stop him from saying more. Reality hadn't set in for either of us.

"This will pass." He said. Those three words were boulders on my heart. I didn't want to think. Not to feel. There wasn't time for me to split my emotions from my thoughts yet.

It wasn't Miyako I cared about. Each second he was trying to hold back, the blade struck, burrowing deeper into my already wounded guilt.

Ji Woon pressed his fingers on my hand, massaging my palm. "Alice…just tell them exactly what you did."

The buzzing sounds stopped, and the flashes of red disappeared. The police station appeared before me again.

He nudged my chin up and stared deeply. "Alice, you'll be fine."

I nodded slowly.

"Take a deep breath," he advised. I followed him as he took a breath. "And another," he said, and I followed him again, filling my cheeks up.

A thin smile tugged his lips. His face turned a sudden rosy hue. He was mesmerizingly handsome with those long lashes, jawline, and pronounced Adam's apple, which I'd been trying not to touch. He was trying to be brave for me and turned my head in the direction of the benches. "We'll meet there later. Got it"

"Got it," I was still reeling from his fingers accidentally brushing my lips.

He patted my head. "That's my good girl."

My cheeks burned up when the policewoman suddenly came over. "Are your guardians here?"

Ji Woon made a call and spoke curtly in Korean. He snapped his phone and looked at the officer. "He's on his way."

"I left my mother messages. I'll call her again in the room," I replied.

"Okay. Come this way." The policewoman gestured to me and walked ahead first.

I grabbed Ji Woon's robe.

He slowly unclenched my stiff fingers from it and then placed his hand on my shoulder above my heart-shaped scar. "You are the bravest girl I know."

Those words meant nothing as I walked straight into the lion's den.

———

The door to the interrogation room opened, and her unique scent wafted in. Her perfume was crafted from the oils of white roses from our garden, with a hint of mint and ginger. My mother believed that all sweet things needed a touch of spice. Life wasn't meant to be a bed of roses because thorns hurt.

I shifted uneasily in my chair. "Okaasan… you're here."

Junko Harris wore her signature frown. Her hair was in a loose bun with tendrils curling on her sharp cheekbones. Pale skin, tanned by the sun, was once worshipped by my father as ethereal, but now stretched like plastic wrap over her bony face. Some might still call her elegant because her pride, like my father's, was untouchable.

Behind her, the tall Detective Lee, whom I met two days ago, walked in. Only he got close to the truth, chipping away at my lies about my father, cornering me till I almost switched. Luckily, Lawyer Kim stepped in and saved me that day, but today, I was alone.

"Detective Lee," I squeaked.

"We meet again." The Detective said as he slipped into his seat opposite us. "I heard you were a hero. They said you and Mr. Park Ji Woon stopped Miss Shima's bleeding till the medics arrived."

"I had to help…" I stared at the table.

He tapped his fingers on his notebook. "The medics said you kept her from cardiac arrest. Where did you learn that?"

I chewed on my lip. "My father's hospital. I was in the ER a lot. I've seen many cases like hers."

His gaze fixated on my face. "Most kids your age hung out with their friends. Dating. Movies. Eating. But you like the ER? With your father? What else do you do for him?"

"Don't answer," my mother growled. Both of us turned to her.

Our gazes met, and suddenly my mother's eyes rolled up to her whites, then she buckled and dropped to the ground.

"Okaasan!" I reached for her arm, and as expected, she was as cold as ice. I dug my nails into her arm. "Okaasan!"

"Alice," She cooed. "Don't take my baby! She's not dead. Don't say she's dead."

"Okaasan," I pleaded. My ears were burning with embarrassment."

"Is she okay?" The Detective came over to our side.

"She's not dead! I'm not crazy! Lying! Lying. Lying. All of you are lying!" Her voice dropped into a whisper. Her face scrunched up in pain; it was hard to watch.

"Mom…please… I'm here…" I held her arm while the Detective reached for the other. Tears welled in my eyes as my mother stared out the window.

Her mind was gone. Again, I didn't exist. Her timing couldn't be worse.

"Mrs. Harris?" The Detective tapped her shoulder, but my mother didn't react.

"She's having a relapse," I muttered.

"Relapse?" He asked. "Does she need a doctor?"

"It's time for her medication." I dug into her handbag and pulled out her wallet and her phone, and flipped her bag over." They're not here…"

"Should I call Dr. Harris?" The Detective walked to the door.

"No, I'll take her there. Are we done?"

He glanced worriedly at me and then back at my mother, who was still muttering to herself. Her skin was a shade of pale blue, and her limbs were stiff as I pulled her along.

"We have many statements from the other eyewitnesses. You

can go now. Please stay in Seoul until the investigation is done." He held the door open as I wrapped my arms around my mother's waist and pulled her out.

"Are you going to the hotel?" he asked us.

"Yes.", I said when my mother suddenly dug in her feet. Her eyes snapped in anger, and she pushed me off.

The Detective caught me before I fell. Both of us stared at my mother as she adjusted her blouse and skirt. She glared at the Detective. "Is my husband here?"

He raised his arm and pointed down the hall. "Down that way, six doors to the left."

"Okaasan, I'm going back first." I gestured to the entrance.

She brushed past me as I held my breath and marched off.

After watching my mother enter Michael Harris's room, the Detective turned to me. There was pity in his eyes. "If you need to see a specialist, I know a few." He pulled out his business card and handed it over.

I crumpled it in my hand and met him unflinching. "I'm fine," I said and left.

16

The summer heat turned the cool air into sweat. As I rushed out of the station, I spotted Ji Woon talking to a handsome man in a suit. When they saw me coming over, the man handed him a bag and left.

"Ji Woon!" I called out, and he waved back.

"Are you done?" he asked, reaching for my hand instantly. Before I could pull away, he threaded his fingers with mine. The warmth of his palm chased away the bitterness of my mother. A small smile stretched over his lips, and I felt myself reciprocating.

A black Mercedes pulled out of the parking lot, and I followed Ji Woon's gaze as he stared at the man driving it till it disappeared around the bend. "Was that your father?"

He nodded grim-faced.

"He looks young. How old is he?"

"He's thirty-eight. We look alike. Many think he's my brother, and they're shocked when they learned he's my father." His mood soured instantly, and he began to kick a pebble on the ground. I pulled his hand, jerking him hard, so he crashed into me.

"Sorry," he held me up to keep me in balance.

"Ji Woon." I took both his arms and wrapped them around my waist. His cheeks flushed, and he murmured something in Korean, trying to pull away. "You need a hug," I embraced him tightly, listening to his strong heart beating against my ear, realizing I needed one just as much.

Seconds passed, and he sighed, placing his head on top of mine.

"People think you look alike, that you're alike. There will always be people who enjoy smacking you down, only feeling good when others suffer. Forget those jerks."

Ji Woon smiled. "I saw a woman in a blue walking into the station earlier, and to your room. Was that your mother?"

"Yes."

"She's beautiful...." He stopped when he saw my reaction.

"I hate her." I gave a withering look.

He didn't look away and matched my anger with understanding. "I hate mine too."

"We're even." I pursed my lips.

"I didn't mean you're not beautiful. You're even more. You're like the sun — fiery, spirited, and untouchable."

"Me? You don't know me. I'm no sun..." My cheeks heated instantly.

He smiled, his eyes twinkling with a secret. "So, are you heading back to your hotel? I left my bag there."

"Yes...my mother won't be back tonight. She's visiting a sick relative." I lied. My stomach rumbled loudly.

"Hungry?" He smiled.

"How about a snack?" We both said at the same time. He chuckled, and both sides of my lips crinkled up.

"But first…" He showed me his shopping bag. "Let's change."

I washed as best as I could and switched to a fresh set of T-shirts, jeans, and a new pair of undergarments. It was embarrassing that Ji Woon guessed my size right. We walked down the street, hand in hand, lost in our thoughts until the traffic light turned red and we had to stop. Pretending everything was fine was hard, especially for him. He wore his emotions on his face. Unlike me, I never left home without a mask.

"Do you like meat buns? Nikuman?" he brushed his eyes when my stomach protested again.

I stared at the street in front, giving him time to compose himself. "I've not had one, but I'll try anything."

"Good. There's a famous shop up ahead." He pointed. "We call them Jjinppang-mandu in Korean."

"Sure." I shouldn't be comfortable. I barely knew him. Still, there was a part of me that was excited to finally meet someone my age, Asian, who was also smart, and a bonus, super hot.

"Are you half Japanese too?" he asked suddenly.

I glanced up at him. "Yes…why?"

He ran his hand through his hair, looking shy. "You knew what Miyako's family was saying."

"Part. I learned Japanese so I could talk to my mother's side of the family."

He pulled me close as we crossed the busy street and stepped to the side and front when the cars came close.

"I don't trust easily." I blurted.

"That's another thing we have in common." He said.

"What else?" I asked.

"Tell you later?" He followed my gaze to our hands clasped together. I was trying to pull away when he squeezed my fingers tighter. Slowly, he looked up till our eyes met and stopped. "This feels right," he said softly.

My face flushed. The tension between us grew. Silence was always my way of avoiding things. However, this time, I lost. I wasn't ready to let him go, either. "Well, then…for today," I tucked a stray curl behind my ear.

He nodded. His pulse against my wrist was racing fast like mine. I wanted to reach out and touch his face, to let him know that he wasn't the only one who felt this connection, but I didn't.

"Okay! We're here." He sighed loudly and turned to the door leading into a small bakery shop. Inside, the wonderful aroma of meat juices and fresh bread made me instantly famished. My lips kept stretching into a smile as I watched him order, gesticulating here and there, probably buying up the entire store.

I forced myself to remember Miyako and her last moments. I feel her body convulsing in my arms. Watching panic race through her body when she realized she was dying.

I recalled feeling nothing then. Ice ran through my veins. The shock of her death didn't wear me down as it did to him. I was used to it. A resident in the ER, watching life and death just a line away.

"Aren't you glad you met him again? He's really cute. A keeper, after you killed her sister." Voices cooed from deep inside my head.

"Find out what he knows. Get him on your side." Others said.

"Shut up…" I growled.

"He can be your first. Do you need my help? I bet he's a virgin. He's sexy." Merle giggled.

"Shut up!" I shouted in my head.

The whispers grew, set aflame by my anger. They taunted, consuming my guilt. Some told me to take what I wanted. They were worse than the bullies at school and more insidious than the adults who manipulated. I imagined myself pushing them out of my head, flushing out the shadows in the fog with light. Yet, their hooks got in, already embedding themselves into my heart, echoing what I didn't want to feel. Then, a strong emotion took hold and blindsided me without my knowing.

Greed.

Being with Ji Woon, I didn't want to let go. I shouldn't be happy by his side. His sister died because of me. Ji Woon was Miyako's, and I took him from her. When I watched him walking back to me with that bag of hot buns and a shy smile on his face, my resolve melted.

I took his food. I laughed at his lame jokes because I knew he wanted to hide. He needed me. I could be his sponge, soaking up his pain.

It seemed vain to believe that only I could save Park Ji Woon. I wanted to believe without me, he'd fall. I was his knight, his protector. And, whether it was his hand on mine, his thigh, or his arm brushing against mine, he drove me crazy.

Even if I were given a do-over, I wouldn't change a thing. All those treacherous roads led to this. Fate drove us here. Miyako had to die for this meeting to happen. Much as I wanted to pretend to be a better person, I couldn't deny my greed.

Park Ji Woon was the first person to incite my interest in the opposite sex. Gravity pulled me to him. With him, I could let go of my past and trauma. To live in the now. For these reasons alone, I stayed because Ji Woon was my raft and my path to salvation.

17

The sky was still bright despite being seven, and the air was less hot and humid. My back cooled with the fresh breeze blowing from the Han River, and after a nice walk from the subway, we felt refreshed.

Ji Woon picked up his backpack at the reception desk, and we went up to my room to shower. I showered first, then he did. With the warm water and soap, the last evidence of today's terrors was finally erased.

We each sat on one of the two single beds in my small room, wringing our hands. A long, awkward silence stretched as our eyes kept meeting, and our bodies kept fidgeting.

"Wanna walk?" He stood up suddenly, and I bolted for the door.

We wandered around - to the gym, rooftop garden, restaurants, shops, but ultimately, our feet still led us back to the scene of the crime.

I could see the scene unfolding. Ghostly images of the little European girl sitting next to me, when Miyako's blood splattered over her face, screaming. The Indian couple who were in the pool closest to where Miyako's intestines fell struggled to get out, adding to the stampede of guests being pushed and knocked aside. The hotel staff, a few years older than Ji Woon and meMe, were frozen on the spot, their faces stark and horrified.

They would never forget this day, and neither would we.

The swimming pool should be closed for the rest of the day. Instead, we found ourselves walking into the humid space, our rubber shoes squeaking on the tiles after passing through the double doors.

There were no signs, no warning to stay away, nothing to show that hours ago, someone had died here. Everything was cleaned up and back in order as if it were any other ordinary day.

Above our heads was the gold oval light fixture, crowning the twenty-meter rectangular heated pool, which reflected its image in the water in blue and yellow ripples. Through the large wall-to-ceiling windows flanking the East and the West sides, the view of the city lights sparkled.

It was eight p.m., and the large pool area was empty except for an American couple soaking in the hot tub in the back.

I breathed in the humid, chlorinated air while Ji Woon knelt and wiped the spot where Miyako had lain earlier. The hotel did an excellent job of cleaning. Every grove was white and pristine. It was unfortunate that Miyako's fate was sealed by the act of chasing after my father. If only she had stayed away, she would be alive today.

Flashes of her last moments appeared in my mind. In slow-mo, I saw her arms cartwheeled, and the knife turning inward, slicing deep into her abdomen before she hit the ground. Seconds split between breaths, the minute difference of life versus death.

I wished I knew her plans. I could have stopped her. But regrets were easy after the fact, and the past was impossible to change.

A sound, raw and guttural, dredged from a place deep within, shook me. It reverberated into my body and out around. His hands were balled tight, and his face scrunched up with tears. When he saw me looking, he tried to turn away. I watched him struggle, pushing back his grief, but his shoulders could not hide his pain.

"It's okay to cry," I reached over and wrapped my short arms around his waist, absorbing the emotional spillage while it burned through my skin, melting my flesh and engulfing my heart with his flames.

No words I said were going to soothe him. After years of post-trauma therapy, nothing anyone said to me ever healed my heart. His warm, angry tears drenched my shirt. I wanted to cry with him, but I could not. As more years went by, the emptier I got. Each time I poured out my feelings in therapy, it became worse.

I had my defense mechanism in my heart to separate the burden of my emotions from my mind. My multiple personalities existed for this. This chasm between them and me protected my core and saved me from the cuts I bore from living with guilt.

"Come, let's sit there." I pointed to the deck chairs hidden in the corner behind a pillar. We moved from the pool floor to the chairs facing out to the city. In the darkness of the indoor pool, the lights from the city were falling stars.

Ji Woon captured my hand as his head dropped on my shoulder and sighed.

"Thanks," he murmured.

I didn't reply.

"Thanks for staying with me today." He continued.

I nodded. Guilt gripped my tongue, and my stomach churned with indecision.

He brushed his eyes with the back of his hand. "I met *Miyako Noona* when I was ten after starting Taekwondo class. My step-mother was busy with my baby brother, so I would hang out at the *Taekwondo dojang* every day after school. *Miyako Noona* was our Sensei's assistant and taught the kids with orange belts…"

I handed him a water bottle, and he took a long drink. I waited for him to continue, watching his shoulders struggle to stay straight. He leaned back in his chair, threaded his fingers with mine, and smiled sadly.

"One day, Sensei told me to pick up some papers from *Miyako Noona's* locker. In it was a family photograph of my mother and *Noona's* father. I was shocked. Growing up, my relatives used to whisper bad things about my father and the woman who destroyed him. The vixen who gave birth to me and died. I realized then, when I saw a snapshot of me in my gi below the family photograph, that Noona knew who I was."

"So those people at the hospital are her family?"

"Yes. My father was eighteen when he fell in love with his Japanese teacher. They were ten years apart. She was Miyako's mother."

"I see." I focused on rubbing his cold arm, not wanting him to see anything in my reaction that might hurt him more. Others might judge, but I had absolutely no right.

"She was pregnant with me the first year my father was in college, and her husband, that Japanese man you met, learned of it and kicked her out."

Ji Woon stared out the window - his hand clenching and unclenching in mine. "My family pulled my father out of college and sent him to military service. In South Korea, the military is mandatory. My mother lived alone with a nurse, and my father was stuck in the military camp when he heard about her complications. He wasn't there when she died giving birth to me."

I climbed into his chair, slipped under his arms, and wrapped myself around his waist. "I'm sorry." I put my head on his chest. This was the best I could do.

He dropped his chin on my head. "I'm a reminder of my father's failure — his embarrassment." He choked up. "*Miyako Noona* isn't easy to talk to, but she is my only family."

"You had a family." I let the painful memories come in with the swirling hurt.

He glanced down and pulled my lip out from under my teeth.

"I have no one. My family hates me. My twin sister died at birth, and my mother thinks I killed her. Nothing I do can change her mind. Sometimes, I wish I were the one who died."

He hugged me.

"I'm making things worse.", I muttered.

"No." He tucked my stray hair behind my ear and stared deep into my eyes. "I wonder why I am born too."

The air between us thinned, and I opened my mouth to breathe.

His gaze drifted to my lips and then finally back to my eyes. "I kept thinking about that day at the market. I wanted to ask for your number too. I regretted letting you go."

His hands were on my bare arms. My body buzzed with his touch. I drank in his scent, filled my heart with his words, and warmed under his sorrowful eyes.

He smiled. "Did you know? I searched the hotels nearby because I wanted to see you again."

"Why?" I asked.

He kissed my forehead. Shockwaves skidded throughout my

body. A soft gasp escaped my lips. We were friends, comrades in tragedy. Grief brought us close. Therapy taught me to let others in. Holding and touching each other to soothe our pain was normal.

"When I first saw you, I felt you and I were the same. It isn't your fault you want to live," he whispered.

I leaned into him till our foreheads touched. The humming of the pool filter and the lapping water receded. The world grew distant as our hearts rose fast, lifting into the clouds. The older couple left an hour ago. There was no one to stop us. No reason not to give in.

His mouth dropped first, closing the gap between us, and daring me to pull away. And when I didn't, he crushed his lips onto mine as we closed our eyes. Sparks rippled across my body, charging every molecule in its path. Desire fueled my hands as my fingers slipped under his shirt and ran onto his smooth back.

He pulled away, sucking in his breath as his hot gaze shot through mine. Before I could breathe again, he cupped my cheeks and kissed me hard. Savoring my upper lip, and when I kissed him back, he groaned and devoured mine. Our tongues clashed, fighting for dominance as his hands explored eagerly. We were opposites. His body was long, strong, and lean, while mine was soft, silky, and curvy.

One of his hands threaded through my hair and held my head while his other slipped under my blouse. His fingers stroked my bare skin under my bra, leaving tingling sensations where he roamed. Drunk by his attention, I let him pull off my blouse and coyly uncovered my hands for him to stare at my breasts cushioned in white lace.

"Can I?" he asked, and I nodded with heated cheeks.

He swooped in to kiss me hungrily and then lifted his mouth

to nibble my neck, letting his tongue trace down my collarbone to my full breasts. Large hands squeezed and massaged, and then took me in turns with his mouth.

"Wait…" I panted and pushed him up. He threw off his shirt and braced his arms, trapping me between him. His pale chest was broad, ripped, and strong. Adding to his face and smarts, he was perfect.

I became shy, but he kissed and coaxed me to untangle my arms, and when I wouldn't, he pointed at my heart-shaped scar on my right shoulder.

"What's that?" The heart-shaped scar curved over the edge of my shoulder like the melting of time. I flexed my arm up and showed him its full puckered state proudly.

He didn't speak. He was staring at it transfixed.

My walls were built back at a rapid speed. He must hate it, I thought. I cursed myself for forgetting. To some people, scars could be ugly. I stepped too close to the sun, and the wax was melting.

"Can I touch it?" he asked suddenly, with seriousness.

I closed my eyes, holding my breath, nodding. The pads of his fingertips gently ran over the embossed skin of my scar. "It feels cold," he murmured, and then he put his lips on it.

I gasped loudly.

"Does it hurt?" His voice was low and sexy. He licked my scar and nibbled my neck.

A flood of warm heat gushed between my legs, and I shuddered at the series of waves lapping over my body. The smirk on his face made my ears burn, but my need was great. I pushed my body against his. "I want you…."

"How much?" He smiled with those bedroom eyes. "Show me."

The heady sensations clouded my mind. I didn't want him to

think I was inexperienced. My hands ran down his smooth, muscled back, and I kissed him hard. "This much."

He pulled away gently, smiling down. "Alice, is this your first?"

My face heated up, and I nodded shyly, for once wishing for Merle's experience. My fingers trembled as I touched him again. Flicking his pebbled nipples and hearing him groan. I was scared, curious, and strangely powerful. Then, I bravely reached down and grabbed him.

He knocked my hand off as if I had burned. "Don't." His voice was hoarse. "Unless you don't want me to stop."

I reached for him again, and this time, he didn't flinch. His head dropped, and he kissed me like he was drowning, kicking off his pants while helping with mine.

I could have said, 'no' to him and knew he'd respect that.

Ji Woon was nineteen, and today, I turned seventeen. Many of my classmates had their first sex. Merle lost her virginity to Ryan, Bailey's intern, and I could have waited till I was ready. Maybe I met a boy I liked enough to be my first. But, he wouldn't be Park Ji Woon. After today, we were soldiers who saw death, fighting with bloody hands and failing.

This overwhelming feeling, this intensity, the fire in my heart — I wanted it to last. For just once, I felt alive. I told myself tonight would become a beacon I could look back on fondly, and I knew this was my choice, not Merle's or any of the others, but mine.

It wasn't out of pity because he had lost someone he cared about. It wasn't to pay back for what I had done to his family. I won't deny that I wanted to ease his pain. To see him smile when we were together before the lies and betrayal pulled us apart.

He swiped a condom out, and I watched nervously as he put it on. I didn't ask him why he had one in his wallet. Maybe it was something that all boys did at our age. Hoping and praying they could get some, never knowing when that might happen.

Again, he retook my lips. The heat from him was a flaming torch in my fog. I ran to it, chased by my ghosts. Then, he climbed above me and spread my thighs. Spit in one hand, lubricating his path, and then slowly, he pushed himself in as I whimpered at his largeness in my tight space. He shifted, lifting my hips and gently pushing in more as he kissed and whispered into my ear. "Alice, you're so beautiful, and so brave. Alicemy Alice."

I arched up to meet him with tears in my eyes.

"You're mine." He pressed his lips on my mouth and plunged in.

I screamed. Pain tore my insides. Another face replaced his — large and red, scarred and menacing. He cackled. Laughing as I cried for someone to save me. Laughing as my little heart tore to shreds, abandoned by the ones who were supposed to protect me.

Ji Woon kissed my lips gently and then my eyelids. The delicious taste of Ji Woon chased away my nightmare. My heart swelled with my love for him.

"Does it hurt a lot?" he asked tenderly, brushing my wet eyes.

I stared right into his worried gaze. I watched his face with arousal and felt him big and stiff in me. Ji Woon's beautiful face had replaced that scary one in my head.

"I'll pull out," he said, leaning back.

I grabbed his arms. "Don't."

He kissed my lips and then my neck, trailing down to my breasts till I moaned and pushed against him again.

"It'll get better, I promise." He began to move, grabbing my hips. Soon, his movements and mine became more hurried, and our moans more frantic. I wrapped my legs and squeezed his waist when the urgency between us reached a fevered pitch. My body, which was torn earlier, hummed with life as his smooth muscles rubbed against my soft flesh.

Suddenly, his lips were on my heart-shaped scar, and he bit me.

My mind exploded. The cord that bound me broke. I flew, shooting off tangent out of orbit and free.

He covered my mouth with his lips as I screamed. My nails raked his back, and he grunted and came after me. We collapsed back onto the deck chair. Our breath ragged, and bodies slick with sweat and the scent of sex.

He threaded his fingers with mine as we fell back to earth. In a ragged breath, I turned to him. "That wasn't so bad."

He smiled, and so did I.

———————

The elevator door pinged, and the doors cranked open. Ji Woon and I stepped out, hand in hand. Although we could barely look at each other without stumbling over our words, he refused to let go. Each breath I took was filled with the scent of him and the memories of what we had done. My face flushed with the memories of his lips exploring what no one had seen, followed by his body joining with mine. My heart raced at warp speed, and his hand accidentally brushed against my thigh, causing me to jolt.

"Sorry," he blurted, his face red as his lips tried on a smile.

I let my eyes trail up his lips to his forehead, avoiding his eyes. "It's okay…." I murmured.

We entered my room and I grabbed my PJs from the dresser, rushed into the bathroom, and locked the door. When I came out, he was sitting by the window with his hands clasped. His gaze locked onto mine.

"Come here." He gestured with his hand.

I swallowed and did as he asked. Barely a foot away, he reached for my hands and pulled me into his arms. With a huge sigh, he kissed my head. "Will you be my girlfriend?"

I choked back my tears. At some point, he would run like everyone because those who saw me change always backed away in fear.

He'd be the same. And, I was the reason his sister died.

My guilt hung heavily around my neck. This was the cross I bore. That was why, when I was in the shower, I came up with excuses, reasons to make him leave.

"Why?" I asked.

«Hmm…" He wrapped his arms around my waist and breathed into my hair. "You're brave."

I shook my head hard. "I'm not brave."

"I'm serious. I've fallen for you." He stared at me like a man craving water after a week of being lost in a desert. At this point, nothing mattered more to me than what he thought. There was power in this. His devotion pulled me up. For the first time in my life, I felt I could change. His belief could make me fly.

"I love you, Alice." Instead of running away, Park Ji Woon was giving me his heart.

I imagined. His heart beating, engorged, dripping with blood. I held it firmly in my hand, gleefully and proudly.

My first confession.

"Lucky you! Congrats on snagging a handsome one! Use him, then lose him," Said another.

Park Ji Woon thought he loved me. He said those words I desperately craved.

Greed. This feeling was new. I'd fight tooth and nail with Merle and the rest just to hear him say it again. For him, I was willing to try anything.

Why? Because really, who else would love a monster?

18

Sleep clutched on the edges of our eyelids. With the shades pulled down, my hotel room was darker than a cave in winter. The sound of the air conditioner hummed softly in the background, lulling us into a dreamlike state.

We made love again and kept talking for hours. He asked me about my life in Kansas, and I told him about my parents, the bullying, and prejudice while avoiding my mind gaps, Merle, and the voices.

Ji Woon told me of his life growing up as the bastard child, always being compared to his almost perfect father, and his promise to himself that he would prove them all wrong.

The tumor in his brain, which they found out about a week ago, was a setback to his plans. It was his father's idea to ask *Miyako Noona* for help. That night, he was supposed to meet Dr. Harris, but his grandmother, the Park matriarch, fainted. Everyone was called to her hospital bed. I could tell from his tone that although he despised that hard, stubborn woman who took him in when his mother died, there was respect in his description of her, who was the kingmaker in the Park Entertainment group, unlike her useless husband and sons.

With Ji Woon's arm around my shoulder and his body plastered on mine, it was easy to fall into a bubble of happiness. His warmth cuddled my empty heart, and his voice filled my thoughts with hope.

I didn't want this to end. But, I didn't know when my parents might come over, and the anxiety of that confrontation churned in the pits of my stomach, adding to the glee of the voices I tried to ignore. I was no longer confident that I could stop Merle, Peter, or the others from coming in my tired state. If I could have one wish for my birthday, it would be to hide the truth from Ji Woon till I leave Seoul.

"My mother might be coming back." I lifted my head from his shoulder and fought with him, smiling as he grappled to hold me back. Throughout this entire time, Ji Woon had been under the impression that my mother was at the hospital with a sick relative. Another lie, which I had to tell to hide the truth.

He sighed, running his finger over my heart scar, adding ripples of desire zapping through my body.

I squirmed, and he cupped my chin, pulling me in for a deep kiss. He knew he got me good; the sexy smirk on his face showed it.

„Ji Woon…please."

"Okay…okay. I'll let you go for now." He kissed my forehead and sighed some more, and then lifted me up and off the bed, gently placing my feet on the ground. "I have to go too."

He picked up his phone from the side table and stood up. His fingers scrolled through his messages and then met my gaze. The sorrow that I thought I had erased came barging back.

"They're going to cremate her today." His voice was soft and tense.

"That quick?" I asked, smoothing the sheets on my bed nervously.

"Yes." He ran his hands through his hair. "I'm going to crash it."

"I'll go with you," I blurted. To hell with consequences and lies.

He placed his hand on my head. "No, don't. It's going to be bad." He stroked my head.

I took his hand and pressed his palm on my chest above my heart. "We can bear it together." I insisted.

His phone beeped suddenly, and his brow furrowed at the message. "I'm serious. Don't come. My father is going too."

"He is?" I mirrored his frown.

He nodded, showing me his phone. Although I couldn't read the Korean characters, I sensed the meaning of the text.

"Why is he doing this?" He looked puzzled at his phone. "He never cared about Miyako. He hated the Shimas."

"How can I help?" I asked nervously.

Ji Woon ruffled my hair and smiled with his eyes. "Alice, you have done enough. I have you. What more do I need?"

I bit my lip hard. Yeah, sure, because I knew I was making it worse. After chatting with him, I could get a sense of what he was like. A guy like him was black and white. A planner who likes things in control, with a box for each little thing. If Ji Woon found out I lied, there would be no forgiveness. The guilt and shame came ten times heavier after we made love for hours. Because of Miyako, I found Ji Woon, and I don't regret it.

My mouth was acidic each time I opened it to speak. The echo of bees enveloped my mind, buzzing as this happiness came to an end. Gravity pulled me down into the depths of my evilness — I was splitting, and Miyako was forming. Her personality expanded to encompass what I knew about her and what Ji Woon had told me, taking shape in my mind as an image of her.

I tried to stop it, persuading myself that her death was an accident. It was my father's actions, not mine. However, as he read through the messages about Miyako on his phone, I saw that he blamed himself.

It wasn't his fault.

It was mine.

And because he did, so did I. The guilt expanded into a massive dark cloud. The storm was coming. Lightning sizzled, and thunder boomed. Fire flared as the heat consumed my thoughts. The final part was completed. Miyako's presence was in my head, and my body reacted to her. The others in my head laughed, rejoicing at my failure.

She was coming out. My skin stretched, and my bones cracked to elongate my limbs. I jumped out of my bed and grabbed Ji Woon's backpack.

"Go!" I rushed to the door. He looked startled for a second and then caught up with me. "Hurry before your father changes his mind. Clear this up. I'll wait for you here."

He took his bag from me in confusion.

I kissed him hard. Our lips made a smacking sound when we parted. Love beamed on his face as he cupped my cheek tenderly. I flung the door open and peered out into the hallway. The coast was clear. "Call me later."

"I will." He smiled and bent down, kissing my lips again. "My dear Alice, *saranghae*."

My face flushed.

He kissed me where he left a hickey beside my heart scar. "I'll call you as soon as I'm done. Naekkeoya." He ruffled my hair before stepping aside.

"Later…" I gritted my teeth against the ringing pitch in my ears and passed on a smile.

He waved and left quickly.

As soon as the door closed, I turned into Shima Miyako.

19

Four hours later

I opened my eyes to the sounds of people talking. Words that I didn't understand because they were Korean peppered the air. My stomach sank as I watched them pass in their black garbs and white sashes on their sleeves. Others in prim suits and black shoes walked softly along the white halls with faces pale with grief.

I wished I were in Kansas. Bailey promised that I was getting better. I thought I was, and now I was back to square one.

Flashes of what she did seeped through the cracks into my mind. I saw Miyako's reflection in a window as she got out of the cab. A flyer from her music hall with an invitation to her funeral in her hand, shocked faces of those who saw her, some people screaming, an uproar in the hallway, some fainting as Miyako passed. Miyako, who was supposed to be dead. Wandering down these halls — a ghost resurrected.

The damage was done. She vanished, and I was back to picking up the pieces. I checked my phone. Four hours. I was gone for four hours. The world spun as I staggered along, searching for the light at the end of the tunnel of closed doors.

"Sorry!" A woman squeaked after the wheels of her cart ran over my foot, and the bowls in the cart clattered, spilled over, and onto my T-shirt and jeans.

I glared at her, and when I saw her tear-stained face, I held back the fire in my breath. She was about my age, but the resemblance to Miyako was uncanny.

Footsteps followed her. "Sayako-san, let me help…" The woman and I turned to the voice.

"Alice?" He froze.

„Ji Woon…" I flushed instantly. He was handsome in his black suit and combed-back hair — mature and powerful, unlike the college student I had been with just hours ago.

We were two worlds apart.

"Is she your friend?" The pretty young teen asked in Japanese and gave me a begrudging side look, making me wish I could disappear.

"I got them from the kitchen. You can take these." He pushed his cart of hot soup to her and grabbed my arm.

I followed him with my heart dropping further after each step, ignoring the mourners who glared at my smelly casual clothes and harsh whispers.

He led me to an empty backroom and closed the door.

"I'm sorry…you told me not to come." I squeezed my eyes to hold back my tears.

He cupped my cheeks with his cold hands and stared into my eyes. "It's okay." Then, he opened a wardrobe and searched through the piles of black cloth. He lifted one. A mourning dress. "This should fit. There's a sink over there. I'll wait for you outside." He gestured to the door and turned to leave.

I grabbed his arm. "Ji Woon…wait." The grey workroom with its yellow-stained windows was creepy. My hair stood on end. Death haunted the dusty corners. "Stay…"

A soft smile lifted his lips, and he bent to kiss the top of my head. "Do you need help? I can undress you if you like." His eyes glinted with mischief.

My ears burned. "Stop it."

He smiled warmly. His eyes dropped to my chest.

I fake-punched him, and he pretended to scowl. "Turn around!" And he turned swiftly. "And, don't…Move!" I heard him chuckle as I quickly but carefully pulled off my food-stained clothes.

I cleared my throat. "I'm done."

He twisted my wavy brown hair into a bun and stuck a chopstick to hold it up. Then, he kissed my cheek and laughed when I missed slapping his shoulder. His fingers threaded into mine, and he pulled me into a tight hug. "No, I'm happy you're here. You bring the sun with you."

"Eww." I scrunched my nose as I washed my hands.

We smiled. Our moods instantly lifted. "Come." He tapped my chin. "I've something to show you." We strode hand in hand, smiling from cheek to cheek. "It's a good thing you came." His words dropped into a whisper.

"Did her father and grandmother chase you out?"

"I dropped to my knees and begged."

I breathed out. "I'm sorry…"

He gave a fake smile. "Why? It's not your fault."

But it was. I lied, and Michael Harris got away scot-free. The voices hissed in my head. I blinked back my tears.

"I should have stopped *Noona* from meeting that asshole. I

shouldn't have told her about my tumor." He pushed the two glass doors out.

I stepped in front of him, pulled his hands to my waist, and hugged him tight.

He kissed my lips, gently at first and then with hunger.

I wasn't the hero he believed I was. I wished I were. For him, I would do anything. For his love, I would be better. Fight harder for my right to exist.

"You have to see this." He turned me around to face the garden. The morning sun lit the pebbled ground in dappled gold, streaming in through a frosted glass ceiling onto the foot of a monolith carved in marble white. Above the stone, a forest of maple trees with pale, veined leaves, ethereal with their thin branches like hands seeking forgiveness in a secret grove spring.

I gasped, my heart warmed in his love. "It's so beautiful."

He smiled and captured my hands. "I knew you'd like it. I'll show you more things like this in Seoul. We'll celebrate your birthday tonight." I was about to reply when I saw them through the glass walls.

Three men fighting — my father, Miyako's dad, and Ji Woon's. The two Asian men pounced on him, and he shook them off like a polar bear, throwing Miyako's father at us. The glass wall shuddered, and my father stared at us in shock.

"Go!" Ji Woon stretched his arms out in front of me as my father stormed through the glass door for us.

The truth was out. I won't be forgiven. My walls collapsed, as the voices screeched and they broke free.

Michael Harris's brows furrowed like curled whips. He saw my change, pushed past Ji Woon, and grabbed my arms. "Why are you here?" His voice bellowed like thunder.

Ji Woon fought back, and my father pawed him off. When Ji Woon attacked again, my father flipped him over like a sack of potatoes. Against the fury of my father, no man was a match.

Injured Ji Woon watched in horror as my father picked me up and tossed me over his shoulders. In less than twenty-four hours, my first love ended.

Alice

20

SAN FRANCISCO
October 2017, Nine years later

My thoughts drifting in the cold, floating in the stillness of the room, were oddly comforting and at peace. Then, breaking my dream-like state came the sounds of sleep interruption.

A man was snoring beside me. I jerked up and scanned in trepidation as I adjusted to the scene of her crime. A chill ran across my naked back, with a thin sheet covering my breasts, wet with musky sweat.

Knowledge was power. Her knowing what I didn't was more terrifying than the stranger with his broad back facing me. Twenty-four years passed, and Merle still knew how to give a good scare. Luckily, my sister always had good taste in men. Appearance mattered when she chose to procreate. Her new conquest had smooth, defined muscles and a tight ass. He slept like a baby, defenseless and trusting. However, from my past experiences, her lovers tended to be monsters when they woke.

I dreamt of Ji Woon again.

The pained look and betrayal on his face as I was lugged away like a piece of luggage. There wasn't time to explain the letter I left behind, so I wondered if he had read it or if he hadn't, and why he hadn't replied. My phone was confiscated the second I got back to the hotel, and Michael wasted no time in packing. My mother and I took the next flight home.

That was the past, almost a decade, and yet it felt like yesterday I was back as my teenage self, hoping for a future that wasn't mine. I should get over Park Ji Woon. The years went by in a snap, and I made progress against Merle and the voices, except now.

The king-sized bed had silk sheets. The walls were gold-patterned, and lacquered wood cabinets held a minibar. On one wall was a large TV, and to the side of it was an open bathtub and shower, as well as an additional living area in the next room.

I slid off the bed quickly, forgoing the sheet tangled with his long legs, and hurriedly put on what I assumed were my clothes.

Red lacy bra and thongs, a slinky, high-cut red dress that clung to my body like snakeskin, and deadly six-inch heels that I would never wear. These weren't the type of clothing for a third-year resident neurosurgeon. Aside from the clothes and underwear strewn on the hotel carpet floor, there were close to thirty wads of cash casually tossed about and a loaded gun on the side table.

This was bad.

Merle liked to push my limits. She relished in taunting my boring life with the risks she loved and raising the bar of my tolerance. The man in the bed must be Nikolai Ivanov, the only son and heir to a Russian mob that governs the Tri-State New York area. It appeared that she flew him over this weekend for a rendezvous.

She made her point. She wanted me to leave San Francisco and finish my medical residency in Kansas, but I kept refusing. Michael Harris was in Kansas. Because of him, that was the last place I wanted to live. So, my sister decided to up her threat.

After a twenty-minute cab ride, I was home. I rushed to my bathroom and forced myself to puke. I got into the shower and scrubbed every pore and every nook of my body till I was pink. It was close to four a.m. I needed to wait till the pharmacy opened at eight to get the morning-after pill. Usually, Merle was careful, but I never knew how far Merle would go. Being pregnant now was more of a disadvantage to me than to her.

My phone beeped. A text came in from Nikolai, whom Merle must have added.

Nick: Babe, where did you go?

Me: Merle's gone.

Nick: Oh. You're Alice!

Nick: Here's the vid Merle wanted you to see.

I tapped on the video Nikolai sent. Instantly, I saw her smiling face in the camera.

"You had a wild night, didn't you, Alice? You and I make an awesome fucking pair." Merle, my twin, chuckled.

Merle's hair was darker and straighter, and her eyes turned black when she was excited. She looked more Asian and was tanner and slimmer than I was. "Congrats on your first one-night stand! How did you like that stranger's dick?" She roared with laughter, with Nick hooting in the background.

"What about me? What's my reward, babe? Watching them go at it makes me horny." Nikolai came into frame bare-chested, showing his broad shoulders and six-pack, giving a sloppy, sexy smile.

"You'll get some soon." She patted his cheek. "Nicky says you liked it missionary. That's so boring." Merle smirked.

"That guy she picked up was a beast! Babe, those angles are worth the Oscars! I'll get a million views for that ass!" They laughed, and the camera shifted to a naked Asian man lying on a bed.

It was dim and hard to make out his face as he was flat on his stomach, but Nick was right about his body. He wasn't as built as Nick, but the Asian guy was lean with broad shoulders and muscled in all the right places. On his tailbone was a blue-grey mark, except mine was a heart shape on my shoulder. Merle climbed onto the man's back and threw off her red dress.

I watched the other videos Nick sent. Trying to focus on the stranger we met. Merle slid into a booth to chat after she spotted his friend leaving. Rainbow lights bounced off the floor and ceiling, and the thick scent of pheromones, musk, and sweat filled the tight, dark room, accompanied by loud music.

The Asian man, who didn't look like a fuckboy, was asking her questions. Handsome with sharp features, with the spotlight wavering, was somewhat familiar and not. Nick came by armed with drinks. Merle downed a glass of hard liquor before switching back with me. When I woke, I was forced to drink, and the last thing I remembered was that both the stranger guy and I were drugged and dragged away by Nick's guys.

"Ready for a threesome, Alice?" Merle turned the camera to the sleeping guy as she ran her hands over the comatose Asian man's firm ass, giving it a good slap. She pulled out a dagger and ran it over his neck. "What do you think would happen if I slid his throat? Think you can get away this time?" Her eyes glittered with malice. "I can go far. Can you? Give me Kansas."

My twin sneered into the camera. "Or next time, it won't just be a one-night stand."

The video ended in a snap. My phone beeped again. Another text came in.

Nick: Call me when you're in New York.

I threw my phone and heard a crack. The threat worked. Merle won. That bitch.

21

KANSAS

November 2018, A year later

Chief Surgeon Dr. Michael Harris's office was stark, empty, and cold as his heart. The past decade did not change his taste. His room was monochrome, from his black table to his white walls and grey couch.

His bookshelf held five books and a glass case containing a blue-white Ming pot of a dragon rising from the water. The ten-grand pot was a set of four — a gift from my mother for each of us. A reminder that even in death, we are chained by our past.

Rumors were that after my parents' divorce, Michael became an alcoholic and admitted himself to rehab. Another said he was in Europe performing brain surgery under a different name. A crazy one said he started a secret lab with billions in funding, using prisoners as live human experiments.

Whatever the story was, it didn't matter because Michael was dead to me. Neither my mother nor I saw him until I graduated from UCSF Medical School Summa Cum Laude, and last year, when he gave the commencement speech for my graduating class.

He aged with perfect ease and confidence. Even my mother, whose wrinkles etched her once porcelain skin, was acting flirty. The incident in Seoul was swept aside, and Harris remained steadfast in his goals. As expected, he rose from the ashes and was more arrogant and stubborn than before.

I was getting better at stopping the voices. A day, a month, or even more of regaining lost time was something I could live with.

But ever since I returned to Kansas, my efforts to keep Merle and the voices out were failing. The closer I was to Michael, the harder it was to remain calm. The signs of them were in my apartment — bags of expensive clothes, a new black credit card, boxes of fireworks, a punching bag and boxing gloves, a wickedly embalmed cat, a coffee maker, a drug lab, and a BMW outside with a gaudy license plate that said "Sweetie." This was Merle's and others' doing.

I clenched my hands on my lap. Today's meeting with Michael, I used the daughter card. I had no choice.

Two lives were at stake, and one was an innocent, unborn baby.

"The risk is over ninety percent that Ellen Han's body would react with that drug," I said.

Michael took off his glasses and cleaned them as I tried not to fidget in my seat. He knew he had the upper hand. I finally admitted that I was his daughter. The hospital gossip spread like wildfire. Our last names were different, and with my looks, it was hard to tell. On my first day at work, I met him here. I made it clear I didn't want anyone to know. I had a father, and his name was David Steeple.

"I believe Dr. Thompson weighed the pros and cons of this prescription."

"Both Ellen Han and her baby could die. We don't know how severely she might react to the drug."

"Her husband signed the waiver and knew the risks."

I dropped my analysis of the drug on the table. He didn't pick it up.

"Solacoyin could cause epilepsy. In her condition and with her expectations, this is extremely dangerous. It's an experimental drug, and the FDA barely approved it last week. There aren't enough case studies to prove that it will remove her infection. We could continue the same prescription suggested by Dr. Kahn and increase the dosage of the two drugs in conjunction to stop the leak." I paused and considered my words. "There are rumors that Dr. Thompson is pushing Solacoyin because of PharmaTech. Maybe you should reconsider hiring him as Head of Neurology."

His brows twitched. Did I push too far? Time made me forget Michael's pet peeve. He hated to be contradicted, especially by women.

He crossed his arms. "Dr. Thompson has been fully vetted. His years of experience and excellent referrals make him the best candidate for the role." He stood up. "We're one of the nation's best research facilities."

I gritted my teeth. "Thompson's in bed with them. Big pharma."

He slammed his hand on the table. "You disappoint me." His words came as a slap. "You're a medical resident. Your job is to listen and learn. If you wish to stay in any department here, you need to follow rank."

Rank. To him, it was always about who held power. Being strong mattered everything. Merle was like him, and I was the weak one and his sole embarrassment.

The heart machine beeped as I made my rounds the next day. The ward was filled with the sounds of patients snoring, and the air conditioner hissed, adding music to the other sounds in a running hospital.

The morning was the best time. Outside, the day was slowly brightening, and if I stepped out, I knew I would hear the birds chirping in the trees. I stifled a yawn and checked my list. A few more to go, and I could call it a day. For three days in a row, I took on the day and night shifts — adding one to cover for a senior, and last night, every resident in neurosurgery was called in for a three-truck pile-up resulting in eight ER patients with head injuries.

I yawned again and peered inside to check on my final patient. Ellen Han was sleeping with an oxygen mask over her face. She was seven months pregnant, and the bulge on her stomach wobbled like a beach ball as she breathed. Last evening, her husband, Sergeant James Han, left by helicopter from the helipad. I overheard him telling his parents that he was trying to delay his posting to Afghanistan next week.

Three days ago, when she was visiting her in-laws with her family, she slipped down the stairs. Emergency medics brought her to our hospital, and our doctors found a brain aneurysm in her prefrontal cortex. The blood leaking into her brain wouldn't coagulate, and my mentor, Dr. Thompson, suggested using Solacoyin, a trial drug used for clotting.

I fought against the drug and loudly voiced the dangers. I wasn't alone. The doctors who sided with me were not as well-connected as my mentor, who supported the Chief Surgeon, Dr. Michael Harris. No one in Kansas City Hospital knew of our family connection till I forced a meeting yesterday.

Ellen's daughter, Sophie, was sleeping beside her. She was petite like her mother. At sixteen, she was the size of a twelve-year-old. Gently, I placed a blanket over the child.

There were rumblings outside, signaling the start of the nurse rotation. Since traffic was terrible and it was too late to rush home, I decided to stay. I stumbled into the doctor's on-call room. Before I could lock my mind to keep myself safe, the buzzing started. My lungs squeezed as I fumbled for my pills. But Merle was faster, and in a flash, she took over.

Merle

22

Merle smiled as she checked herself in the mirror. She was definitely the better-looking twin. Her dark hair cascaded down her back instead of Alice's unruly curls. Men were drawn to Merle's mysterious black Asian eyes, whether lined with kohl or a wingtip. Alice never bothered with makeup. Her sister didn't care to wear the right clothes to accentuate her curves, which Merle sometimes wished she had.

She frowned as she snagged a makeup bag from the nurse's station. It wasn't fair. This body should have been Merle's. She dabbed the blood-red color on her pale lips, adding more black eyeliner to highlight her almond-shaped eyes and some tasteful contouring.

Gorgeous. She puckered her lips and searched the hallways for the hot GS doctor she saw the last time she was here. It was thrilling to make out in the linen closet, and having sex on a surgical table was on her bucket list after the Mile High Club.

She toured the wards with her doctor's coat unbuttoned, showing off a tight white turtle-neck she had taken from someone's locker, revealing her flat midriff. A few nurses and a doctor gave her a second glance, but she didn't care. Daddy was here today, and she was planning to have him treat her to lunch. As she waited for the elevator, a nurse with strawberry blonde hair came rushing out.

She glanced at Merle over and narrowed her eyes, then she spotted the name tag on Alice's doctor's coat — Dr. Steeple. "Dr. Steeple? I've been paging you! It's Ellen Han! She's relapsing."

The nurse caught her sleeve and dragged her to the patient rooms. Merle snatched her arm back.

"Get someone else! I'm off duty."

"All the doctors are in surgery." The nurse frowned. "Dr. Thompson said to give her Solacoyin, but the patient's report said Ellen Han is your patient. What should we do?"

Merle stared at the vial and syringe on the nurse's tray. She knew better than to deviate from Alice's directions. She knew nothing about medicine. Things could easily go wrong. That's why she fucking hated the hospital.

"Dr. Kahn is out sick today. Dr. Steeple?" the nurse asked.

"Did Dr. Kahn say you could increase the current dosage?" Merle was going out on a limb with the doctors' jargon. Daddy said to go with the same drugs if Merle couldn't get out of work. Also, she promised Daddy not to get involved in the hospital.

The nurse checked her tablet. "We can't give her more. It'll be dangerous for the baby." Her pager beeped. The nurse sprinted, and Merle followed closely. They dashed into the ward to the blast of screaming machines. Another nurse was trying her best to assist. Ellen Han, who was the size of a giant beach ball, had blood coming out of her nose and lips as her face turned a shade of purple.

"Doctor Steeple!" The other nurse shouted.

Merle grabbed the nurse's tablet and scanned through the notes on the Solacoyin prescription. Death was a fifty-fifty chance for the mother, who was allergic, but an eighty percent chance it was safe for the baby. She couldn't let the baby die. "Did you say Dr. Thompson and Dr. Harris approved this?"

The nurses nodded.

"Where's the prescription?" Merle scrolled through the side effects of the drug again.

The blonde one showed Merle the tray with the syringe. "It's here." The beeping was driving Merle mad, like nails on a chalkboard. Fuck.

"Do it!" Merle pushed the nurse to the patient. "Give it to her, now!"

The nurse administered the drug. Seconds later, Ellen's heartbeat slowed, and the noise stopped. More seconds passed, and the blue color was leaving Ellen Han's face.

Merle and the nurse looked at each other and smiled when Ellen's daughter came rushing in.

"Eomma!" the daughter cried, sliding to the patient's side. The moment the teenager held her mother's hand, the monitors shrieked again.

Ellen Han flapped, clutching her throat as red spots blossomed on her face, neck, and arms.

"Help! Someone help her!" the teenager cried.

Dr. Harris barged in with two more doctors in tow. Merle backed against a wall, gasping in horror as they tried to save Ellen.

"The baby!" Merle shouted, but no one heard her. "Daddy, save the baby!"

In less than thirty minutes, the mother and the baby were dead.

Ellen

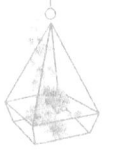

23

The next day

Ellen hugged her stomach and smiled when baby Noah kicked. Her cheeks were sticky, and the camera in her other hand was rolling, capturing the evening sky as the sun slowly set along the horizon, leaving a trail of pink, fluffy clouds.

The view from the rooftop of Kansas City Hospital was beautiful. With autumn here, the treetops were a riot of yellows, oranges, and reds.

Baby Noah kicked, and Ellen smiled lovingly. Her hair was in a tangled loose ponytail, and her hospital gown was crusty with blood.

She studied the cell phone she stole from Dr. Thompson's desk and dialed her husband's number. The phone kept ringing, but wasn't picking up. Sergeant James Han was notified of her death when he was at camp for an emergency meeting yesterday. He was probably here, somewhere.

In her hand was a bottle of wine. Hidden in a stack of medical books in Dr. Thompson's office. She giggled as she emptied it over the side.

She sighed. That was perfectly good wine, but she didn't want to risk hurting baby Noah. The scent of it was giving her a heady buzz. She was celebrating, yet the Han family was at the funeral home.

There was a number labeled Dr. Harris on the caller ID. Ellen stabbed at it. In two rings, it stopped.

"Hello?" A man answered in a low voice.

"Dr. Harris?" she giggled.

"Yes?" There was a pause. The sound of heavy breathing. "Who is this?"

"Ellen." She smirked.

"Ellen Han," his voice dropped.

She pressed her wet lips on the phone. "I have Alice. I'm taking her. This is goodbye." She crackled.

Baby Noah kicked again, sharing the joke.

She pulled her arm back over her head, looped it, and tossed the phone up and over the edge.

It was suddenly night, and a cold wind began to pick up. Ellen shivered and tottered to the edge of the roof. Below, a man in his white doctor's coat rushed out of the building with his aides to meet the emergency crew pushing a person on a stretcher. Ellen tossed the wine bottle over the guardrail right above his head and sauntered to the elevator with a smile.

Peter

24

A week later

The fire burned gleefully. Peter danced, scooting sideways and clapping his hands, grinning from cheek to cheek to the music in his head. His blonde hair was sculpted up, reflecting the flames in orange spikes. Standing straight with his pale, bony shoulders squared, he moved his arms like an inflatable dancing man. He loved the feel of the heat as it ran its fiery fingers across his skin and warmed his heart.

The fire ate the little shed in the backyard. The Shed of Horrors was Merle's and the others'. It held their morbid collection of bones and jars of preserved flesh, Mrs. Johnson's embalmed cat, some toy collectibles, and racks of clothing from many seasons. Flames rose in the air in languid waves, spreading fast in the dry air, engorging themselves on the wood, bones, animal skins, and cotton.

They would be furious. The thought of them shouting and cursing made Peter happier. Happy enough to say burning this shed was the best present he could ever give the girl he loved.

Alice. Sweet, kind Alice who wore her heart on her sleeve. Merle and the others didn't treasure her as much as Peter did. The messages he left behind, the notes and drawings he sketched, professing his love. Although she hated Peter lighting things up, he knew deep down she loved his gestures — his grand show of affection, unleashing revenge on those who harmed and insulted his precious girl.

No one cared for Alice as much as Peter did. If it made Alice happier that she didn't want to thank him, that was okay. Peter didn't need much. Dad gave him whatever he wanted, and being able to sleep on Alice's bed and breathe in her scent was enough to keep him going.

Alice was now an adult, while he remained the same. He wished he could love Alice like a man loved a woman. He often imagined them together and left a little of himself behind. That made Alice scared, and Peter knew she hated him leaving his body fluids, but his impulses were hard to control. After all, he was a hot-blooded young man. Things usually got awkward after she woke, and then, they were no longer friends. But Alice always forgave him after he did something good. They were tied together, like it or not — now and forever.

His mind wandered to Alice's plane ticket to San Francisco and her resignation letter on her desk. He was disappointed in Dad. Hurting Alice was hurting Peter, too.

Why was Dad always mean to Alice when he loved the rest of them? It was a sore point that always bugged him over the years.

The fire exploded and rained onto the rooftop of their farm home. Rainbow sparks lit the air, and the sizzling sounded like a cat purring between his legs. Now their old childhood house was burning too. The gazebo with those wisterias that Okaasan loved fell in one swoop. It raced at breakneck speed, boiling Dad's precious carp into fish stew.

Peter hooted and danced. Singing and humming a birthday tune. It wasn't Alice's birthday, but it should be.

"Goodbye, Kansas! Ashes. Ashes. Gooooobyeee. Alice, say goodbye." Peter sang.

"My cat!" Mrs. Johnson, in her tiny space, screamed. "Kitty! Save Kitty!" She fought Peter.

"Ashes. Shut the fuck up. Fuck you all!" And when the old lady took over, Peter jumped into the flames. "Goodbye, Mrs. J! Hello, San Francisco!"

Fire ate old Mrs. J as she screamed and fought to get out. Beams fell, trapping her arthritic legs. Down on her knees, cradling her melting, glued-together cat. Marbled eyes melting in the heat. White hair lit like lint. Her thin, waxed skin was turning into gel. Someone else took over, dragging their communal body out of the licking, hungry flames as Peter danced in their head.

Secret's out. Alice is watching. She knows now. There was a way out of this madness, and Peter showed her how.

"Here we come! Here we go! Happy Birthday, dearest Alice! One mind, one body, always will be."

Alice

25

SAN FRANCISCO

October 2021, Two years later

The waves crashed onto the shore, leaving tendrils of seaweed, foam, and brine on the blackish sand. The patterns left behind were inky swirls reflecting my life as it was swept over and over again, often out of my hands.

The smell of salt and unwashed seagulls lingered in the air as the wind blew with gusto, flipping umbrellas and chasing the brave women and men off the prickly sand who thought getting an autumn tan was a good idea.

I came searching for respite, away from the hustling and bustling of the hospital, after my lectures, and the constant, ungrateful whining of my mother. A few months ago, she called, finally telling me she had cancer and was divorced again. The divorce I knew. My stepfather was the first to inform me. We had a good talk and parted ways with my blessings for his new wife and baby on the way.

Ovarian cancer, stage four, she said. Her doctor was a

no-nonsense type, which suited my mother just fine. After close to three decades, my mother was still hard to read and beautiful even without hair. We never got along, and she treated me mostly like I didn't exist. If there was one thing Junko was sure of, it was that men who loved Junko never left her. It was Junko who decided when to end the relationship, not them.

My stepdad, David Steeple, was not much of a looker, unlike the man who made half of me, but David's love was loyal. Over the ten years, despite Junko's terrible temper and the ups and downs of their relationship, he stood by her.

David was tricked into marrying his secretary after he was drunk and accidentally slept with her, according to my mother. He wouldn't have left if not for that cunning bitch.

Under the afternoon sun, I felt myself recharged. My mother wasn't the only reason why I had to leave. Seeing my peers in the hospital, who had been promoted and were achieving their dreams of becoming an ER doctor or a surgeon, made me envious. It was hard not to be reminded of my failures and my disabilities.

My phone rang. "What's up?"

"Where are you? I've been calling you!" Eli was shouting through the noise of metal screeching as the BART approached its station.

I checked the fifteen missed calls and messages from Eli and the hospital. "I'm at the beach." I yawned, spotting a seagull creeping closer.

"The hospital called. Junko's not doing well." He raised his voice. "I'm on my way there."

I picked up my shoes and stumbled through the sand as fast as I could to my parked car. "I'll be there in twenty minutes. Video me when you get there."

The day had come. My mother was leaving us. I should be happy, but instead, I felt sick.

Eli was sitting by her side with his hand in hers. Growing up, I sometimes caught glimpses of Mom staring at me with eyes that seemed to convey envy and, more often, jealousy, especially when Michael Harris looked at me more than a glance.

I watched from the door as my mother smiled at something Eli was saying. My best friend stayed by my side and helped me navigate those difficult days. He was a constant ray of sunshine with boundless positivity.

It was Eli Randall who kept me alive and going. If there was a point in my life that I was grateful for, it would be the day everything clicked when I relented to his endless pursuit to be work partners and best friends. Eli never needed anything from me. His being gay meant I didn't have to worry that he was trying to get me to bed, and his sensitivity to my moods matched us to the T.

When Eli first witnessed my switch, he went MIA for a week. It was one of my lowest points after Ellen Han's death. Then, Eli returned with a box of my favorite whipped cream strawberry shortcake and a curiosity about my personality, and that was when I swore we would be best friends forever.

He raised his head and gestured for me to come over. My mother followed his gaze, and the smile on her lips dropped to a frown. I didn't speak, walking to the side table and picking up her empty flask of water and flower pot. She hated the sight of wilted flowers.

"Dr. Lopez said she's better now." Eli patted my mother's shoulder.

I checked the monitors for her vitals and reviewed the reports on the laptop located on the pushcart. There were some abnormalities, but I didn't want to comment till I spoke to her doctor-in-charge. "Did the nurse come by?" I asked Eli.

"She just left," Eli replied, handing over a book for horticulture to my mother, and grabbed the potted plant from my hands and followed me out the door to the nurse's station.

"Thanks for coming," I said as my shoulders fell.

He gave me a side hug. "If you need me, I'll stay."

I checked my phone. It was five p.m. "You'd better get going. Didn't you say your blind date was at six?" I took the pot from his hands.

Eli ruffled my hair. "Nah, I might not like him."

I crossed my arms. "You never know. He could be that soulmate."

He smirked. "Didn't you say if we're single at forty, you'll marry me?"

"Since when?" I laughed. "I have time. My soul mate could be around the corner."

I scanned the nurse's station and spotted Dr. Lopez talking to my mother's nurse.

"First loves don't last." Eli grinned. "I'm telling you this from someone romantic. Forget that guy in Seoul. It's a needle in a haystack."

A male nurse with a blue mask, checking his chart, lifted his gaze. Our eyes met, and we stared at each other, not willing to concede. A blush grew on my face. Obviously, he had heard us.

Eli glanced at our exchange. "Now, this one I approve," he winked at the nurse.

"Okay…" I pressed my hands on Eli's shoulders, shooing him off. "Time to find that true love of yours."

Eli sighed. I watched him leave before searching for that nurse again, but he was gone.

After filling up my mother's flask, watering and pruning her potted plant, I headed back to her room.

Suddenly, I couldn't breathe. My instincts were right. Earlier, I sensed it, a storm approaching. The pit of unease grew. Behind me, a man was speaking, and there was no mistaking that baritone voice. The flashbacks struck like lightning bolts.

"Death happens all the time," he said.

"But, we're supposed to save them, not kill them!"

"Supposed? The hospital will deal with the lawsuit. No child of mine is a coward."

He tore my resignation letter. "There's an opening in Neuro Critical Team 1. You'll join that surgical team on Monday. You've proven yourself with Han's case and come highly recommended by ER Team 7."

Vomit rose in my gut. I hated it when he brushed off my words as if I were inconsequential.

At present, my hands tremble. Water in the flask sloshed, and the pot was slipping from my wet palm. Harris's power and his reach were always omnipotent. Even this far across the states, I'd heard his name more than once. His reputation preceded him. Nothing could hurt him. Not then, and especially not now.

Each room I passed was either occupied or locked. My heart thundered when footsteps came closer. The flask slipped out of my hand and dropped with a clank, splashing water everywhere. A nurse saw and rushed off to get a towel, and I dashed into a room with an open door. Someone was coming out of the supplies room, and I pushed him in, slamming the door behind me.

"Sorry!" I squeaked and pressed my body against the door. The room was small and cramped, with shelves on both sides piled high with blankets, pillows, toilet paper, and other cleaning supplies.

The male nurse whom I saw earlier frowned. I was blocking his way out.

"Just wait," I whispered.

"Why?" His voice was smooth and a little accented.

Up close, he was a head and a half taller, with wavy honey-brown hair. His uniform was snug across his chest, revealing his muscles, and fitted along his long legs. Although he had a mask on, I could tell he had a chiseled jawline and knew by the shape of his eyes that he was Asian and handsome.

He crossed his arms, making the veins on his lower arm stand out, and this made me even more nervous.

"Just a little longer…." I flipped the lights off and placed my ear on the door, hearing Michael outside talking to the nurse about cleaning the floor, and then his conversation with Dr. Lopez about my mother.

The male nurse reached for the knob, and I placed my hands on his chest and pushed him back. "Please, just a few more minutes?" I tilted my head, giving him a pleading look in the small, dimly lit room before putting my ear back on the door.

He placed both his arms over my head and crushed me as he leaned in on the door too. He was warm, and his hair brushed my forehead. Heat shot through my body, and with him on me, I felt his heart beating, strong and fast.

"Why are you hiding?" He snapped off his mask and mine. His face was inches away as I looked up at his lips.

My face was on fire, my ears even hotter, as our heated breaths stopped time. Flirting was Merle's arena, and my first was with Park Ji Woon.

His scent was intoxicating. I wrapped my arms around his neck, plastering myself against him. I was soft to his strong, hard body, obviously wanting me. He lowered his face to mine and as he was about to kiss me, I turned away.

"He's gone," I slipped under him and turned the knob.

He held my shoulder. "I'm Jason. What's your name?"

I turned. "Alice."

"Alice." He repeated. "Alice….which department?"

«Neuroscience, Berkeley."

"Wanna have dinner?"

His words were simple and laced with meaning. My throat went dry when he brushed his fingers on my earlobe. My cheeks burned.

With the other hand, he opened the door and pushed me out into the hallway. "Meet you at the nurse station in an hour."

Later, an hour passed the appointed time, and he didn't show. I waited one more, just in case. Ghosted. I should have known. My father was an excellent case study. Handsome men were liars.

26

Four days later

My mother was dying. Her lungs were ragged with short breaths. Pain slashed across her gaunt face, and there was a perpetual sheen of sweat running from her forehead down her temples and pooling at the V where her collarbones met.

"Do you regret marrying him?" She held onto my hand like a vise. Her nails dug into my skin and pierced through my flesh. Beads of blood formed in slashes of red, and they hurt. She didn't care how I felt. Right to the end, she was selfish.

"You think I don't know?" she muttered, ignoring my question about Michael Harris. It was obvious I wasn't talking about her second marriage.

David was as gentle as a lamb. How could there be regrets? Regrets were for the tumultuous emotions born from heartbreak and anger, a whirlwind storm that destroyed every good thing in the past. Dorothy would know.

"Know what?" I was confused. Mother was not the sort to

speak in riddles. Her curt words were meant to cut. She wanted to break me, and so she did.

"You are not Alice..." Her voice was a whisper as a wave of pain crashed into her, and she sucked in, holding back her tears, squeezing out the last bit of sympathy I might have for her like a well-washed piece of rag. "You took my daughter! You killed her!"

That one hurt. I was hers just as much as the one she lost. We were twins. Why didn't she love me as much as my sister? I tried to tell myself it was her guilt that made her mad. She chose not to remember. Somewhere along the way, when she was pregnant, Junko was under the impression that she was only having one child, even though her gynecologist had told her repeatedly that she was having twins. I wondered why she chose to shut that out. The ultrasound pictures showed two. There were two baby names, although in the end, only one lived.

"I'm not crazy." She gulped some air and squeezed my hand till it turned purple. "Both of you made me this way!"

I pulled my hand off from her loosening grip. Everyone had their limits. "Fine." I played along. If this helped her to pass on in peace and lowered my guilt, so be it. The last thing I wanted was to manifest into her.

Mother heaved. The monitors were dropping. The shrill began as her heart began to race erratically. Her doctor and nurses, waiting outside, came rushing in, and I was pushed out. They knew it was too late to take any action. Michael Harris emerged like a magician.

I stepped away, looking for a place to hide.

A hand grabbed my arm and pulled me out and into his embrace.

The beep of death rang from the room and out into the hallway.

I cried into his chest. I still didn't know what he looked like. Today, it didn't matter. Jason's familiar scent and strong arms were what I needed.

27

The funeral parlor was small, about twelve by fourteen feet. On a stand made of recycled wood from sequoia trees, newly varnished, was her casket. My mother — Junko's eyes were closed, her face heavily made-up like an old forgotten geisha.

The white cherry blossom kimono that she wore was wrapped snugly over her bony frame. Cancer ate away her flesh and left her thin as a reed. It was hard to see how she had changed and shrunk.

After a second marriage, my mother still loved the man who was sobbing at the podium. Unfortunately, my biological father was Dr. Michael Harris, Chief Surgeon at Johns Hopkins Hospital. A prestigious title for a criminal.

Gossip said that my stepdad, David Steeple, a law firm partner, liked women and wine too much. When my mother was diagnosed with ovarian cancer two years ago, David left her and took on a new wife, fifteen years younger, and was now expecting a baby. He was not here today as everyone expected.

I didn't blame David. He tried his best. My mother was a case even he couldn't handle. The wolves were watching, and seeing these people made me wish I wasn't here as well.

The mic dropped on the podium, and the sound reverberated through the room. The twenty-plus people who came to send my mother off — relatives, work colleagues, and too many of Michael's friends- shifted and muttered in their seats.

"Sorry," Michael spoke with his mouth close to the mic as he fumbled to place it back on the stand. He shuffled his notes, taking a deep breath. Always the cold, confident, and intelligent man, this vulnerable side of Dr. Michael Harris was hard to believe.

I made a move to stand up when Eli grabbed my wrist. He shook his head and held me down.

Michael wiped his face and cleared his throat. "I…" He pursed his lips and straightened his back. "I met Junko when I was twenty-six during my medical residency in Tokyo. I was in the ER at Tokai University Hospital when Junko walked in with a bloody hand and a finger in an ice bag."

He pointed his index finger in the air and stared at it. "She asked how long it would take to attach her finger back," and I told her, "Have dinner with me, and I'll tell you." His lips curved up. "And so Junko gave me another finger—"He lifted his third finger. "That one was still attached."

Everyone laughed, and his smile broadened.

"It took ten tries before she said, 'yes,' and that was just for coffee." The room chuckled, already charmed. People were always quickly taken in by Michael.

I crossed my arms and glared at him. I heard this story a million times, except my mother told it differently. She said Michael ignored her. He was rude and told her to go away. Bad luck made him her surgeon, and then, after she filed a complaint against him and a few more arguments later, hate turned to interest, and from interest, it became affection, and then they fell in love.

"I extended my term in Tokyo. We dated for two years while Junko finished her degree at Nodai. We got married after and came back to Kansas. Junko was special, different from the rest. With her…" He stopped and covered his eyes, choking back a sob.

Part of me wished he were telling the truth and that he, deep down inside, loved her more than himself. However, lies came easily to this man. The mask he wore was layers thick, hiding something grotesque beneath.

Yes, my mother was special. She was special because she was Michael's salvation — the supposed angel who loved the beast.

"Junko was my soul mate. We thought nothing could break us and that we could weather any storm." He looked up with unshed tears, and the crowd cried with him. "It was my fault she left, and I regretted every single day that I let her go."

Regret. A word I never thought I would hear him say.

Michael did not regret making me his alibi. He did not regret it when that Japanese woman, Miyako, died. He did not feel remorse when he left his teenage daughter alone to deal with the backlash of his crimes, and when he didn't back me up against Dr. Thompson after I warned him about Ellen's allergies, I knew we could never be family again.

I regret that I once trusted him.

"She was all that mattered…." Michael was sobbing. His words were muffled afterward.

Again, I was forgotten, left behind. Anger crouched on the surface, ready to explode. I did not want to make a scene. It would be disrespectful. With gritted teeth, I grabbed Eli's arm. "Get him off."

Eli, whose gaze was transfixed on Michael at the podium, did not reply.

"If you don't, I will, and I won't be nice."

Eli was softly sobbing. "Let him talk. He loved her. You had her for years. Give him this…."

I stood up fast, tipping the chair. "That's enough! Crying is not going to bring her back!"

Eli grabbed my arm, and I struggled against him. "We can't change what happened!" I shouted and accidentally punched Eli in the face, and he fought back.

Chaos broke. Chairs were pushed aside as people scattered from us. I pushed Eli off and fell onto my mother's family from Japan, knocking down my grand aunt. Blood dripped down my neck from the cut on my cheek. Michael's doctor friends rushed to help my grandaunt, who probably broke a rib.

I stood confused and lost.

Michael stood at the podium, staring blankly ahead through it all, tears running down his chin. His hands were gripping shreds of paper in a vise.

Nothing changed. Guilt was for the living.

28

SEOUL

January 11, Three months later

The room was a shoebox with no windows, one long desk, and two metal chairs. In the dark, I floated in space, no air, no sound, alone. The scent of cold surrounded my body. Cocooned, I was at peace.

My head dropped onto the edge of the table with a loud thud. "Argh!" I cradled my throbbing forehead with my hands.

"You okay?" A man with a black mask popped in from the doorway.

I looked up and our eyes locked. "You."

Jason, the male nurse with whom I had a fling two months ago. I didn't believe in coincidences; I only believed in bad fate. Seeing him here meant the worst was yet to come.

"Well, good morning, Alice." He slid into the tight room and rolled a bottle of water to me on the table. "This might help." He pointed to my head.

I rubbed the cold bottle of water. Our eyes kept on each other.

He reached to flip on the switches.

"Don't." I shook my head.

"Oh yes. I forgot. You like the dark."

"Why are you stalking me?" Immediately regretting what I spoke.

He laughed. "This is what I do. Your host coordinator is sick, and they need a translator."

"Right…"

"Okay. I wanted to see you." He chuckled.

I'd call him a liar, but I was past the moment of calling him out. "What do you want from me, Jason? You're not a nurse, are you?"

"I was doing my internship," he said. "And you didn't ask me. You assumed."

"I didn't want to know," I replied. True. We barely talked. Our mouths were used for other, better things, and sharing feelings was the last thing on our minds.

"I'm a psychiatrist, and my patients don't like shrinks."

"Take that mask off."

"You had no problems fucking me with my mask on. I remembered your fingers in my pants…"

I smacked his shoulder. "Stop it."

"Ouch." He reached over and ruffled my hair.

I tried to smack his hand off, and he backed away just before and chuckled.

"You can't tell anyone about us."

"Why? We're both single. We can date. I miss you, my pet." I could hear mischief. "And…just to let you know, any woman would jump at the chance of spending more time with me."

"I'm not any woman."

"I know, and we're not over yet." His voice dropped to a whisper, and he tipped my chin up to his face.

"I'm done." I pulled back and crossed my arms.

My laptop rang, and Zareen's face appeared on the video call. I tapped to unmute the mic, and he flipped on the light switches.

"Alice! How's Seoul!" Zareen was sitting on a bronze-patterned couch, and under it was a colorful Persian rug. The walls were dark orange with Burgundy curtains.

"How's your father?" I asked, feeling a pang of guilt that my first messages to Zareen after arriving in Seoul yesterday were venting about my panel.

"Hanging by a thread. There are good days and bad." Worry lines puckered on her forehead, and dark circles cradled her swollen eyes. "Our families have gathered. It's any moment now."

"I'm sorry…." I breathed out, recalling the last hours of my mother's death. That week, I wouldn't have made it without Jason.

He must have caught me glancing because he reached out under the desk and held my hand. I could feel his eyes softening and the warmth of his fingers as he squeezed mine. I looked away and brushed my lashes quickly.

Zareen was tearing up, and my throat grew tight. I didn't know what else to say. I never let anyone in.

"This will pass," Jason said. "He lived a full life with love and no regrets."

Zareen perked up and bent close to the screen. "Oh! And who's this young man?"

Jason took off his mask.

"Yes, a very handsome man," She smiled. "Are you with Merced?"

He returned a smile. "I'm not with Merced. I work with Salinger, and Dr. Ed Bailey is my supervisor. I'm Dr. Park Ji Woon."

"Ji Woon?" My jaw dropped. He gave me a side glance and smirked. I pulled my hand from him, but he held on. It was a tug of fingers for a few seconds before I relented. Zareen was studying us, and I didn't want her to know.

Now in the bright light, his features were unmistakable. After my mother's passing, everything went in a blur. He said his name was Jason, and I took it at face value. When we were making out at UCSF Medical and the hotel beside it, we met at night.

I should have recognized him.

"Oh! You're the one Eddie's talking about! Jason! Ji Woon?"

"You can call me either." He smiled.

"Ed and I went to college together. He was my senior when I started at Johns Hopkins." Zareen added.

"I'm an alumnus too."

The rest I didn't hear. A bubble grew around me. Thick walls muffling their words. Their voices bounced against my walls. All I could hear were my thoughts.

This was planned. Ji Woon knew who I was. And I fell right into his lap. Literally.

My heart was suddenly deliriously happy. No. I shouldn't be like this. For months after I got back to Kansas, I searched for him online. Years pining and wondering if he got my letter, I left it with the hotel reception. Or he hated me.

This was revenge.

I peered at him as he chatted and flirted with my boss. It was hard to believe this man was the same boy I had met, my first love. We were both broken and hated by the world.

"I'm working for Eddie." He turned to me with another of his killer smiles.

"Eddie?" I blinked. "Wait…Ed Bailey?"

The noose was growing thicker. "That Dr. Bailey?"

"Bailey told me all about you. He said he's sorry he can't come back to see you, Alice."

"Such a small world…small world!" Zareen chuckled. "So is the old dog a good boss?"

"He shaved his head before the trip there. Did you see him?"

"Yes. Two days ago. I dropped by Hopkins and sat in his lecture. His class on Dissociative Identity Disorder was fascinating. It's amazing how you can use hypnotism to penetrate through this disorder."

I was glued to my boss, worried that she might recognize me in those videos. Bailey signed a non-disclosure and pixelized my face. No one knew about my multiple personalities except Bailey, Michael, Eli, and Nick. And now, Ji Woon.

"Did you know I put that study together?" He smiled proudly.

Of course, he did. All my secrets lay out in the files, ordered, researched, and analyzed. A cadaver, splayed for the whole world to see. And the last person I wanted exposed to was Park Ji Woon.

"Really? You did?" she said excitedly. My heart fell again.

"D.I.D. is my specialty. We have several patients with that disorder in Seoul. If you come by, I'll be happy to give you a tour of our office and my beautiful city."

"Wow!" She covered her mouth. "Handsome, smart, and slick." Zareen grinned and glanced at me.

Each breath I took was acid.

"You're in danger, Alice. This one knows what he's doing." She leaned into the camera. "Dr. Park, are you single or married, and how old are you?"

"Why? Are you bored with your husband? How could he let someone as beautiful as you go?"

Zareen roared with laughter and wagged her finger. "No, no, not me! Alice is single and needs to loosen up a little. If you don't mind, could you please bring her out for some fun? Introduce some of your friends, especially those single men!"

He placed his arm over my shoulder. "Alice and I have a date tonight." He beamed.

"Oh, you do? You're fast, boy."

He laughed, and I nudged him hard in his side. He smirked. "Only the best. Don't worry. She's in safe hands. I've got everything planned."

Zareen gave two thumbs up. "Excellent! I told you, Alice. This trip will change things."

"I can get around fine," I muttered.

"I know, and that's why I believe you'll represent us well in this conference." Zareen sat up straight.

I heaved a sigh of relief. "Yes…about that, the panelists…" I shot Ji Woon a look, but he purposely didn't catch the hint. "Erumph."

"What?" He grinned innocently.

«Alice…I still think…" Zareen spoke first.

I cut her and spoke quickly. "I think two guests on my panel are enough. I have many people coming."

"The Hidden Psychopath and Psyche of a Psychopath sound like book titles, not serious panel discussions," said Ji Woon.

Zareen nodded. "See? That's what I told her, too. I promised to give you free rein, but this time, Alice, we have to listen. Merced personally asked us to put Dr. Harris on our panel."

"Dr. Michael Harris? He's famous. He'll bring in the crowd," said Ji Woon.

Instantly, I saw his hand. Michael was the big fish, I was the bait.

"No." I stood up. I didn't come to Seoul to sell myself, and I definitely didn't come to meet my nemesis.

"Alice. The Dean called and said he wanted to use the funds for something else. Your research into the early intervention on children with psychotic brains was rejected." Zareen said.

"Isn't there interest in LA? How about the partnership with UCLA? Or the bond measures for Berkeley? Can't we carve out a little from their research funds for my work?"

"It is not enough. That's why these sessions are critical."

"You said the funds were in place. You made me come to Seoul thinking that. The panels are supposed to recruit professionals who are interested in my project. How can I convince them if it might not happen?"

Ji Woon raised his hand. "I'll do it. I'll clear my schedule this summer to help. I know lots of people. I'm sure we can pull some money for the trial."

I whipped around, glaring at him. "Why are you helping?"

"Because I want to. This project is worth looking into," he replied too quickly.

"You changed your name. No one would know who he is. Treat him like a stranger. Please?" Zareen clasped her hands.

"Sometimes you do things you don't like." Ji Woon crossed his arms.

My hands itched to choke him. This was a trap. My rational mind told me to run. But my giggling heart wanted to stay.

"It's either me or Michael." I gritted my teeth.

That was what I was afraid of. The stress of Michael is in the same room as me. I could hear the voices cheering. Merle was packing up. She was filing her nails, getting ready to sprint.

They were my secrets, and I wished I could take them to their graves. I'd been good about knocking them off. Only a handful remained. I was getting close.

All I wanted was to live that normal life. And now, with Ji Woon, this secret was coming out.

How many more people knew I was a freak? Park Ji Woon should never see me switch.

Disaster was here, and it was calling my name.

29

Two days later

I didn't want to be here. Never thought I would ever come back, but here I was. Corralled into doing everything I didn't want to do. My life was always a string of nooses pulled by everyone. Even my mind wasn't a place I could hide.

"Welcome to my session, The Hidden Psychopath. My name is Alice Steeple, and I am a Neuroscientist at the Helen Willis Institute at UC Berkeley." I placed a smile on my lips.

"Today, it is my pleasure to share with you our panel of prestigious guests — Dr. Michael Harris, ex-chief Surgeon at Johns Hopkins Hospital; Professor Samantha Durham, a Forensics Psychologist; and Dr. Xu Meng, Professor of Traditional Chinese Medicine and Acupuncturist from Beijing University."

My panel smiled at the crowd.

I gestured to my first guest. "Dr. Harris is one of the leading surgeons in awake craniotomy. He has an unheard-of ninety-nine percent success rate and has helped many US Army veterans regain functionality in their hearing, vision, and movement. Thank you for being here with us today to share your insight into the neuro-logical functions of the human brain."

Dr. Harris nodded and uncrossed his arms.

"The next member of our panel, Professor Samantha Durham, is a New York Times bestselling author of 'The Psychopathic Neighbor,' a psychological thriller, with over four hundred thousand copies sold worldwide. Professor Durham is a forensic psychologist who specializes in understanding the minds of psychopaths. Her latest project is the study of behavior patterns in serial killers incarcerated in the State of Texas. She will be holding an informal book signing at the end of this session."

Professor Durham smiled and waved her hand limply.

I gestured to our last guest.

"And this is Dr. Xu Meng from the Beijing University of Chinese Medicine. He is a world-renowned acupuncturist, mentoring over ten thousand students from thirty-six countries. Dr. Xu comes from a long line of Chinese physicians, and his ancestor treated an Emperor in the Qing Dynasty. He is known to treat psychological cases using acupuncture and has shown significant breakthroughs in molding the minds of mental patients. Thank you for taking the time to share your unique perspective in our session today."

Dr. Xu nodded and took a drink from his bottle of water.

I straightened my shoulders and spotted Ji Woon in the crowd. He smiled encouragingly. I focused my gaze on the exit sign above the door. With the microphone close to my lips, I began:

"When we think of psychopaths, the image of a cold-blooded killer, charming and manipulative, comes to mind. The film industry and media paint psychopaths as criminals, dangerous predators who show no remorse and enjoy killing to fulfill their sadistic, warped sense of reality."

My slides showed movie images of famous murders and horror films — black and white, and some colored photographs of notorious serial killers with gruesome images of mutilated corpses and body parts.

"According to the FBI bulletin devoted to this disorder, the psychopath is an intraspecies predator, found in every country, belongs to every race, and the majority are men. Several studies show that roughly 1% of the men in the United States are probably psychopaths and almost all show signs of conduct disorders with risks of antisocial personality disorder at a very young age."

I placed my elbows on the podium.

"Over the years, as neuroscience advanced, through functional magnetic resonance imaging, we see differences in psychopaths' brains, especially in the reduced connections between the prefrontal cortex, which governs stress and risk, and the amygdala, which governs empathy and emotions, in comparison with an average person. Before brain scanning technology, psychopathy was seen as a behavioral personality disorder, but now, some experts think psychopaths are born, not made."

I turned to my guest speakers. "My question to the panel is: Is psychopathy an inherited genetic condition? Should people born with different brain structures be labeled as a threat?"

Michael took the microphone. "With the right chemical treatment, we could reduce some of the traits of psychopathy. For example, abnormal neurochemicals such as monoamine oxidase, serotonin, testosterone, and other hormones can affect impulsivity, hostility, and recklessness. It is possible to increase and decrease dosages to change the chemical makeup of the brain and reduce those psychopathic tendencies."

"Are you saying you can cure the psychopathic brain?" I asked.

"Possibly, I have been leading several kinds of research over the years on this study. Together with surgical manipulations and chemical interventions, it is possible to change the human brain map. Mental disorders such as schizophrenia and dissociative identity disorders can also benefit from the research I have done. We could change the human mind to bring back balance and normalcy."

"You found a way to stop them?" My voice echoed in the room.

"Yes." He stared at me.

The audience was whispering, wondering who 'them' I was talking about. Ji Woon was trying to tell me something with his urgent gaze, but my eyes kept darting back to Michael. I shouldn't think about the children who died. Those little faces added to the growing horror as my mind pieced together his actions with the dates I was sick growing up.

Professor Durham pulled the mic to her mouth. "Psychotherapy and Neurofeedback are just as important as chemical treatments. Dr. Harris." She sneered, and Michael glowered at her.

"The mind is a complicated organ. It can't be 'cured,'" She air-quoted. "It is impossible to measure the conscious and sub-conscious states with pure science. Long-term psychotherapy is far more effective in helping people with a mental health condition than merely taking parts out of their brain."

Michael looked ready to murder Durham. I picked up my mic. "Thank you, Dr. Harris and Dr. Durham. Now, back to my original question. Are you born a psychopath? Is there hope for those with psychopathic tendencies?"

Durham adjusted her black-rimmed glasses. "Miss Steeple's question earlier was whether psychopaths are threats to society. A smart psychopath could easily feign the treatment and pretend he is getting better while hiding his plans. He could also manipulate the therapist to get what he wants, for example, a job recommendation, or play with her feelings and make her second-guess her judgments. I would suggest, in addition to behavior therapy, also considering hypnotherapy and increasing law enforcement. Psychopaths are different from other mental disorders. This is an issue of intention."

"I see and now…" I spoke, but she cut in.

"I'm not done speaking." The microphone close to her mouth magnified the sounds of her breathing across the room. Several people shook their heads, and others shifted in their seats.

"The one in a hundred people who are psychopaths blend in easily among all of us. The percentage of those caught is small. The intelligent ones never get caught, and they are relentless in their goals. It only takes one to do massive, terrible damage. Although psychopaths make up fifteen to twenty percent of prisoners, they're usually the most serial killers and sex offenders, scoring high on the PCL-R Hare, and three times more likely to re-offend. The laws of society don't affect them. These people enjoy the game of evading and manipulating, while thinking they are the cats playing with us, mice."

"You think they are dangerous?" I asked.

"Yes. Psychopaths need to be tracked." She gave a disdainful look. "Firm regulations and monitoring are the ways we can keep ourselves safe. A psychopath is supremely selfish and only loves himself. Without a conscience, he would do whatever he likes and justify that he is right. Many of them crave attention to show the world they are better than all of us." Her eyes burned with fervor. "Control them, or they will control us. They could be here in this very room, sitting right next to us." She turned to Michael and raised her brow.

I ignored the almost tangible animosity between the two and picked up my microphone. "Robert Hare said, 'Nature provides for all sorts of diversity.' Autism or psychopathy, which show different brain formations, are part of the same spectrum of evolution. Some people are on one end, super-empathetic, and others, like psychopaths, are on the other extreme side. Most of us, as Hare said, are somewhere in between."

I paced the stage away from the professor's piercing look, trying my hardest to control the sarcasm in my voice.

The door opened, and the woman in the white stepped in. My throat became dry. Suddenly, a spot of red bled out from her waist, staining her suit. Growing bigger and redder until her clothes were soaked in blood.

I held my breath, staring at the pool of blood under her white shoes.

My audience shifted uncomfortably with my silence. I closed my eyes and opened them again. That woman in white disappeared, and the door to the exit was closed. Heart beating fast, I gripped the microphone between my hands. I spent too much time preparing for this session to fail.

"Fear begets more fear." Biting hard on my lip, I continued. "It is natural for us to fear the unknown and to want to control the environment we live in, abiding by rules to feel safe. But, if we were to place every one-in-a-hundred person in prison or to put an anklet on him because of his brain scans and write him off as 'us' versus 'them', it would create more criminal psychopaths."

I returned to my podium. "There are eight billion of us in this world. We can't all be the same. Judging a group of people solely by their brain imaging or a psychological checklist is biased. Some studies show much to support our inaccurate beliefs that psychopaths, in reality, have low self-esteem. They know they are different from the rest of us, and they are trying to fit in. However, when society rejects them or recluses themselves after failure, you'll reach a low point like any other human being. However, when psychopaths react in vengeance, their criminal acts are crueler."

Durham snatched up her mic. "And you're expecting us to show empathy to these people?"

"We are not here for a witch hunt. We're here to discuss our different minds, to find commonality and understanding." I ignored her anger and turned to my last guest.

"What do you think about our discussion, Dr. Xu? Have you met a patient with psychopathic tendencies, and is there a role for traditional Chinese medicine in changing a psychopath's mind?"

Dr. Xu took the mic and spoke in Mandarin first, and then his translator spoke next, 'Normal' people commit the most crimes. Being charming, intelligent, adventurous, confident, ruthless, and cool under pressure are seen by my people as good traits. In China, our history is marked by famous emperors and leaders who possess these characteristics. We admire them and want to be like them. I don't see why psychopathy is a problem."

He studied the audience.

"We can use Chinese medicine and acupuncture, the same as what Dr. Harris said, to reduce impulses, anger issues, and other behaviors. We can help our patients become the happiest, most peaceful, and most productive individuals in the world. But..." The Chinese physician pointed up. "I cannot make a psychopath feel kindness. A leader needs to be kind sometimes. If we give a psychopath the rewards he wants, then he can mimic kindness."

"Isn't that giving in to their demands? That makes it worse!" Durham interjected angrily.

Dr. Xu spread out his hands. "Don't we reward people who excel? Why not make these psychopaths valuable members of society? Many people in my country are trying to survive. We have billions of people and cannot waste our precious resources on one percent of the population when we have ninety-nine percent to feed."

"So, what is your suggestion?" Michael asked.

"Leave the psychopaths alone. Give them constructive rewards. Evil exists in all forms. If it is that person's fate to kill, it is the other person's fate to die."

"Easy for you to say because your country has two billion people! What's a few thousand missing or dead?" Durham was livid. "I have a suggestion. Why don't we send the world's psychos to China? Let them turn these monsters into respectable human beings!"

"The definition of respectable is subjective. The brain can change given the right tweaks and medical attention." Dr. Harris spoke up. "The US Army Veterans have given up their lives and bodies for my country. After the war, some soldiers returned, displaying areas of psychopathic strains. These people are not monsters. We have the technology and medical know-how to fix them and include them in our world."

I lifted my mic. "Criminal behaviors can come from anyone and anywhere due to many circumstances. It is unfair to judge someone based on their brain makeup or DNA and assume they lack the will or desire to be good simply because they lack empathy. It is not up to us to call them monsters."

I wanted to believe that everyone deserves a chance and more. I wanted to believe that monsters deserved the right to be loved. Because my father had his soul mate, and although he took the wrong path, made terrible choices, and refused to believe he was like the rest of us, I still wanted to hope.

Thirty minutes later, after a long, rambunctious discussion with the audience, my session was over. As the crowd filtered out, Michael came to my side and slipped a USB into my pocket.

He held my hand down from checking my pocket and glowered at Ji Woon and three plainclothes agents who were sifting through the crowd to get to us.

"I'm..." Michael's lips moved against my ear, but the crowd was loud.

"What?" I turned to him and put my hand on mine.

FBI agent Odeh Amir appeared with Ji Woon by his side. "Dr. Michael Harris, you're under arrest."

The agent pulled out a pair of silver handcuffs and cuffed Michael's wrists. "By the jurisdiction of the United States of America, you are charged with twelve counts of murder, eight counts of sexual assault, money laundering, collusion, and price-fixing. You will follow us to the US embassy and be extradited for your crimes."

"Wait!" I grabbed my father's arm. He brushed my hand off, "Wait..."

Ji Woon pulled me into his arms. I fought him as everyone watched stupefied, as the FBI and Korean police led Michael out.

"What did he say?" I cried. "What did he say?" I struggled against Ji Woon's grip. Tears streamed down my face. I didn't care what people thought.

That asshole. Why did he say that? The Michael Harris I knew would never apologize.

—||—

30

Hours later

The large neon sign of the hole-in-the-wall barbecue restaurant flickered blue and green. Smoke rose in waves, swallowed by rumbling silver vents above. When the door slid to the side, the smell of delicious, seasoned, burnt meat engulfed us, followed by the noise of chatter and laughter inside.

Michael's arrest was still sending shockwaves to everyone. The conference hall was filled with reporter ants, and it wasn't easy to escape their scent.

To cheer me up, Ji Woon, Eli, and Lief, his new Norwegian therapist friend, insisted on a feast and getting drunk tonight. It had recently snowed, and the paths along the street were covered with a dusting of white. At seven p.m., the sidewalks to the popular restaurants were littered with footsteps and people rushing up and down the subway stairs, hurrying to their meetings with their friends and home.

Ji Woon walked over to a pretty girl in a blue polo shirt and black apron with red Korean characters and pointed at us. The other Korean customers ogled at my boys. I was a queen with my entourage of hotties.

"How about somewhere else?" I asked. Feeling eyes on my back. The guys were giants on the tiny stool seats and looked good enough to eat.

"No one knows you here." Eli shared a smile with Lief, who reminded me of an elf in LOR.

"Alice! Did Eli tell you about the girls in the men's bathroom?"

Eli was retelling his story. He was trying hard with that overly big smile. He wasn't shocked when Michael was taken away.

I learned of Ji Woon's callous side days ago. To his FBI partner, Agent Odeh, and the people who knew him on the business side of things, Ji Woon was no-nonsense and efficient. When he was in therapist or host mode, he was affable and kind.

Ji Woon was right. We both changed. Time eroded our innocence, and those promises we made long ago, after my betrayal and lies, were gone. He knew Merle was Michael's partner in crime. I played along because I was waiting.

My secret. My strange disease. Wasn't he going to tell the world? Why wasn't I arrested like Michael was?

When my mom died, he was there to distract me. Our one-week fling of crazy sex left another hole in my life when he ghosted. Never did I consider he could be the same guy as the teenager I met. Maybe I didn't want to. I needed him, and because of him, I got over Mom's death fast.

I gestured to the pretty girl with my chin, "So, what did you say to her?"

Ji Woon gave a side glance to the serving girl and then smiled at me. "Triple meat, *Bibimbap*, *Soju*, and beer."

I chewed on my lip. I knew from the way she was giving me those mean girl looks that it wasn't anything. "She said something."

"What did you think she said?" He dragged my stool closer. The guys watched as he casually plucked my lip off my teeth, and Lief joked about us getting a room.

I scooted back, and Ji Woon smiled. "What did she say?"

"She asked if I was single. I told her I'm planning to make many babies with you tonight."

Lief hollered, and I glowered at him. "What the hell?" I tried to punch his arm, which he avoided with ease.

Eli frowned. "Aly and I made a pact. We're getting married if we're single at thirty-five."

"Forty," I corrected.

Lief patted Eli's butt. "Lucky you. You don't have to now."

Eli pulled my stool to him, and Ji Woon hooked his foot on the leg.

"Guys!" I grabbed my stool and sat back down.

The pretty girl came with a large tray of small side dishes and tofu soup. She brushed her hand on Ji Woon's arm "accidentally".

Ji Woon scowled at her. "We'll leave if you want."

"No, we'll stay."

Ji Woon tucked my hair behind my ear, ignoring the girl. "You're so cute when you're jealous."

He leaned in. "You did well today. My good girl."

Those sweet words, which he loved to say in San Francisco, still have an impact on me. I shuddered, and from the corner of my eye, I spotted Ji Woon smiling.

The marinated meats and *Bibimbap* sizzling stone rice pot came next. The girl slapped the cuts of beef and spicy pork on the charcoal grill, with arms moving fluidly over the flames like a conductor. Peter chattered in my head, whispering in envy. Food cooked over a strong fire was his favorite kind of meat.

I nursed my drink. The sounds of my friends' laughter and their faces glowed in rosy hues. Buzzed with beer and *soju*, we were normal people enjoying a dinner in good company. The world began to spin, and I hugged Ji Woon's arm. He kept giving me side glances and stroking me casually.

"Do you think a parallel Universe exists? If you get to choose again. Would you make a different choice?" I asked.

"You think that before you sleep?" Lief chuckled.

"Yes. To Aly. Party pooper." Eli raised his glass and chugged.

"Don't you ever regret?" I asked.

"All the time," said Ji Woon, and he took a shot and flipped the spicy pork.

"What's the point?" Eli slammed his fist on the table. A bottle jumped and beer poured onto the table in lapping foams.

The waitress came with towels and napkins.

"If you have twenty-four hours left to live, what would you do?" Lief asked.

Eli patted Lief's cheek. "I'll spend the night with you."

Lief laughed. "I'll tell my boss to screw himself and spend the night with you!"

"And you?" Eli accepted Ji Woon's offer to fill his shot glass. Their first impressions were not great; however, after we hung out with Ji Woon's K-pop producer brother one night, Eli warmed up.

Ji Woon turned to me. "I'll spend the night with Alice, make breakfast when she wakes, take her anywhere she wants, and stick to her till she dies."

Both Eli and I stared at him.

"Hear that? Ji Woon wants to marry you!" Lief slapped Ji Woon's back.

"Hurt my best girl and you'll wish you were never born." Eli made a slicing motion with his tongs.

"Whoa…is he always like this when drunk?" Lief shook his head.

"Eli gets moody", I said.

"You guys are all no fun," Lief glanced at all of us and winked.

"Alice is mine." Ji Woon wrapped his arm over me and kissed the top of my head. "And, Eli, I'll treat her right."

Eli tossed a hot grilled steak at Ji Woon, barely missing my arm.

"Ashes! Eli Randall!" Peter shot out from my mouth. "Don't waste a perfect piece of meat!"

Lief burst out laughing, and the other two men cracked a smile.

I shrugged Ji Woon's arm off and stood up. "I'm going to get some air."

"Wait…Alice. Your turn…" Lief gestured. "What would you do if you're about to die?"

I stared at Ji Woon. "Why wait? Silence myself."

Those seconds rolled into a minute, and then smoke rose from our barbecued meat.

"The meat!" Lief grabbed the tongs.

"Dark…this girl is always dark?" Lief turned to Eli, who rolled his eyes.

"She's not always like that," Eli glanced at Ji Woon. "It's been a rough day."

"Don't pity me." I plucked the tears from my eyes.

"Never." Ji Woon poured water into my shot glass. "My Alice is a fighter."

"I'm tired. I'm heading off."

He caught my arm as I stood up. Everything around me turned into streaks of orange and red lights. "I'll take you back." He said.

My world tipped. I stubbornly stood on sea legs.

Last night, I found another photograph in my coat pocket. Children standing in a row. A man in a doctor's coat in the middle. Faces scratched out.

Who were they? The minds and I were unsettled. They said it wasn't their doing.

A note was scrawled on the back.

I came to Seoul to find him. The person who left those pictures in my pockets through the years. It wasn't Ji Woon. Wasn't anyone I knew.

My work to clear the mud in my head was a never-ending quicksand. Disaster seemed to always follow me.

Seoul. I wish I had never come.

I longed to be back home and to the mundane life at college, teaching aspiring students, and my notoriety as my father's genes, no one knew.

No one knew my face, but the bitter gut feeling was retching up. Premonition laced my time. Acid was clawing my legs.

"Alice, are you okay?" I heard Ji Woon speak.

"I gave you Michael Harris, that stupid USB. What more? My blood, my bones? What? I'm sorry. I can't stop her." I raised my voice.

The patrons were watching. I hated the spotlight. I wanted to drown in the mediocre. Fade into nonexistence.

Eli took the fork from my fingers. "What the fuck did you say to her? Why is she crying?" His arms sheltered my breakdown.

"She's tired." Ji Woon took my coat and his. "Come, let's go."

Eli snatched my coat from him. "I'm done being nice. I'm bringing her back."

I slipped away as the two men argued.

The snow came fast in flurries. I stuck my tongue out to taste the sky. The ice crystals tasted of the night, coupled with dirt and car exhaust. The automatic doors opened, and Ji Woon stepped out with a credit card in his hand.

"Yay…" I gave a lopsided grin. "You won."

«Alice…come here." He pulled me to him.

A gust of wind blew out, slicing through my thick wool jacket and sawing into my bones. I was naked against the onslaught.

"You have me now. I won't let you be alone again. Never." Ji Woon's eyes held mine with a bright zeal.

It was these times that I wanted to let him in. But I'd fallen for his act so many times.

His phone kept ringing. Then the rings stopped, and the texts came in endless beeps.

"Pick it up," I said as we hurried down another busy street. It was almost ten, and the paths were filled with more people. Cars were crushing ice as they charged by. Snow was pushed to the sides, forming dunes of *Bingsoo*. Puffs of vapor left people's mouths as they spoke.

My coat couldn't keep me warm. Ji Woon's arms over mine melted into my bones, and our three-legged walk was dragging with each step.

"Pick it up." I glared at him.

The ring and beeps were now interchanging. He turned it to silence.

"Who is it?" I asked.

"You have to trust me. I'll fix this."

"Fix what?" I asked.

He cupped my face. "I swear I will make it up to you. My life for yours."

"Ji Woon. What are you saying?"

"Just give me a little more time. I promise."

"Time? You're worrying me." I grabbed his arms.

"I'll show you." We stopped in front of a crowded bakery, and he led me to a patio chair on a deck outside the store. He pulled my phone out of my handbag and placed it in my hand.

"You're safe here. Don't move."

I grabbed his coat. "Ji Woon. Please. What do you mean by your life for mine?"

"It'd be fine." He scanned his texts. "I'll get the car. Just don't talk to anyone."

"Don't go," I held his hand, and he pulled away.

"I won't take long," he said, touching my cheek.

I scanned the people walking by. My head buzzed. It was hard to decipher who was my enemy when I didn't know who they were.

He kissed my forehead and lips.

The more I saw him fade from my view, the more scared I was. The unexplainable feeling that this was the last. A dread reaching up.

"Wait!" I shouted.

There was never a goodbye between us. He would leave as suddenly as he came. The years that we lost, and the bridges we made each time we met, would break. And even though those mortars did not, I always thought it was the end.

This time, I thought we could stay. To finally be together.

Yet, the feeling was back. Urgency took my legs, and the voices were strangely silent as I ran after him. Ji Woon understood us. Accepted us in its entirety.

The red thread stretched taut, and my legs took off after it. The sidewalk was slippery and wet, with snow coming down heavily.

Ji Woon was moving fast, silver fish swimming against the current of fate. Growing smaller and smaller as he pulled away from my sight.

The ground was shifting. I struggled against the snowy quicksand. Ahead, I saw Ji Woon crossing an alley between two buildings, his phone glued to his ear as he talked to someone.

A tall woman appeared from the alley leading out to the street. She had long, straight hair that reached her waist, and despite the cold, she was wearing a thin, white suit. In her hand, something glinted bright.

A dagger!

He didn't see her. He was on the phone, and she was within throwing range.

"Ji Woon! Watch out!" My voice broke from my chest.

I dashed and tackled his attacker. A bright beam flared from my side, blinding me. I raised my hand to my face and turned to the black sedan in the alley. The woman in the white suit pushed me off, and I realized then that it wasn't Miyako.

In my cloudy mind, I thought it was her, and instead of a dagger in her hand, it was a syringe.

Her arm raised and cut through the air.

I felt it pierce through my skin. Emptying its poison.

My knees buckled, and I slipped, crumbling onto the icy ground. The car drove up to us at high speed and then screeched to a halt right before it hit.

Ji Woon swiveled around. His face was a mask of dead horror.

I was dragged to the open back seat.

In stop motion, I saw him. Ji Woon was sprinting for us. His mouth was moving. His eyes were burning with fury.

The headlights turned off, and the door slammed shut. The car rumbled loudly. The last I heard before losing consciousness was the sound of the car careening against the ice and the smell of burnt rubber.

Alice

31

Yellow Sea

I woke up to the rocking of a boat. Nauseous from the combination of undigested *Galbi*, *Soju*, and a stale cloth bag over my head.

"How much did you give her?" I was startled by the voice of a girl speaking in English.

"Not enough to kill her," replied a woman with a nasal voice.

"You think she's awake?" the girl asked.

There were the sounds of footsteps coming toward me. A foot landed hard in my stomach. I grunted, and tears exploded from my eyes.

"She's awake."

I grabbed her foot and missed catching air.

"Who are you?" My voice scratched against the strands of canvas.

One woman slipped behind me. Her nails came down, piercing like talons through my thin cashmere sweater.

"What do you want?" I struggled against her grip. Her kicks

and punches came at lightning speed. I cried with each strike, clutching my sides. "What do you want?"

"Are you filming this?" The girl panted as I fended off her attacks with my bound hands.

Pinpricks of light formed patterns on the threads, but I couldn't tell who she was.

"That's better." The nasal voice replied.

A boot slammed down on my left side. I tried to get up on my knees and was sucker punched in the head.

My world spun. "Why are you doing this?" I cried.

The sound of metal dragging across the floor sent chills down my spine. I braced myself, but the ropes that bound my ankles gave me little room to move. The boat rocked and I slipped on the wet floor, my heart in my throat. "Let's talk this out…."

"Talk?" A girl laughed coldly.

I heard her swing and raised my arms over my head.

"This is for *Eomma*!" The bat came down on my shoulder hard.

I screamed. My arm dislocated. Pain scorched my skin and tore through my veins. I sobbed, cradling my arm against my chest.

Then, the bag was ripped off with a fistful of hair. Light blinded my sight. The world was rays of white, and the ringing grew. I was losing hold. The voices in my head were clamoring to get out.

I heard a familiar click of a camera, and when my eyes could focus, the first thing I saw was her phone pointing right at my face.

"Say your name!" the nasal one ordered.

I glared in defiance at their masked faces in matching beanies and black waterproof tracksuits. It was hard to tell who was who, other than their sharp difference in height.

The shorter woman, whom I called 'the girl,' raised her baseball bat. "Say your name!"

I glared at her.

She jammed her bat into my stomach, and I grunted.

"Look, you have ten thousand likes, and counting. You don't want to disappoint your fans, do you?" The taller nasal one sneered, pointing to her camera.

Disappointment. The one word I hated. It meant a lot of things. None of them brought happy memories.

The girl raised her bat again as I raised my bound arm.

"I'm Alice Steeple." I closed my eyes. "I'm an American. A neuroscientist at UC Berkeley. Eli, Ji Woon, I'm on a boat!"

The bat came and struck the side of my temple. I saw stars, and the taste of blood on my lips. "You won't get away with this..." I recalled being stabbed with a syringe and panic written on Ji Woon's face, and him chasing us down the icy road as the car swerved and screeched. "The police will hunt you down."

Behind the black mirror pointing right at my face, I saw hundreds of messages flooding through the forum. The women weren't lying. I was on live.

Faceless people watching me behind their screens — Gleeful, cruel, relishing in my pain. I didn't get the Korean characters, but some were in English, Spanish, and Japanese.

I was on display. Like an animal. An oddity.

"Kill them!" The voices inside me yelled.

The boat arched up, lifting ten feet and then dropping into the pounding waves. The rain sloshed in from above, cascading in a waterfall down the metal steps, flooding the below deck with its foamy brine.

We fell and rolled on our sides. My kidnappers helped each

other up, and the taller one with the phone kept the camera rolling. Crouched with my tied wrists behind my back, I glowered at them. "You won't get away with this. You're gonna regret today."

The petite girl strode over and, with surprising strength, dragged me up.

I fought her, but the throbbing pain of my dislocated arm and spinning head numbed my movements.

She pulled my sweater over my head, wrapped it around the rope that bound my wrists, and stepped back. Her partner stepped forward with her phone, snapping pictures of me in my bra, and zooming in on the purpling bruises, hanging arm, and broken ribs and chuckling as she assaulted me with her camera.

"Is that all you got?" I taunted. Madness crowded my thoughts. I was fighting both battles inside and out.

The girl slapped me across the face.

Blood dripped from a cut on my lip. "Why?"

"You murdered my mother! Harris, all you fucking doctors! Ellen Han is my mother!" The girl screamed and slapped me more.

My ears rang, and my vision crossed into doubles.

The girl grabbed my hair and pinched my chin up. "Michael Harris. I know you're watching this. Noon at her hotel. Or this bitch dies."

I shook my head and laughed. "He won't be there. You lose."

The girl screamed and swung the bat right at my face.

Red exploded. Fuck it. Let the monsters come.

Ellen

32

The rope cut Ellen's wrists. A chill clung to her exposed pregnant belly, leaving a clammy feeling on her skin. The smell of salt and brine, with voices rebounding on the walls, disappeared up the deck. In the dark, her breath was labored as Baby Noah woke and stretched his foot out, pushing at her skin till she could see every little toe and heel.

Another surge lifted the boat and smacked it down. More seawater and rain poured down from the deck, sloshing against her ankles. The chill clung tighter, adding pinpricks to the goose bumps already scattered over her arms and legs. Again, the boat surged forward, bouncing against another crest.

A beam of light lit the metal stairs and trailed down to the bed of grey tarps. Ellen spotted the silver tip of a screwdriver tucked under it and wobbled with her thirty-six-weeks-pregnant weight and the roll of the boat to get it. Luck was with her that the boat tilted and she slid to the side and rammed her dislocated arm back into her shoulder. The popping back of her bone into the socket was excruciating, but the pain was gone in an instant.

With the screwdriver, she worked on her bindings, snatched

Alice's winter coat from the foldable cot, and then snuck up the stairs.

The midnight sky was littered with stars as the winds and rain receded to the north. Adding to it was a bright horizon where a stretch of city lights blinked like rainbow dust. The two women were standing at the pilot's helm under an arched awning. Ellen watched as the tall woman bent down to kiss the petite girl.

In the shadows of the rotating high beam of light on top of the yacht, she waited. With swollen ninja feet, she edged up the steps onto the pilot's helm.

The women pulled away, and the tall one kept her hands on the girl's shoulders. "We can't drag her around Seoul. The CCTV will catch us."

"We'll leave her in the trunk," suggested the girl.

"Honey, there are eyes everywhere. Let's toss her over now and tell him she's still alive."

"Michael Harris isn't stupid. He'll want evidence. And, what about Oppa Ji Woon? He said to leave Alice alone." The girl pouted.

"Honey, he likes that bitch. He's a traitor. Men think with their dicks." The tall one kissed the girl's head. "Let's throw her over now."

The beam left the helm, and Ellen moved in. Neither one saw her. She stood up behind the tall woman and drove the screwdriver deep into her back. The boat lunged forward with another high crest, and the woman fell onto the wheel.

"Gina?" The tall woman gurgled and slumped to the floor. "Gina!" The girl screamed. She glanced over at the hulking shadow of Ellen in Alice's thick coat.

The waves swelled, and the wheel spun, throwing the boat sharply left, tossing the girl and Ellen back. Ellen caught the railing and cradled her stomach, heading down to the deck while the girl struggled to steer the boat afloat. She crossed over the pile of ropes she had laid earlier and picked up the boat paddle. Targeting the dark spots, she avoided the rotating high beam and waited.

A gun cackled, and a bullet whizzed by. It grazed Ellen's cheek. Two more shots came closer. If not for the waves trashing the boat, they would have met their mark.

Ellen squinted in the rain. The spotlight lit on the girl's face. "Sophie."

She stepped out into the spotlight and revealed her protruding stomach.

"Eomma?" Sophie dropped her gun, skipped down the steps, and hugged her mother. "Why? How are you here?" Sophie pulled away and felt her mother's stomach. Noah pushed under her hand. "Noah…" Tears ran down her cheeks. "Noah's here, too. Eomma. Appa died in the war, and Grandpa and Grandma were in an accident. The Parks came and took me to Korea."

"Sorry I took so long, nae ttal…my daughter." Tears ran down Ellen's cheeks.

"Eomma…" Sophie hugged her tight. "It's just..just…I was so mad! I loved Pearl. I didn't mean to push you."

"Pearl?" Ellen stiffened. "You can't like girls, my dearest! You'll go to hell!"

Sophie snapped her head back. "Hell? Why do you always say that?"

Ellen placed her hands on Sophie's shoulder. "It's okay. You're young and confused. God will understand. You haven't met the right boy yet."

Sophie pulled her hair, eyes glaring. "No! No! Stop telling me what to do!" She froze. Confused, she stared at Ellen. "No. I'm, I'm twenty! You left me first! All of you left me." Her eyes dropped to Ellen's stomach. "Can't you love me?"

Sea water struck them, mingling with hot tears. "Noah. Noah! It's always Noah! I came first!"

Ellen reached out as Sophie backed away and picked up the gun. She pointed at Ellen's stomach.

"You never asked me if I wanted a sibling. You always did what you wanted. They made me a Director at Park Holdings. I'm in Forbes! They loved me now. Why can't you?"

Sophie wiped her grubby nose, pointed the gun at Ellen's face, and dropped it back to her stomach unsteadily. "I hate him."

Ellen backed away from Sophie's gun, covering her stomach with her hands. "Sophie, you're scaring your brother."

"I'm not going to change. I always liked girls. It's not a sin! The world's changed. You're the wrong one!"

The rotating spotlight shone on Ellen's face.

Sophie rubbed her eyes. "Alice? What did you do to her?" She lunged for Alice and pushed her against the railing of the boat. "Bitch!"

Lightning flashed above their heads, followed by the quick sound of thunderclaps. The yacht heaved and tossed. Ellen's face appeared again.

"Eomma?"

The spotlight appeared again, and the face returned to Alice's.

"You tricked me!" Sophie screamed.

"Sophie, it's me. Eomma." Ellen cried.

"No! Eomma is dead!" With inhuman strength, Sophie tipped Ellen. Noah kicked fiercely in Ellen's stomach. "Die!" Sophie pulled the trigger.

The bullet went through her ribs. Ellen grabbed Sophie's arm.

Ellen fell. Alice fell. Sophie screamed.

The waves rose like giant hands. Silver lightning darted between clouds. Down, down they fell into the churning waters of the endless ocean. Dark depths stretched up to drag them in.

Ellen. Alice. Ellen again.

The waves arched high and crashed into the boat amidst the cries of a woman.

Alice

33

4:44am, The moment of death

Water stole the rest of my air. Shutters of a camera, nanoseconds flashed. The rest of my life zipped by.

People huddled in their jackets, scarves, and ear muffs. Four feet of snow and slush lined the roads, splashing onto cars and buses. The night market was bright and noisy. The scent of whole fried potatoes, donuts, and the sweet, spicy, tangy smell of *gochujang. Tteokbokki.* Pop-ups were selling those spicy rice cakes. I chose one. Someone was watching. I dived into the crowd. Filtered past a family of four with a stroller. The man in the black hoodie followed.

Sounds of skateboards along the Han River. I ran, and they crashed into me. His hand reached down. His coat was grey, not black. "Jason!" The male nurse. I heard he left San Francisco. He never said goodbye. Not saying meant I was nothing to him. Alone again. That was my life.

Mother dying. A black mask over his nose and lips. He stood at the back of the room and watched as I made a mess of her funeral.

Photographs in my coat pocket. Children dead in beds of white. Was that Michael in the lab coat? Who put them there in my pocket? Were they real or photoshopped? I didn't want to go to Seoul. Too many bad memories. Instinct told me not to go. "Go to Seoul." The note said. Was it Merle? No. It wasn't her style.

The man in the black hoodie stood across the street. In the shadows with his face hidden, staring at me through the window. He was there on campus, at my lectures, where I liked to eat. I told the police. Eli got me a new alarm security system. No one believed me. They think I'm crazy.

Michael, my mother, step-father David, and the faces of people I met along the way. Those whom I thought we could be friends, only to be tricked and used. There was Park Ji Woon, Miyako's ghostly pale hand, which landed on the floor with a thud. I saved no one. The barn burning, a spark of heat rising to the sky. God's wrath at the man who took me and the boy who gave his life to save mine. "Peter!" I shouted for him. My friend, my brother, the son my father never had.

"He wants you dead." The tall woman said. "Ji Woon could have caught up with the car." Like my mother, he kept still, his legs refused to move because his heart didn't. Those seconds he pondered, those seconds he let them have me, made all the difference.

"He left you for dead." A man said.

My voices were panicking, cajoling me to wake up. If I loved them, they'd love me too. A life for a life, they said. If I opened up and gave in to them, I would be stronger than I'd ever been.

No one could kill me. No one could kill us. I am immortal.

But the ocean was too vast. Too much water to swim in. The watery grave was pulling me in.

It was easy to let go.

Ji Woon left me here, in this ocean, my grave.

Lies. They were all lies. Everyone was a liar. The psychos in my head were no better.

I didn't deserve love. I wasn't good enough. I'll never be good enough.

Okaasan never forgave. She never forgot the wrongs Michael and I did to her. Couldn't she see we did it because we loved her?

Maybe I didn't. Maybe I wanted her punished because her hatred burned my heart.

"Three, two, one. When I snap my fingers, wake up." I know that voice. Ji Woon.

The pressure of the sea was too great. My tears mixed with salt. My eyes hurt. I could see no more.

«Alice…*Saranghae*." I watched the muscles on his back flex as he put on his shirt and buckled his pants. Young Ji Woon was the best birthday gift a girl like me could get.

He kissed my lips and dropped his tongue in for a final taste. In the dim lights of the hotel room, centuries ago, it was hard to make out his features. Teenage me still longed for him because his voice stirred my soul when it should have been hate.

My heart twisted for the boy I betrayed.

"Did you get your revenge?" I asked him, and the shadow that covered his face answered what his lips could not.

Bodies clamoring over bodies. Writhing shiny black worms.

"Three. Two. One."

Heavy ashes were drifting from the sky. Ballooning smoke and red flames were rushing in.

He's choking me.

She's choking me.

They're choking me.

Light pierced through my mind fog, and a hand reached out.

I grabbed it.

34

A minute after dying

The sea glowed gold. In the warmth, I felt cold, locked in a bubble of nothingness floating in space. Orange lights seep through my eyelids as my fingers lie dead on my chest.

Let me fade, I told them. The voices whimpered. Their fear grew as I gave in to dark peace. My mind was released from the vestiges of my past, emptied as their memories kept seeping through, leaching, hoping to latch onto mine.

Their buzzing was pinpricks compared to the booming of the golden light. I knew it wasn't heaven. A girl like me didn't deserve one.

Then, all of a sudden, hands grabbed under my arms, and an oxygen mask was placed over my face. Two divers in seal suits wrapped straps across my waist and legs.

Snatched up to the surface by a hovering helicopter. Wind blasted my hair against my face. The sounds of the blades were like wet rubber suits slapping together. Ahead, the city's lights dazzled on the horizon.

Three Coast Guard boats and a helicopter surrounded the area for this daring rescue. Someone reported that *Exodus* — the yacht the kidnappers used- was found.

They were talking amongst themselves now. An anonymous call tipped the police that the American woman, Alice Steeple, was last seen taken aboard this boat at the marina. I was trending online, and the whole of Seoul and the surrounding provinces were involved.

"Your vitals look good." The doctor shook his head and muttered to his nurse and rescuers. "This is the first I'd seen. No hypothermia or injuries. How long was she in the water? What about the American? Did they find her?"

I was afraid to speak. Afraid to look. And most of all, scared to know.

One thing was sure. I wasn't Alice.

───────────

Forty minutes later,
Seoul Gangnam Police Station

The room was tiny, with four white walls, one of which had shades drawn down, a table in the center, and two plastic and uncomfortable chairs chairs.

It didn't matter what I said or didn't say. The biggest lie was on my face.

I stared at her. In the looking glass, marbled in the shade of black.

Her face. Not mine.

They tell me my name.

Sophie Han.

My killer. The murderer.

"Where is Alice Steeple? What did you do to her?" They asked. It had become an International affair. The terrorist kidnapping. Their video shot to millions. The world is watching. The US Secretary of State was involved. Hurting the American was a slight to the US's face. Urgency riddled in their voice. Whispers between the investigators. Was Alice dead? No one could have survived those waves and that storm.

Gina was dead. Stabbed in the back.

"Miss Han, your guardian will be here soon." The cop in blue said. My prints weren't in the system, but they knew who I was.

Her face was plastered on the bus stops and billboards. I'd seen her several times in my few days in Seoul.

Sophie Han. She was on the cover of Forbes in January, top thirty under thirty, and the youngest member of the Board of Directors in the Park Entertainment legacy. The *cheobol*. Heir to a media mogul's throne.

The resemblance was slight. Ellen had a mom-next-door look, while Sophie had a superstar's makings. Or it was the Korean beauty industry at its best.

I stared at my reflection in the interrogation looking glass — a black and crystalized sheet of rock like the winking glimmers in my heart. The drowning earlier consumed my thoughts as I weaved through the newfound memories of those personalities who died for me.

In their death, the throes were the same. Each time the lungs struggled for the last breath, the heart stopped pumping, and the brain shut down. The countless times I had to die so I could live.

Behind the glass, the interrogators were staring back. To them, I looked like Sophie Han — Pixie haircut on smooth, pale, blemish-free skin.

The police came to my interrogation room. One at a time and then two. Like the people on the rescue boat, they kept asking about Alice.

Sophie Han was the prime suspect. Dash cams and CCTVs at the marina caught Sophie and another woman, Gina Chen, dragging Alice out of a car and onto the boat.

"Alice is dead," I said.

"Where's her body?" They asked.

"I don't know," I replied.

They gave me a grey tracksuit and *gukbap* — stewed beef with soup and rice. I ate it and then crouched, grabbing my stomach.

"What's wrong, Miss Han?" The cop in charge asked.

"My stomach." I cried. "It hurts."

He radioed his supervisor, and I dropped to the ground, curling my legs in. "I need the bathroom."

He showed me the way, standing by the door.

"I will wait here."

The toilet stall was grey and narrow, and the porcelain sink was small, barely the width of my waist. The smell of urine and chlorine stung my nose as I scanned for something I could use. I grabbed the mop and broke off the bristles.

"Miss Han, are you done?" The cop called out.

"Yes." I swung open the door. The cop looked up from his phone, and before he could react, I struck as I'd learned.

One in his stomach, another on his shoulder. I was careful not to hurt his major organs as he groaned and slid down the wall.

In a blink, I was on the streets.

—||—

35

Cars honked as I dashed across the icy road. A winter morning in Seoul was dark, gloomy, and extremely cold. I couldn't feel my toes after sprinting past with only socks and indoor slippers. All shops were closed, except for a chain coffee shop, which opened at six o'clock.

I touched my straight, silky hair, brushing the sides away from my jaw. I missed my warm, wavy curls and my body, which was taller and curvier, and not easily blown by the wind.

Running around Sophie's four-foot-eleven body made me feel childlike. This was the first time I felt disturbed in someone's face, and the first time I was aware that I was someone else.

I frowned and gritted my jaw, mimicking the look Sophie gave.

A gust of winter wind ruffled my hair, plastering my bangs over my eyes as emotions barraged my heart. A manhunt in a foreign country was too much. Like a buoy, I bobbled with no land in sight.

I wrapped myself up in a long gray coat I found in one of the offices and searched for the Korean won I took from that table in my pockets. The money was enough for some food.

"Can I borrow your phone? I lost mine." I asked the woman in the Korean bakery. I learned some Korean before I came.

"Hello?" The phone picked up. "Eli?"

"Who's this?" My best friend Eli sounded tired.

"It's me, Eli."

I heard a rustle of sheets. "Aly?" His voice dropped to a whisper. "Is that you? Why do you sound different?"

"Something's happened. Eli."

"Did you turn again?" He cut me off. "No. No. Where are you?" I heard the sounds of clothes rustling.

"Stay there. Give me the addy. I have to tell Ji Woon. That guy's freaking insane! When your video came out, he went psycho, dude. Ballistic! Aly, he yelled at everyone, and punched the US Ambassador!"

"Is he with you?" Was Ji Woon just pretending? The woman said he planned it. Ji Woon wanted me dead, too.

"He's out with that FBI dude...Odeh. They've been searching the waters. I just got back."

"Does he know what you can do?" Eli asked.

"No. Only you do," I said.

"Good. Good. Okay, where are you"?

"Gangnam. Take this down." I gave him the address of the coffeeshop.

"Got it. Stay there. I'll come alone. Wait for me, Aly."

I was eating *jjinppang-mandu* and waiting for Eli when I noticed a black car with tinted windows returning to the light again. The window of the car rolled down, and a shadow of a man stared.

No, I can't be caught.

—||—

36

A woman in a maroon suit got out of that black car, followed by a large man in a black suit. "Director Han, please come with us." The moment she walked into the store.

"Who are you?" I backed into the corner, and the maroon woman snatched the phone from the bakery owner's hands. The man moved fast despite his girth, and soon, both had me against a wall.

"He is waiting for you in the car." The woman gestured to the door. Not wanting to cause more trouble to the owner, I stepped out and followed them to the Rolls-Royce. The scent of musk and man's cologne plagued my nose when I got in.

His eyes caught mine. They had the same look — annoyed and hard to read when they meant business.

Ji Woon's father could pass off as someone in his late thirties, and if someone said they were brothers, I'd believe them. Unlike Ji Woon, his father was stockier and in a tailored suit; he wasn't a guy to mess with.

"Chairman Park," I said.

Before I could buckle up, he grabbed my shoulder. His fingers dug in like blunt claws. "What did you do?"

I didn't reply. Watching his face turned red as the muscle in his jaw twitched. It was a staring contest, and this was something years of therapy taught me well.

"What the hell is wrong with you?" He threw his iPad at me. "The President called. The Blue House is telling me to hand you over."

"Ji Woon is calling in all his favors for that American!"

He rubbed his eyes with the palms of his hands. "The US Ambassador wants this settled fast before it becomes a bigger scandal."

"We're going to say it was a prank. AI Hackers. We have your alibi. It wasn't you who tortured that woman. You followed Gina Lee. Submit your apologies today!"

"It wasn't a prank," I muttered, and I picked up the iPad and caught the picture of me tied up with my bra exposed and my face bleeding with cuts. My left arm hung in a weird angle to my side, and on my right shoulder was my heart-shaped scar.

"Did you take your meds? When was the last time you saw Ji Woon?"

Just hearing his name was enough to stoke my flames. "I don't need him."

"Gina is dead. We'll pin it on her and the guard at the marina."

"Secretary Choi." He tapped the seat in front. "Call Ji Woon. Tell him to meet us at Sophie's apartment."

I wasn't ready to meet Ji Woon. I hugged myself tight. Everything was scorching through, a race of flames through dry tinder. My heart struggled to beat, and my head tried to make sense.

Forgiveness. Did that exist?

Which were lies? Which was the truth? Everything he did was calculated. That boy Ji Woon in my dreams died.

The fact was, this Park Ji Woon did not love me.

———————

"Where are we going?" I finally asked when the car stopped at a red light. I tested my door, and it wouldn't open.

"It's a child locked." The secretary sneered. Other than the old driver in his seventies, Secretary Choi was there, imbued with hate. I could feel anger coiling up her neatly styled hair and slithering to the car's roof. Peter would say, "It was nice and toasty."

"Where are we going?" I asked.

"To the airport," she snapped.

"And then where are we going?"

"Change of plans. Costa Rica. Stay for a year till the gossips die."

"And if I want to stay longer?" I asked.

"Where are the stock certificates?" She asked.

"I tore them up."

She whipped around and pierced me with her eyes. "Ms. Sophie Han, this isn't a joke."

"Oh. So, I'm not a director anymore? Are you speaking in *Banmal*?"

"You don't deserve the promotion. I told Chairman Park you'll not appreciate his efforts." She snapped.

"And you do? You're in Mistress, aren't you?"

She reached for me with her painted talons, and I scooted away. The car swerved, and she was forced to turn around.

I stared at the scarf around her neck. The voices in my head were gleefully giving me ideas. My fingers itched. What was one more?

I was riveted to the fluttering cloth.

The car stopped at another red light. I grabbed both ends of the silk cloth and tugged it hard. She fought and scratched my hands. I laughed as she choked.

The driver panicked. The car skidded across the ice and crashed into a tree. He fumbled with his handle, flung his door open, and stumbled out.

I followed, climbing over to his seat, grabbed the secretary's handbag, and made a dash across the road. I glided through the slush and ice with my bare feet.

Ice burned like fire, but I didn't care.

There was little time left. I had another date to get to.

Ji Woon

37

January 12, 2022,
Two days before the drowning

She wouldn't stop screaming.

The Alice he knew wasn't explosive. The girl Ji Woon remembered in Seoul and the woman he followed in San Francisco, whom he dated for a week, were both confident and complicated. Seeing her this way was very troubling.

"You broke her." Guilt spoke from the inside.

"Alice. It's okay, it's okay. Everything's okay," he coaxed her. "I'll count down to one, and you'll wake up."

She slapped his hands away, and when she couldn't unlock the car door, he purposely locked it; she slammed her head against it.

He reached out to cushion her head with his hand, and she kept hitting the side repeatedly and making dull thudding sounds, mumbling in a child's voice.

"He can't hurt you. You're safe with me. Dearest, you're safe..."

With a heavy heart, he pulled the sleeves of her coat over her hands and tied them together into a straitjacket. She thrashed against him — fighting the bonds, gnashing her teeth, and crying. Her arms poked and bruised his sides, but he kept blocking.

"You're safe. You're safe." He kept repeating. "Three, two, one." He snapped his fingers.

He deserved to burn in hell. As a psychiatrist, what he did to her was something he'd never consider doing to his patients. He toyed with her when he knew she needed help. Yes, he caused this. He pushed her too far, and her mind was lost. Blinded by his revenge, he couldn't let it go. He blamed her for Harris's crimes, even when he knew with D.I.D., it wasn't Alice's fault. And, knowing her case, he was where the blame went.

"You're safe." He breathed deeply. "Alice, wake up. It's me, Ji Woon."

She whimpered. Tears streaked her face like fallen stars.

It was easy to get to her. Her shards were obvious, and with her prior history, he had many places he could pick. He took her when he could, drilling through her memories and searching for clues. Before, she betrayed him, but now it was his turn.

He knew he would meet her if he were at UCSF Medical. In fact, with his investigator watching her moves, he knew exactly when and where to catch her. Using a project as an excuse to assess D.I.D. patients, he persuaded Ed Bailey that it was a win-win to go to San Francisco. Salinger was starting up, and there weren't enough patients to test their hypnotherapy skills.

Those who depended on him for their revenge kept pushing him forward. Finally, Michael Harris wasn't going to get away. His detailed, coordinated plan with the FBI was to uproot every part of this man's life and erase the foundation of his beliefs. He would betray his partners who believed in Harris, and the lives of those whom this man remotely cared for would be destroyed.

With each action and tweak, Ji Woon made his pawns move, and for Alice, the more he observed and spoke to her, and the more he touched her, the more obvious it was. As much as he tried to eradicate Alice, she was buried like a thorn into his bleeding heart. Wrapped and melded into his flesh with a decade of longing, she was impossible to extract.

Seeing her again, breathing in her scent, tasting her fears and reliving her anger and insecurities, holding her close and being part of her life had made him realize — he would own her. In his mind, the more time he was near her, and that Harris knew, the father would hate it.

Ji Woon sent pictures of Alice and himself to rile his enemy up and rejoiced in seeing Michael Harris flinch at Ji Woon's actions on his only descendant. The father-daughter relationship was estranged, and any word from Harris would worsen things.

However, months later, days before Ji Woon's grand revenge, watching Alice fight with her mind, he wondered who the bigger fool was. Hurting her was bashing himself. Many times, he wanted to take off his mask and love her. Just be a normal couple and live that simple life they wished for.

The storm finally relented, and her energy was spent.

The car was quiet again. Her chest heaved gently, and her eyes fluttered in her sleep. During her restfulness, Ji Woon picked her up and returned her to her room.

38

Ji Woon was in shock. There were chains and cuffs anchored to her bed. On the bedside table was a silver box of syringes and pills. Her disorder was worse than he thought. It was debilitating and affecting her everyday life.

Alice was sweating and tossing in her sleep. The cuffs he put on her should keep her safe. He wiped her wrist with a cool, wet towel and watched her stir in her sleep.

"Alice?" Her eyelids fluttered but remained closed. "How are you feeling?" He gently checked her forehead.

"Hmm?" she answered. Her body gestures were languid. The chain and cuffs jingled when she lifted her hand. Her mouth moved, muttering something.

He bent closer to listen when suddenly, she grabbed his sweater and pulled him down. Their mouths collided, and her teeth cut his lip. Her hands were fast and hooked over his head, and she spun the chain around his neck. She kicked him to the side and jumped onto him. On instinct, he stuck his hand through the gap between the chain and his throat as her arms stretched to tighten the links.

Coughing and choking, he fought for control. Her thighs

squeezed his sides as his vision blurred. He forced himself to look up. Black irises seized his fears. Twin faces are similar but not entirely the same. If the eyes were windows, Alice was the melting of snow, and in Merle's, a tornado bent on destruction.

"Merle." He gasped.

"Where's the key?" She shook him hard.

"I don't know…"

She pulled the chain tighter.

"Wait!"

She tilted her head like a doll with a broken neck. "You're new." She smiled, revealing straight, overly white teeth. She lowered her lashes, opening her mouth slightly as she slowly licked her plump, red lips. "A friend of Alice?"

He slammed his head on hers and tried to push her off. One hand attempted to unwrap the chain around his neck.

Merle jerked her elbow down, and his neck snapped back. He gagged for air. Together, they wrestled like two gladiators in a ring. Each tried to get the upper hand, fighting for a leg up.

Ji Woon panted. The metal chain links scratched the sides of his neck, cutting his skin. "I have the key."

Merle laughed, a deep, hysterical laugh as she straddled him, tightening the choker chain when he didn't comply. "Liar…liar pants on fire…" She sang. "You know what? I changed my mind." She smashed her mouth on his, coaxing him to open his. With finesse, she slid her hips up and down his torso as he struggled.

The scent of Alice in the sheets was too tempting, and his body reacted. With Merle pressed against him, it was hard to focus. She giggled when she felt him respond. Except that the sound of Merle's voice was jarring against his ears.

He turned his head to the side as she kissed his neck and

hovered over his collarbone. Her hand found the top of his pants and slipped eagerly beneath his buckle. He flinched from her, but she kept attacking till she got what she wanted.

"Didn't Alice tell you? We share everything." She jerked his chain and caused him to spasm with coughs.

In between breaths, Ji Woon forced himself to stay calm as she stroked him.

Her breath was hot against his ear. "You can pretend I'm her. Fuck me good, and I'll let you go."

He sighed and turned to face Merle, kissing her back hard, telling himself this meant nothing. This wasn't the time to be a stickler. He had to bide his time. His mouth trailed down her chin and nibbled her neck. Slowly, he unbuttoned her sweater and slipped it off her shoulders, teasing her warm skin with his lips as she moaned.

"I will…" he whispered, and Merle smiled, hurriedly unwinding the chain from his neck to pull his sweater off. The second the chain came off, he dropped a foot to the ground and tossed her on the carpet. Merle hit the carpet with a loud thud. Ji Woon pounced on her, tucking the chain under her back and spreading her arms apart, anchoring her with his weight. "…never hurt Alice."

She laughed as she playfully struggled. "You like it rough? Me too!"

"Where are the graves?" He pressed her wrists down. "Where are the children's graves?"

Merle stopped moving. Her breath was panting as she closed her eyes. "I don't know."

"You're lying." He pushed her arms up above her head and grabbed both wrists with one hand. With the other hand, he grabbed her face and made her look at him.

"Where are their graves? He killed them. Took their brains…"

"No! You're wrong! Daddy won't do that! It wasn't him!" She tried to push him off.

"The oldest was twelve and the youngest three. It wasn't just the skulls he cut. He took their limbs and their organs. He left them in pieces. Merle."

Tears clung to her lashes. Merle's face paled. "It's not him! Daddy saves lives. He won't kill those kids! He promised me!"

"We found specimens in his Muir Woods cabin. Carefully labeled and stored with his research papers. There were videos of him conducting his secret surgeries. You cleaned his messes. You knew about his experiments."

"What are you talking about? What Muir Woods?"

"You're not the only one he has?" He asked.

"Shut your mouth! I'm his only one! Get off me!" She fought his hands. But she had the chains, and he didn't.

Unlike Alice, there was no forgiveness for her. Merle manipulated the evidence. She hired that gigolo and caused Miyako's death.

"You helped him kill children."

"No!" She screamed. "It wasn't me! Daddy doesn't hurt babies! He won't. He'd never, not after what happened to us…"

"Us? Who? Nikolai? Was he part of it, too?"

"Don't you dare touch Nick!"

"Nikolai Ivanshov is a criminal. Did he help Harris dump the bodies?"

"No! He washes Daddy's funds. It's not him!"

"What about the graves, Merle?"

"Maybe it's him?" she cried. "Cyrus? No. Not that traitor or the man with a black hoodie…"

When Ji Woon was in San Francisco, he heard about that man. FBI Agent Odeh told him about Alice's stalker.

Twice, Ji Woon saw the man in the black hoodie, too — once in an alley, with their informant dead, and then another time in Alice's home. The man stood by the window, looking out with the shades apart and a hoodie drawn over his face.

Odeh said the SF police came and did a search. They checked Alice's security feed but found nothing. After that, Ji Woon sent his people to protect her. No one saw that man in the hoodie since the day of her mother's funeral.

Seizing his distraction, Merle tried to knee him. Ji Woon snatched the syringe from the nightstand and stabbed her arm.

Merle's angry eyes flashed in a fury and then fluttered closed.

He tossed the syringe and placed his fingers over her throat to check her pulse. When it slowed, he got off her and staggered to the window, away from her reach. With his forehead and hands on the cool glass, he breathed loudly, counting his breaths to calm down.

The chains rattled, and he recoiled. After checking, she was still asleep, so he took another deep breath. He should have been more careful. His shoulders shook as he laughed. A cold ache washed over him. Damned, he almost died.

———

Alice was slumped on the carpet again. Her brown, wavy hair covered parts of her pale face. He knew he would find the crease between her brows if he looked. On her bare shoulder was her heart-shaped scar. It appeared when Merle vanished.

She was back — his Alice. He recalled their wish upon the stars. When they were of legal age, they would elope and marry, running away from people who used them. That night, they made many promises that he looked back on, and Alice knew they would never come true.

Sorrow hung like a cloud. He often wondered if she meant them. Suppose they could drop everything, turn their backs on this world, and be happy.

That was a long time ago. After fighting Merle, he should have left the room.

Why couldn't he leave? His heart ached from a thousand wounds. Not a day went by that he didn't think of her. He loved Alice, but could he forgive Merle? And forgive those who came with her?

God saved him. He was going to get burned.

39

Cold hands pressed the base of his neck, followed by a cool jell against his skin. Ji Woon bolted from his chair with his fists raised to his chest and blinked with his crusty eyes.

"It's me," she stepped back with her hands raised. "Ji Woon, it's me, Alice."

"How do I know it's you?" He frowned.

"If you see me as Alice, it's me."

He shook his head.

"Fine, ask me something that only I know."

His pulse raced as flashes of last night's fight with Merle juxtaposed with Alice's face. He had a brush with death. A realization that only came after Merle slept. Because they looked alike, he let his guard down.

"White," he said.

"Shroud," she replied.

"Red," he said.

"Hands."

"Blue-grey," he said.

"Stormy clouds," she replied.

"Black," he said.

"Ash."

He lowered his fists. "Pink," he said.

"Baby's foot."

Ji Woon ran his hand through his hair. It was a game he and Alice played that night Miyako died. It was something Alice learned in therapy to help with grief.

She approached him carefully. "So, can I?" She showed him the cloth bandage and pointed to the first-aid kit on the table. "I'm almost done."

Slowly, he sat back down, eyeing her warily before gesturing her over with his hand. Heart hammering fast, he stared at the top of her head as she wrapped the bandage around his neck — the familiar scent of her masked his worries. Merle didn't have that scent. Another marker that will help him identify.

"I've checked and cleaned the cuts. There will be bruising for a while."

Alice stepped aside, walked over to the mini-fridge, and pulled out a bottle of honey lemon tea. "Here. This will help your throat." She offered him the bottle and studied him quietly as he drank.

They both sat in their spots — his by the window and hers on her bed. Together, they watched the sunrise. Winter clouds gave way to a hue of orange. The heater in the room kept the frost off the glass, and the Han River, with its plates of ice, was beautiful in its stillness.

"What time is it?" he broke the silence.

"Seven," she replied, sounding sad.

He turned, and their eyes met.

She tucked her hair behind her ear. "Why didn't you leave?"

"I was worried."

She sighed. "Who did I become? What did I do?" There was no asking if he knew of her multiple personality disorder. With Alice, all it took was a glance. They were connected. Words need not be spoken.

His eyes dropped to her lips, and a flush of heat warmed his face when he remembered what he had to do to distract Merle.

"Merle?" Alice asked when he didn't reply.

Alice read people well. They spoke about it that night long ago and were surprised at their similarities. Throughout her life, she was taught to gauge how her actions impact people's feelings, and to survive with her disorder, she had to lie and pretend her way out of what Merle and her other personalities did.

"I'm sorry." Alice wrung her hands on her lap. Gloom settled over her shoulders, and her hazel greens were dulled with blunt pain. "Do I want to know what she did?" She closed her eyes, and he resisted the urge to soothe her brows.

"Merle is not you." He pressed his hands on the glass.

"Please don't make me call her out," She panicked.

She remembered what he said in the car. He couldn't promise her that. He had more questions for Merle. Getting Merle to betray Harris was tricky. However, until Harris was brought to justice, the dead and their families would not leave him alone.

Closure. He owed it to those who were suffering. "How sorry are you?" He rubbed his shoulder, which was aching from when he fought Merle. Silence stretched between them, and Alice didn't answer. He wondered if she knew he would do whatever it took to get what he wanted. "I've been working with D.I.D. patients for years. Like Dr. Bailey, I use hypnotherapy. My success rate is ninety percent. Better than Bailey's."

She gripped the bedsheets till her knuckles turned white. "How many personalities do you have?" he asked.

She bit her lip. He thought she wouldn't answer. "About five primary? The rest come and go."

"Do they have psychopathic tendencies?" He asked.

Her eyes widened in shock. He needed her to trust him again, as she had done when he was Jason before he left her and broke her heart. "Nothing you say will surprise me. I have a patient with twenty constant personalities that fit every type in the MBTI."

She raised her head till their eyes met. There was fear in them, but also fierceness. "All of them. Psychopaths. My neurofeedback changes when I'm one of them. Their brain patterns are identical when I'm them, but it is in the average range when I'm myself."

"Ji Woon…I don't know how much longer I can hold them back."

"What do you want?" he asked.

"I want them dead. Gone. I want to forget all about them. Bailey tried. Can you do better?"

Ji Woon didn't want to be her mountain. But a shred of tear from her eye was enough for him to move one. One thing's clear as it always was. Being with her was a disaster. Alice was waiting for a landslide to happen.

Alice

40

January 14, Present time

"Miss? Miss? We are here." The man in the cab tapped on his plastic shield. "Grand Hotel Solaris".

I shrugged off the last vestiges of sleep and pulled off my hoodie.

"Fifty-one thousand, six hundred won." He took the credit card and pushed it into a card machine.

The cab driver stared at my blood-stained hand and my face, and then dropped my credit card in my hand. The moment both my feet touched the concrete, he sped off.

A blast of wind slammed into me, and I shuddered as I wrapped Secretary Choi's scarf over my face and zipped up my coat.

Rows of vans and people made it impossible to walk in. Like many, I wore the basic black winter coat, scarf, and mask. No one noticed how the clothes were too tight, or the boots were not for my small feet, because my reality was what I wanted them to see. Besides, the reporters were either on their phones or chatting with their colleagues.

Snow pelted against my hair, forming shavings of red ice sliding down my cheeks. My bloody hand smeared the ivory stone lion guarding the hotel as I mistakenly leaned on it to tie my bootlaces. My mind was still fuzzy as I tried to recall how I'd hurt my hand.

"Sophie Han!" Someone shouted and pointed at me.

"Damn it!" I swiveled and dashed.

Sophie's face flashed by as I ran along panels of glass in the lobby. A truck was offloading produce as I snaked past the delivery staff and their boxes. Suddenly, a hand shot out and caught my arm, pulling me to an open door.

"This way!" I caught a glance to see who it was before we slipped inside. Ji Woon and I sprinted up the stairs. The people chasing us banged on the one-way-out fire exit, and their voices echoed in thunderous drums. We kept climbing the endless steps. Our panting ricocheted until we stopped on the floor. He pressed his card key on the key panel. We stopped at a random door, and he pressed a master card key and checked the room before pulling me in.

"Sit!" He tossed me onto the king-sized bed and flung the curtains apart. The late morning light killed the shadows in the room and blinded my eyes. I sat up with my arms crossed. "Why the fuck are you here?" His voice was cold and gritty.

I flinched.

"Where's Secretary Choi? Your flight's in…" He checked his phone. In my mind, I was thinking of words to hurt him.

He ran his hands through his hair. "Okay…fuck it. Sophie. Where is she? Where's Alice?" His voice instantly lost its edge and hung with worry.

He strode to me, arms raised, hands reaching to grab my

shoulders, and stopped. He backed away, pulling at his hair. "What did you do to her? Please. Tell me she's still alive. Please…" His voice broke.

Tears formed in my eyes and ran down my cheeks.

He shook his head. "I know…I know I owe you, but don't say you…" He swallowed hard. "I told you not to hurt her. It wasn't part of the plan. You weren't supposed to hurt her!" His eyes flashed with anger, and he looked away. "Look, I'll pay you back. Whatever you want — anything except her. I'll take her away from here. If the sight of her makes you mad, you won't see her again. It wasn't her fault. She has D.I.D. She has no control over what Merle does…"

„Ji Woon…"

Tears welled in his eyes. "I beg you. I just want to know she's alright. Just tell me she's alive. Please, she wasn't part of the bargain. We agreed. She was just bait. I don't want to hear…"

He sat down on the bed. His hands covered his face.

"She's still breathing. I'm not too late. I can't be too late…"

„Ji Woon…" I gripped his hands.

"I was at the station. I rushed over when I heard they rescued a girl. I thought it was her. You filmed that fucking video! You got what you wanted." His grip tightened. "You punished her enough. Come on. It wasn't all her fault! Harris pushed for that drug! You knew Alice didn't want to. The hospital sided with him. They killed your mother. You can't blame Alice for all of that…"

"I know," I said. "Alice is alive. She's fine."

He breathed out deeply. His eyes met mine. "Where is she?"

"Ji Woon…I…"

His gaze narrowed. "Why are you calling me Ji Woon?"

He dropped his hands and paced the room. Glancing at me every few seconds. "No…it can't be…but…Sophie calls me Jason Oppa."

"It's me, Alice."

He froze. "How? Why are you awake? How…"

He snatched my hoodie and slapped my hands away as he unzipped it and pulled at my sweater over my shoulder.

We both stared at my heart-shaped scar.

"How's it possible? Your hypnosis is evolving…" he muttered. "Your mind is awake…"

"Maybe it's because I died…" Tears began to form.

"What do you mean?" He held my hands.

"I drowned Ji Woon. I thought I was dead for sure. But they…" I tapped my head. "Ellen left and another too…they bought me time before rescue came."

He hugged me tight. "All I care about is you're here."

"But I'm wearing her face."

"We'll figure it out. And one day, I'll be stronger than what you put out. I'll break your hypnotism."

He kissed me. Our lips knew each other, even when our eyes didn't. Our foreheads touched, and we both smiled. "And I'm never gonna lose you again."

"Come." He pushed me into the bathroom. I caught the edge of the marble sink.

The lights turned on. My vision spun; the bees buzzed in my head as I stared at my reflection of Sophie in the mirror.

The lights turned off. It was pitch black.

The lights flipped on again. My mind stuttered.

Lights off. I was shocked, and before I could process it.

On. His fingers flashed in front of my face.

Off. "On my count...three. Two. One." A voice whispered.

On. Fingers snapped. My world turned white. Time stood still. I froze as the world turned, and then,

"Close your eyes."

Then, I was asleep.

41

The hotel lobby was deafening with the murmurs of many people talking at once. The tide of heads swallowed anyone who entered, and I quickly hid among the Asians. Large white screens and bright spotlights were positioned in makeshift areas for the reporters, covering minute-by-minute updates on the American kidnapping situation. Videos and pictures of my torture were plastered on the screens, with the more graphic parts pixelated.

Again and again, assaulted with visuals of my face, naked body, and large purple bruises for everyone to see.

The boat swayed in the storm. Flickering light. Fists. Legs. Claws gripping my scalp. My arms were screaming from blocking their attacks. Each hit thundered through my body. Mine exploded as pain rippled out in concentric waves.

My heart sped up. The voices were growing louder in my head. They wanted out. Someone had to pay for hurting us. Sophie and Gina believed they were right. What about me? Did I deserve this?

I felt someone coming. The buzzing as the red thread was pulling us closer. I scanned the crowd of heads, searching for her.

And then, I stopped.

Found her. Her face was hidden beneath a black hoodie. My breathing sped up the closer I moved towards her — the rush of adrenaline. The voices in my head were buzzing, warning me to stay away. Why? Their fear reverberated through me, telling me to stop.

I took a step forward eagerly when a hand clamped on my shoulder.

"Alice." My exhilaration snuffed.

Michael Harris took me down the escalator to the basement level and a row of small tables. In less than a day, he aged twenty years. I forgot this human god was mortal, and the mask he showed the world and the smiles he shared with others were iron-thick. If there was one thing to admire, it was that he was always cool under pressure. With millions of people watching him, he acted as if it were a day in a park.

I glanced at the FBI and NIS agents in the crowd and crossed my arms.

"You just called me Alice." My lips quivered.

"Because you're my daughter." Our eyes met, and I caught the flash of sorrow in his. "I see you as you, always."

I pushed him hard, and he staggered back. His hands clenched, but he didn't retaliate. He would never hit us. Not to me nor my mother. The rest of the female population wasn't so lucky. "Liar." I stepped away.

He ran his hand through his shorn hair. The cut was uneven, and the cuts and scrapes were done intentionally. The prison was already reenacting its revenge. It was the first time he'd worn it really short.

"I should have protected you..." He sighed.

"Isn't it a little too late?"

"Maybe. Where's the USB?"

Chit-chat was over. I knew he didn't leave it on me, for me.

"Why?" I asked.

"Where is it?"

"I gave it to the police."

He crossed his arms. "That USB had my entire research. They won't know what to do with it."

"You can't expect me to believe you've found a cure for my illness."

"With surgery and the right drugs, we could fix brains like yours. When you're done, you can submit my journal. We can be co-authors."

"You think I'd subjugate myself to your stupid experiments? It's over. They caught you. No one's going to read your work. You won't get that Nobel prize. You're a murderer."

He clamped his jaw. "I was framed. Those were cadavers."

"They were children!"

"They were bodies. Their parents signed them off for science."

"You're fucking insane! You're a doctor. You swore to protect them. Organ trafficking? They aren't pieces of meat!"

"I am the Chief Surgeon of two reputable hospitals. Organ trafficking? Why would I risk everything I built for that?"

I laughed. The whole situation stank. "What about those women you fucked? Miyako and those women!"

He stood up. Towering over me as I hid in his shadow. Once again, I refused to follow in line. I was his disappointment. The daughter that shouldn't have lived. The son that I was not.

"They attacked first. All I did was punish them."

We were too different. He'd changed so much. Once long ago, we were father and daughter, united for my mother.

The day he raped Miyako and when she died, I couldn't forgive him, and the day my mother divorced him, he stopped being my father.

A bullet grazed my cheek, striking the window behind me with a resounding crack.

"Gun!" Someone shouted. The conference-goers ducked.

I lifted my eyes without moving my head and fixed on the person in a black hoodie. Across the room, the hand rose with the smoking gun pointing at me.

The gun exploded again. Michael lunged forward, knocking me down. The bullet struck his back and lodged straight into his heart. His head drooped on my shoulder. Body convulsing against me as life bled out at warp speed.

"Dad?" I choked back a sob. "No. Daddy?"

I felt him smile against my cheek as his last breath curled his lips. "You called me Daddy...."

His heart stopped.

"No! No!" I didn't get the last word. I sagged, shell-shocked with the weight of my father on my shoulders. He was still warm. However, the doctor in me knew it was too late.

Two hundred pounds of human flesh, with an IQ of a hundred and ninety, the world-famous Chief Surgeon, was gone. His blood pooled at my feet. The scent of his death and acid in his body, already breaking down, invaded my nostrils.

Onlookers watched with silent, thundering hearts. And then, time drew a breath, and the screams began. Jarring scenes of people running. Faces of terror as every man was for himself.

My father's body slid to the ground. His sky-blue eyes, turning dull, stared up at me. "People die all the time," he always said.

"Daddy..." The more the crowd panicked, the cooler I got. Dissociation was what I did best. Cameras flashed in rapid-fire.

The onslaught of people speaking over one another and the rush of medics to my father's body was like watching TV.

Ji Woon came to my side and threw his coat over me. "Alice! Are you hurt?" He ran his hands over my body quickly and met my shaken gaze. "Talk to me. Alice! Are you shot?"

I heard a gun drop. The crowd parted like the Red Sea — a girl in the hoodie. I stared at my feet, soaked in my father's blood, and back at the girl in the hoodie, a smoking gun in hand. Our eyes met, seconds snapped, and then she took off.

I reacted instinctively, slipping under Ji Woon's arms in a flash. Like an arrow that left its bow, I ducked through the crowd and camera lights, pinning my sight on the girl's head bobbing in the masses.

Ji Woon was a little behind, held back by the swarm of reporters as I snaked past arms and shoulders sharp like mountain peaks.

Anger was my fuel. The fire torched my insides. My tunnel vision was narrow and grey. Red bled the walls as I honed in on her black hoodie.

She stumbled through the icy, snowy sidewalks across the street ahead. The afternoon sun, barely peeking through the clouds with flurries, was masking my sight. Traffic was high, and I saw her body flitting back and forth between the cars, buses, and trucks. I lunged forward and saw her scrambling up some crates, throwing her leg over a plastic barrier atop a slope leading down to an underground expressway below.

"Get down!" I crossed to the mid-section.

"Get off!" I shouted again, waving at her, and dashed across. A loud beep resonated in the air; something metal hit my side. I felt bones break, flung in the air as a rush of wind combed through my hair.

Down, down, down. I was an angel with broken wings. Fallen,

hitting the roof of a silver SUV. My head burst into the colors of a rainbow. The ringing of a gong echoed in my mind, followed by the shouts of my alter-egos as my consciousness split. In the background was screeching, banging, and metal crunching.

"Alice!" Blood rushed down between my eyes. A fog glazed over my vision as his voice grew louder. "Alice!" Ji Woon slid down a pebbled slope, grappling with rocks and plants. I could see panic in his face as he staggered through the crowd of groaning people.

I lay on the rooftop with my hair splayed out. My legs spread-eagled, with a mask of pain stretching across my brow. My chest heaved as I shook my head and clambered off the vehicle. Those who saw me were shocked — parting and letting me through, no one lending a hand.

"Alice! Wait!" I heard Ji Woon shouting. Fire exploded from the SUV. Everyone ducked as shrapnel flew at projectile speed. I dragged myself away, escaping the apocalyptic mess. Ji Woon's heading bobbing in the madness. From the mirrored windows, I saw the hoodie girl watching as I struggled onward to her.

It must be her.

She, who left the rose cards. She, who was stalking my windows. The polaroids of orphan kids in a row. She left them behind. Hints. Terror.

I glanced at a window in passing and saw my reflection.

Sophie Han was finally gone. It was me again. Alice Steeple.

I touched my face and smiled. Rose red lips stretched as pain laced my brow.

Flakes of snow drift onto the bloody mess of metal and glass where the accident stood — crowded with people struggling out of their cars. Smoke rose to the sky. The sounds of shattered cars beeping as dirty, icy slush turned pink.

I kept going, limping and hurrying away. My body mended in seconds as I absorbed another one of my personas.

Cars drifted to the sides as the ambulance came minutes later. The paramedics pushed past me, rushing to the most injured. More rescuers arrived. Two out of the four lanes were blocked, and others waited as more ambulances and fire trucks came for the rest.

No one saw Sophie Han after that accident, and to those who thought they saw a woman through the lens of a camera, it was Alice Steeple, the missing American, who was hit by a truck and took a nosedive into traffic.

Rumors were that Alice was rescued from the sea, and those who saw Sophie Han had seen a ghost. The fingerprints and blood samples collected belonged to the American. The videos were stark proof. It was Alice whom the officers were talking to. The clothes she wore belonged to Alice. All evidence pointed to the American.

The rescue and search for Alice was called off in less than twenty-four hours — a waste of national resources for a notorious, rich doctor's daughter.

Speculations a-plenty.

Dr. Michael Harris was shot down in plain sight. Dead at the scene. Some said it was Sophie Han, some said it was Alice, his entangled daughter.

Gina Chen, a security guard, a friend of Gina who rented the boat, and a driver, are all dead. Some bodies had Polaroid pics, roses carved to throats. Was there a serial killer on the loose?

That American would know.

The mind believed what it wanted to believe. Soon enough, more reports would come in — another body had been found.

Someone

42

January 15, 2022, The next day
Eulwangni Beach

Rays of sunlight skimmed across the rough, salty waves toward the coast. A jogger in his mid-thirties, dressed in thin winter gear, panted in rhythm to his steps as he did his five-kilometer daily run before heading to his high-flying job in the city.

Today was no different. The sun was barely visible, and last night's snow added a thick layer of powder to the beach. His legs sank as he ran, adding more cardio to his workout, burning fat from the alcohol he had consumed the night before with his clients and host girls. His breath added steam to the air, and his small searchlight was like a star in a lonely galaxy.

A call came in from the US, and he missed seeing the lump of black ahead until he tripped and fell in a resounding offed.

"Mr. Kim, are you all right?" asked his American customer on the other line.

Mr. Kim, the jogger, coughed up a clump of ice and turned

around. He snatched his phone from his shoulder strap and flipped on the light.

Seaweed wrapped around her like an emerald-laced dress over her partly decapitated body. Bluish white flesh was chewed away with teeth marks and embedded with pebbles and sand. Her small, heart-shaped face marked fear, and her bow-shaped lips stretched in a silent scream.

Mr. Kim turned to the side and puked. His gut wrenched, heaved, and tossed all of last night's sushi, soju, hard liquor, and beer in a projectile display. Food stains dripped from his lips, and the drool of partially digested alcohol ruined his thousand-dollar running shoes, but even that was nothing compared to the memory of her gouged-out eye.

Despite the mutilation, he knew that face. He met her once at a dinner gala. She snubbed him, and that annoyed him.

Sophia Han. Her face was everywhere, but he never imagined she'd be at his feet.

Merle

43

Same morning

Sweat trickled down her temples and pooled in her collarbone. Merle smiled in the mirror. Ever since Alice drowned, the walls began to crumble. Years of separation were thinning into webs clear as light. Alice's greatest fear was coming true, and this was the day Merle was waiting for.

Merle planned to win this fight. Soon, she would be the primary as she should be, and Alice and the rest would disappear.

Steam burst out in clouds when the door swung open, and a pair of naked women in their sixties sauntered out like models on a catwalk, except they were old and wrinkly and yucky.

Merle scrunched her nose as she sucked her banana milk. Those images of them were buried in her brain, impossible to unsee. If it weren't for Alice and her flying trapeze into traffic yesterday and then losing her phone, Merle would be at her five-star hotel and bubble bath.

Her daddy was dead.

Merle wasn't sure how she felt. Sad. Yes. But sad? Daddy was her north star growing up. Maybe because he said he loved her and gave her anything she wanted. Thinking back, though, wasn't that part of the agreement?

Through Alice's eyes, she saw Daddy slip and feel the warmth of his blood in Alice's hands. The gun dropped. That man in the hoodie again. Fuck. Who was he?

Merle shook her head. Alice was such a coward. She always needed someone to rescue her. They should have taken the bullet.

Once she got a hold of that hoodie fucker, Merle would serve justice fast, hard, and painful, the way Daddy taught her.

A man cleared his throat and spat into his plastic cup. Yuck. COVID might be almost over, but still? Merle sighed, tossed her empty banana milk into a bin, and scanned the general resting area.

Jjimjilbang Yonsei, a neighborhood bathhouse, wasn't Merle's choice of spa and relaxation. She cursed under her breath. With winter buffeting snow and cold temperatures, this was the only place she could hang out till the stores opened. Banana milk and sauna egg were the highlights here.

What was she thinking? This place was the dumps. Where was the scent of cucumber and lemon water, coupled with the perfumes of aromatic lotions?

Merle missed the soft chimes, elevator music, and gentle, smooth hands of a patient masseuse. The scrub lady — dressed in a black tank shirt and wet shorts ruled the women's arena. Just a few minutes earlier, Merle casually passed the couple and studied the scrub lady slapping her hot pink gloved hands on a naked plank of flesh, working on scraping off every bit of skin till it was clean and baby smooth.

Merle didn't need that. Her skin was silky and taut, and thousands of dollars had been spent on perfecting it, proven by the rally of men at her feet. And the men in this place were no better. They were the first she looked for because the thought of male and female naked bodies separated by a wall got her horny. What a disappointment because the men here were like the women, old, wrinkly, and fugly.

TV was blaring with news updates and live coverage on the missing Alice Steeple and the rising body counts. The famous deaths were Sophie Han and Dr. Michael Harris, whose hours of news coverage talked about every detail. The rest of the news was background noise about a marina security guard, Gina Chen, Sophie's lover, and the Chinese spy, a friend of Gina Chen, who loaned the boat, and Chairman Park's driver, who crashed a car.

The manhunt was on. Every new channel was talking about Alice Steeple, who was last seen alive escaping the car wreckage by the Han River.

It should be Merle taking the spotlight. If only Alice had let her out, that torture video wouldn't have been made; what terrible lighting and angles, and those two bitches would have been strung to the boat and fish food.

Merle grinned at the blurred pictures of Sophie and her lover, Gina, making out on the beach. She was proud that Alice was getting better at letting her freak out. Who would have thought that Alice would post lesbian porn and suckered punch the Chairman?

She agreed with the rest of the others. Screw the Park family. Vengeance was a two-bladed sword. Ji Woon played a dangerous game, and naive Alice was lured into their nest of vipers.

Daddy shouldn't have jumped right in. Daddy shouldn't have died. Daddy didn't like seeing them cry.

No. Dr. Michael Harris wasn't dead. Until she saw his body, to Merle, Daddy was alive. Lying in some bed in the hospital, waiting for Merle to come and get him.

Everyone's wrong. Dr. Michael Harris wasn't a killer. Someone or somebodies took the time to frame him. The only parts of his crimes that were true were the women he punished and the money he made. Organ trading, what a fucking joke. Daddy would never taint his career with that. The experiments were done legally at hospitals. Nick funneled the money. Merle dealt with his women and witnesses.

So, who was it? Who betrayed them? Cyrus? That bastard. Weak, chicken-hearted Cyrus?

Merle slammed her milk carton on the table and glared at a pimpled young man who had been ogling her for the past hour. The man-boy took that as a yes and finally came over with another banana milk. He spoke to her in Korean, which was useless, while Merle gave him a once-over. He was slightly taller than her, with decent shoulders, not skinny, monolid eyes, and lips soft and defined. From afar, he was hot. Someone like him could get some action. His skin could be better, but it was fine because banging him wouldn't matter in the dark.

She grabbed his hand, startled him, and dragged him to the ice room. Until Eli got her messages, she'd eat this boy.

Alice

44

The ice room was freezing. Clouds puffed from my mouth, and the young man was asphyxiating with the towel stuffed in his mouth and the key ring cord around his neck.

I didn't need to help him and would have stayed to watch if it wasn't for the police and the spa lady searching the rooms for me. Someone saw Merle earlier and thought she was me. It won't be long before they find me.

I decided it was time to switch. My abilities were growing stronger as my personalities melded into my mind walls. As Merle had said, we were merging, and somehow, I was no longer afraid. The second death, when I was knocked down and flung into traffic, took my Sophie's face away and changed things.

A life for a life. I had plenty to give.

The pervert who attacked us got what he deserved. His phone was filled with pictures of naked teenagers peeing, rapes, and penis shots. When Merle was done with him, we switched minds. She gave him a taste of his own medicine after we saw some sadistic videos he took of some of his victims.

I stared at the man as he slowly turned blue. His eyes bulged out, and he scratched at his neck at the stretched rubber cord tied to a pillar.

"Need help?" I asked. He shook his head and mumbled something into the towel. "You won't die. I'm a doctor."

His face paled more as if I said I was the devil.

I shrugged and studied his face, eager to test my new abilities. Sophie was my first, and this guy was my second. No longer was I manifesting new personalities from my guilt; I could become anyone I wanted.

My bones cracked, elongating as my skin stretched and nerves tingled. Changing used to hurt a lot when I was younger. I was accustomed to the pain and enjoyed the endorphins that each body switch brought. Now that I had control, I felt omnipotent.

He shouted into his gag. Terror was written all over him when he saw I had changed into him. A puddle marked his underpants as he cried.

Any camera or video would show a woman watching a man tied up and gagged. But anyone in the same room or within a good twenty to thirty feet radius would see me as I wanted them to see me.

Him. The peeing pervert man.

It was going to take lots of therapy to get him back. I pulled off the cord and locker key from his neck.

The voices in my head told me to let this menace die, but the coldness in my heart melted the further I got to the door. Sighing, I returned and took off his towel. He slipped to the ground and puked.

I gestured to the police detectives to the room, and left.

—||—

 Someone

45

KANSAS

Twelve years ago

There was no end to their crying. The continuous wailing came in waves. However, in their voices, there was a hint of celebration. One had to die for another to live.

Lying on a surgical table, a child was dead. A black cloth hid his carved-out head. Hiding away his scrawny shoulders and slashes, needles pricked in every vein to medicate and give life to the boy whom Allah did not allow to live. In the following table was a young girl, about three years younger. Throughout her life, she was despised for smiling. Happiness was not hers while he suffered.

In the child's clasped hand was a plastic white lily — one of many faded flowers in a vase at the reception desk.

The girl was wheeled out into a VIP room. Like the boy, there were lines across her scalp, but the surgical lines were neatly stitched up, unlike the boy's old head. Her heart monitor was beeping strongly, and the other flatlined for the old body.

The parents signed the waivers. They knew the risks. This was their only chance to save their boy, the genius and their pride and joy. He didn't deserve a life of sickness. He was the oldest and favored. This was the first of a series of operations to come. He would get a male body in a few years. One that would suit him better than his sister's temporary husk.

A son carried his father's name. His sister, the thief, lived the life that should have been his. The poor boy spent most of his days within the white walls of a ward and the scent of chlorine instead of flowers and fresh morning air. At fourteen years old, every doctor they consulted told the parents to say their last goodbyes.

The black screen of the one-way mirror brooded. Today, many people gathered on the opposite side to witness a famous brain surgeon performing his experimental brain graft.

The switch graft was a success. The boy lived on, and his vital signs showed promise. The girl wasn't meant to die, but complications happened after. People die all the time. The waivers were signed. The doctor was indemnified.

A person in a black hoodie stood over the skinny child. He reached over to adjust the cloth over the gaping head when the child's golden eyes suddenly opened, and her mouth dropped in a silent scream.

Alice

46

The sky was pregnant. Heavy with snow, blanking the world in a shroud of white. Thick clumps came down, patches of ice like a *bingo* that decided it was too cool to melt.

"Namsan Tower, please." I adjusted my face mask.

The cab driver stared at the rearview mirror, and my heart stuttered. "Cable car station?" he asked.

"Yes." I lifted my phone and kept my eyes on it.

I am that bathhouse guy. I am that *Jjimjilbang Namja*, I am that bathhouse guy, I told myself.

The cab driver took another double-take, and I nodded at him. He sighed and sped up, cutting through the streets like a pro.

I used the phone I stole from the guy at the bathhouse to text Eli again and check the news for the mayhem I caused.

Fake news and confusion lit the Internet. My face splattered in articles, and the trolls had a field day. The pictures they got were snaps my kidnappers used, or my only headshot from the program sheet at the conference.

I didn't want to think about my old life or whether anyone cared enough to trust I wasn't the maniac that the Internet and the world painted me as. Other than Eli, I didn't care what anyone thought. Still, my fingers called Salinger, and I left a message on Ji Woon's voicemail.

I never thought it would come this far — my presence in this country. With every step, a mine exploded — bodies littered, blood like acid rain. Every person I met was dead.

The search for Alice Steeple through the omnipotent eyes of CCTVs snapping my hour-by-hour movements and the Netizens sending sightings of me helping the police meant they were close.

I was as elusive as Bigfoot.

My voices agreed for once; helping me escape was the priority.

Twenty-five minutes later, I arrived at the cable car station, and after another ten minutes of climbing, I was up in the clouds with a three-sixty view of Seoul city. Winter continued its assault on the buildings and trees. The temperatures were ten degrees below freezing. No one in their right mind should be out.

Leaning on rows of colored love lockets, a black beanie, hiding his wild curls, and his arms crossed in a black turtle-neck, in sleek Korean fashion, was my clumsy, messy, lovable gay best friend. It took a few double-takes.

"Eli!" I pounced on him and hugged him from behind.

He turned around and hugged me back before pulling my arms apart. "This is some crazy shit. Our President and the South Korean President know your name."

He dropped me back on the ground and stepped back, giving me a once-over. "It's you, Aly, right?"

I took a deep breath and let my body return, switching from the Korean bathhouse man to myself. Then, I pulled off my black mask.

"Yes, it's me." I smiled and watched warily, expecting a look of some disgust.

It took him two weeks after he met Merle and another week after he saw Peter to come back to me.

He came closer. "How are you doing this?"

I crumpled my mask into my pocket. "This? It's new and, yes, a long story, but later." I looked around. With visibility dropping, I could only see three feet around us. "Did you get the train tickets? When are we going to Busan?" I asked.

"Michael wasn't supposed to die." He sounded sad.

I studied him, looking up at the sky. Snow tackled his face like everything around us. Our few minutes were up, and we were being buried.

There was a time when Eli adored Michael like everybody did. Everyone in our field wanted to be touched by the Brain god. Michael's thesis was the most widely read and featured a sardonic humor that the others lacked.

In our four years of friendship, I dumped all my hatred and insecurities about that man onto Eli and got him on my side.

"What do you mean?" I asked.

"Now, we'll never know." He brooded.

"I was almost shot!" I frowned.

He patted my head. "Yes, yes. I'm glad you're okay." He kissed my forehead and placed his hands on my shoulders.

"Aly. Did he tell you? Where are the graves?"

"Graves? Not you too?" I shook my head. "Why would I know?"

"Did Michael leave a clue in that USB? Did he give you a hint?"

"Hint?" My heart raced. "Dude. Why?" His grip was like talons biting into my arms.

"I don't know. I gave the USB to the FBI. I am done." I wrenched his fingers off.

"What about the money he took?" His eyes locked onto me. "That money was supposed to be mine." He said.

"What are you talking about?"

He pushed me off, and I slipped on the ice. The locks on the bridge braced my fall and cut my palms.

"My gold. He stole them!"

"What gold?" The pain from my cut palms was nothing compared to what his revelation was doing.

Eli slammed his hand on the handrail. "I was supposed to watch you. He must have told you. I'm talking millions of dollars…"

"No. Watch me?" Reality was honing in. Just when I finally found someone I could trust, I was betrayed again. Naive, desperate to be loved. I was so stupid. Falling into the same trap over and over again.

Everyone used me.

All this time, I was rebelling, thinking I'd escaped from Michael; he was still the master.

"You hung out with me because he paid you?" I clutched my chest. The cold air did nothing for my lungs. The voices in my head laughed.

Hate exploded, and I grabbed a large piece of ice and threw it at him. Eli didn't shun it. The ice shattered on his chest.

"How could you! How could you!" I shouted, but my voice squeaked and sounded pathetic. "How could you do this to me!" I screamed a voiceless scream.

Eli grabbed my hands and folded them behind my back. He let me trash. He let me cry. He took the onslaught of my emotions and sighed.

All the men in my life were jerks. The ground where I stood cracked, and I imagined dropping into an endless dive.

He stepped away. His face was a mask of calm and calculation. They might look the same, but this detached person wasn't the warm, beautiful guy I knew.

"Enough, Aly. I'm hurt as you are. I waited five years for this. Michael was close to a cure and promised me his first dips."

"I did as he said. Protected you from harm. And I failed. Those bitches. It was hard to hide from those CCTVs. I had to find you fast. That friend told me where Gina lived. And Gina, she's such a piece."

He pulled out the dagger I gave him. He always liked collecting those things. He loved carving out the designs on the hilts.

I always thought it was a quirky hobby for his pacifism until I saw him twirling the blade in his hands.

He ran his finger on the edge and sliced his finger. Bubbles of blood pooled, and he sucked it.

"Eli… you're scaring me." I backed away.

He breathed out and watched the cloud evaporate from his mouth. He smirked, stretching those pouty red lips over his teeth. In a flash, he was beside me again, grabbing my waist and pulling me backward to his chest.

"I'm sorry. I need you to call him up."

"Call who?"

"Michael's in there."

"What?"

"You'll remember what he told you. He must have told you something."

"Eli. Don't. You're scaring me."

"It's okay. You want them gone, too. I know you'll live. I've seen you poison them."

"Wait, wait." I struggled in his tight hold. "No, please. Eli, no. It's not the same."

"See you on the other side." His lips touched my cheek, smearing his blood onto me, and then, he slid his hand around my throat.

Pain flared instantly. The voices screamed, and I sagged into him. One rushed forward to keep us living. Like a flower blooming, I felt myself change.

"Why?" I gurgled and staggered away from him. My body mended at lightning speed. "Why Eli?"

"I'm sick of your whining about them: your blackouts, your locks. We can't ever have fun cos you worry so much. I told you. I'll deal with them." He watched me and smiled.

"This one is that bitch who died of an overdose, right?" He waved his bloody knife. Poisoning is too slow. You want results, you have to take that leap."

The buzzing grew to a fevered pitch. Eli sneered and grabbed my arms as I fought and slammed myself against the wall of locks. "Next!" He stabbed my heart. Once again, I switched, taking on another of my personalities, an Indian boy from school who jumped off the tallest building because he couldn't ace all classes.

"Stay still," He pulled me to him.

I felt Eli's knife slide through my ribs again. The pain was nothing compared to the cruelty of him.

"Why? Why?" That was all I could say before he made me switch again. Tears ran down another face as my gaze fell on his stony silence.

"Eli...where's my Eli..." I choked on my blood.

"I don't go on dates. I don't have friends, Aly. They were paid actors!"

He scratched his nose with the tip of the blade, letting my

blood drizzle down his chin. "Your voices are the only thing interesting about you."

He grinned and sliced my throat, watching without emotion as I held my neck. Once my blood dried, I was a black girl in her barista apron. She was cursing in my head, and being an MMA figure, she fought Eli back.

"Five! This is getting tiring. Where is he?" He shook his head. "Call him up!"

"You never cared for me?" I rubbed my hand over my wet face.

"Wrong!" Eli sighed heavily. "I care about you a lot. You're my Soulmate! Can you imagine how much I hate Ji Woon? How I had to swallow that shit feeling each time he touched you? How much I hate seeing that fucking dopey look in your eyes?" He grabbed my hand and placed it on his chest.

"I'm right here, Aly!"

"But, you like guys," I said.

"Except you."

"I thought...I didn't know. Eli, stop this. We can leave this place and go home. Put this in our past. Lock it up and throw the key."

"You and your fucking keys. I don't want to go on like this. I'm fucking sick of pretending, Aly!"

"My real name is Cyrus Matel! I was supposed to die that day of this incurable disease, but my fucking parents couldn't let go, couldn't let go. Michael Harris used us. My sister and I were his puppets."

He shook his head, and I backed away, scanning for a way out. Eli was a great runner.

"And what did you know? It worked. That damn man was a genius, and his DNA is in you, which makes you a genius too. He cut me up here." He gestured to head. "And, he took my brain out and put it in her body. Toss her brain, keep her brain, I don't know. He won't say. My beautiful sister, Nadia. I took her body and lived for a couple of years till they found me another and transplanted me again, and voila! Many bodies later, here I am!" His eyes glowed with unshed tears.

"I'm that real Frankenstein freak! Not you! Me, Aly. I'm his living prototype. His genius."

"I didn't know," I said.

The voices fought for control. Selfish, psycho, bastards and bitches.

"And now I want my billions!" He plunged his knife into my abdomen. Again, the light faded, and I transformed.

"Call Michael up!" A swarm of a million locusts followed by the cracking of bones. My limbs stretched to his six feet two, filling out his large frame of muscle and bones, and my long dark hair was shortened into a buzzcut with the color of corn. Like paper torn apart, my face stretched, replaced by Michael Harris — the one Eli wanted.

„Michael Harris!"

"You looking for me?" I spoke in my father's voice.

Eli clapped. "Dr. Michael Harris, the man of the hour! So where's my gold? My money? Where's Nadia's bones?" He did a spin, and when he turned back.

I grabbed the closest rock and tossed it at Eli's head.

The rock hit with a dull smack, and Eli dropped to his knees. I dashed down the stairs.

Five men in black clothes waited. Father was a black belt, and I learned from the best. I knocked them down with my size, and those I didn't, I flipped them off.

Ahead was the castle stone fortress leading down to the city. Bullets ricocheted against the stone walls. But thankfully, in this impending snowstorm, no innocent bystanders were around. I ducked and lunged for the walls. My heart pumped as my momentum built.

Hail the size of marbles pelted on our heads. For once, the gods were on my side. A surge of Korean police appeared below from every corner of the trail — close to thirty people, uniformed and plain clothes, Asians and not. FBI Agent Odeh was in the crowd. They were staring at me, shocked. Barely hours ago, they witnessed my father's death.

I scaled the castle wall. The hollow sound of a gong rang loud in my ears, followed by the same buzzing of voices. Flashes. Bullets struck my back, and I flipped over to the other side with gritted teeth and fell.

47

Hands clamped down on my lips, dragging me deeper into the snowy foliage. I struggled with my assailant's grasp, an assailant who was stronger and determined to make me do his bidding. His hot breath brushed against my ear.

"Alice, don't scream. They can't see you."

I caught his steel gaze, nodding so he knew I would be calm.

Dressed all in white, with a white beanie, Ji Woon was invisible in the snowstorm. "Take off your coat." He helped me into a white snow jacket, pulled another white beanie and scarf from his pockets, and tucked my hair in it.

"Are you hurt?" He"asked.

I shook my head and hugged him.

He breathed heavily with relief. "Are you okay?"

I nodded and glanced at the long wall in the distance, amazed at how much I had run. Visibility in the storm was impossible. I could barely make out the police and FBI agents, all wearing bright orange vests, as they combed the area.

"They won't find you", Jiwoon said.

"How did you find me?" I asked.

"I had Eli followed," He smirked.

"Of course you did," I placed my hand on his face and pulled him down.

"You got your face back." He smiled.

Our eyes met. His irises were dark and dilated. And it took a second before he smashed his mouth against mine. I drank him up, exploring his lips with mine, tasting his tongue as we tangled ourselves into legs and arms.

I pulled away first. Our breaths mingled as one. "I don't trust you yet, Park Ji Woon." I placed my hand on his chest, and he grabbed it tight.

"It's okay. So long as you're"safe." He looked up at the slope and trees ahead. "It's about a mile." We stared at the small pavilion, barely visible. Strong winds buffeted, and snow came down in chunks.

"Come," he pulled me along.

We hiked up the slope through four feet of snow with Ji Woon in front, clearing a path for me until his legs gave way.

"What's wrong?"

"A little more…" H"s teeth chattered.

I reached for his legs. He tried to push me away, but I grabbed his pant leg and checked his calves. They were purpling and stiff.

"You've got frostbite." I bent down, ready to carry him on my back.

"No, no…I can walk""

"This is pretty bad. How long were you waiting for me?" I glanced down the mountain where the castle walls were. The search must be called off.

Ji Woon sagged on my arm. His eyes were closed. It took three tries to lift him on my back. He was over six feet, and I was only five feet five. We sank a foot more into the snow as I staggered forward. My muscles screamed. I had to keep going. I gritted my teeth and dragged him along.

"Don't sleep." I turned to his cheek. "We're almost there." I slapped him up. "Where's your car?"

"Passt thhhhee papapaviviliiion, dddoownnn thththee ppaaath bbbeeehhind thththoooose trrreees."

"Ashes, I'll take over." The fire burned through my veins as Peter assumed my body. My limbs grew long and bony. Although thin as a reed and taller than Ji Woon, Peter was stronger than I. With Ji Woon on his back and almost delirious, he didn't notice our change.

When we arrived at the pavilion, Peter brushed the bench clean of snow and slowly laid Ji Woon down, and searched for Ji Woon's keys.

"Stay here. I'll get the car," said Peter.

He sprinted down the path leading to the car park when Eli appeared.

Eli grinned. "Peter! It's you!" He reached for a hug, and Peter scooted to the side. "Eff you! Eli! Traitor!"

"Whatcha talking about, bruh? We're best buds, right?" Eli grinned.

"I ain't no eff-ing friends with you! Ashes! Aly and I are a pack."

"Hear me out, Peets! I can give you what you want."

"You don't know what I want!" Peter spat. "You tried to kill her!"

Eli wrapped his arm over Peter's shoulder. "Dude. You want Alice. You wanna touch her, love her like a guy loves a girl, right?"

"You're fucking crazy!" Peter looked to the side. Alice was reading his mind. He was struggling to hide his thoughts. Eyes not meeting Eli, who was smirking.

"Dr. Harris transplanted me into my sister's head, and I've been in others. His experiments worked, I'm proof. His assistant works for me. We can pull you out and put you in a body of your own. So, join me. Aly will come around. She wants this too. Everyone in her head gets their own body. We'll get the best. Trust me. This was Harris's grand plan."

The others in my head and Merle were listening eagerly. A shadow of doubt was growing, and I could feel them turning to Eli's side.

Eli was lying. It was scientifically impossible. A horrible thought amassed, and guilt grew into a monstrous, toxic cloud.

The walls that held us separate began cracking when I drowned. Greed.

It didn't matter if those living bodies belonged to someone else. Those personalities in my head had no qualms about getting the best for themselves. Eager to hunt a new body for their own.

Blood thirst.

"Did you help him?" I spoke through Peter. "You killed those children."

Eli stepped back and clapped his hands. "Is that you, Aly? Speaking through Peter? What else can you do?"

I took over, and Peter vanished as my features and body returned to mine.

Eli smiled with a gentleness in his eyes only reserved for me. "Now, this is the you I love."

He reached to hug me, and I stepped away.

I caught a flash of anger, replaced by his skillfully crafted smile, which I had thought was real all that time.

I was such a fool.

Eli reached over and gripped my chin, pulling me to him. "I told you we'll always be together."

In the past, I thought nothing of this act. Eli and I were very close, and I trusted him completely. He liked men and stood by me. I didn't think much about him touching me.

But now, I saw desire in his eyes. He spun me and grabbed my arms behind my back. His hot breath on my ear.

"You didn't know...those summer camps at the Helen Retreat. Harris was operating on you. But he wouldn't do what he'd already done to me and the others. You are his blood, after all."

The snow stopped suddenly. The sky was clearing up. The fog was lifting. I heard a groan, followed by a grunt.

Ji Woon!

"Where are your guys?" Those whom I thought were people were trees or lampposts. Worry mounted. Ji Woon.

Eli pulled out a new dagger with a rose hilt — silver with red roses.

"Who?" he smiled. " stared at the hilt on the blade. Silver with red roses. This was the one painting he was most proud of.

The news showed the markings on the bodies. They thought the psycho was me. Bent on revenge. Gina was found dead on the boat — a slice to the throat with the same markings.

"You killed them. You shot Michael!"

"He wasn't supposed to jump in. I wanted to scare him," he made a sound. "That money. That gold. I earned them! Nick and your father took my share! I want a fast, sweet ride, too. Vacation to exotic places. Enjoy life, a new body." He glanced at the pavilion where I left Ji Woon.

I struggled against his grip. His body tightened around mine. Hard and insistent.

I stepped on his foot, and he grunted, not letting go. "Nothing you do will stop me. Give up, Aly. Everyone will pay for what they did."

I struggled more. I elbowed him, pushing until I found the weak spot and threw him off. His knife clattered on the ground.

"You can't get away with murder, Eli. They have CCTVs everywhere."

He laughed. "You don't know me."

"Nick was begging in the end. Swore he'd leave you if I left his dick. He was screaming when I took his balls."

"No! Liar!" Merle burst forward and charged at him. Eli side-stepped, as Merle screamed and charged again. Eli struck and aimed for her heart, but missed when I took over and fought back. My sister wailed and cried, but the time to mourn wasn't now.

A gunshot rang out in the air and struck Eli in the arm.

Ji Woon was pointing with a smoking gun. His face was paler than ice.

I dashed to the pavilion.

Ji Woon was wrestling with the gun with one of Eli's men. The weapon landed in the bushes beside a steep drop. Although shorter in stature and more diminutive, the man was well-matched to Ji Woon, who was weak and bleeding.

I lunged for the bushes, fighting off one of Eli's men. Behind, I heard Ji Woon's grunt and slip, and Eli grabbing Ji Woon by his hair. A knife pressed to his throat. A bead of blood bloomed and trickled down his throat.

"Eli, take me instead," I begged. "Ji Woon doesn't know anything. The Park family, the Koreans won't let you go. We'll leave together, and I'll help you find your money."

Eli sighed. "Aly. You think he won't find us?" He hooked Ji Woon closer, pulling him down to his level. Ji Woon stumbled, and Eli laughed. "What do you see in this boy?"

He turned to me. "I wanted to do you a favor. He'll be my next. If that makes you love me more, I'd do it for you."

I shook my head. "No. Eli. No."

Eli pushed Ji Woon off, and two men grabbed Ji Woon and pulled him aside. "You'll thank me."

"I'll tell you. Let Ji Woon go — the clues. I've figured them out," I looked away. "And." A thought suddenly lit in my head. "I can show you, Nadia."

"Nadia?" Eli stepped forward, and I stepped back, feeling with my feet for the snow-covered, graveled path leading to the drop where we had climbed earlier.

"You saw her? When? How?"

"I've been dreaming about her. Yesterday."

"Show me." His eyes teared up. "Show her to me!" He rushed to me, and I stepped back more.

"Let Ji Woon go. Tell your men to leave us."

Eli gestured, and everyone left the pavilion and headed down the path.

"Now. Show me."

"I'm sorry, Nadia," I whispered in my mind. "Please, help us." The girl whimpered.

"Nadia…" Eli moved, sheathing his blade back into his holster. Coming closer. "I miss you, my dear sister."

"Stop." I raised my hand. "She needs her space."

Eli nodded. "Yes. Yes."

I dove into the mist as voices cried out, demanding I take them instead. Avoiding the tendrils of fingers, chilly and moist, and then dipping my feet into red lava, sticky and hot, melting into my consciousness when I found her.

Nadia. Crouching in a corner, dark and dusty in the recesses of my thoughts. A beautiful girl with lush black hair and eyes filled with stars.

The scene changed. She was screaming, straight-jacketed on a bed. Fighting the inevitable in a stark white room. Behind a black mirror, the spectators filed in, ignoring the girl crying as they chatted excitedly about what was coming. Another bed rolled in. A scrawny teenage boy, bare-chested with concave ribs, brown-skinned and shuddering breaths, wrapped in tubes.

Time flowed. My heart was detached as I watched my father take her brain out and replace it with Eli's. She must also know — the sacrifice she was giving. The buzzing was music to my ears. Nadia was coming.

Eli caught me in his arms as I changed to his beloved sister.

"Nadia? Nadia? My Nadia?" Tears flowed down his cheeks.

"Peter! Now!" I shouted in my mind.

"Yes! Fire them up!"

Flames shot out through Peter's fingertips, and Eli's men waiting by the sides screamed as the fire hopped, consuming one person after another at rapid speed. Men screaming inhuman sounds, as the human bonfires ran in circles that no snow can cool.

Eli, Peter, and I lit. Burning together in agony. Eli dropped his arms, and I dove for the gun in the bushes, and he lunged forward, and stole the gun from my hands, and shot Peter.

"Alice!" Peter gasped. Flames unfurled like the wings of a phoenix. His last sparks fizzled like ashes between my fingers. "Alice." His voice whispered, and he was gone.

"Again! Nadia! Give me Nadia!" Eli foamed. There were sounds of fighting, and Eli glanced over.

This was my chance. I rammed into Eli, and we both leaped off the slope. His arms stretched out as we fell, crashing into a tree, embracing his right arm around my waist as we were caught by thin branches.

The tree sagged with our weight, cracking as our bodies slipped, seconds to our deaths.

Eli smiled, unwrapping his fingers around my waist. "What are you doing? Eli! Hold on!"

"Let Nadia out once in a while…Aly…"

I grabbed his hand, tears streaming down my cheeks as my head hung close to his. "Eli, I need you."

He brushed his lips on mine. "I was happiest with you."

"We'll get help together."

"I'm a freak. I should have died. I'm living her life," He sighed.

I felt cold hands on my ankles. "Alice!" His hands are pulling me up. He grunted as he dragged me back.

"No! Wait, no!" Eli pushed me away as the branches broke under our weight.

He glanced at Ji Woon and smiled.

"I love you more than you'll ever know," Eli said, and his shoulders arched back, and he threw me forward.

The tree snapped into two just as Ji Woon caught my waist.

One moment, Eli was there, and the next, he was gone.

Tears blinded my vision.

I felt nothing.

Saw nothing.

I was empty inside.

Alice

48

Four days later

The air in the morgue was sterile and probing like a rod entering your sternum. Sister to the hospital ward, except in here, the people lay in permanent peace. Time meant nothing to these bodies. Ultimately, the world continued to evolve, eventually forgetting.

It wasn't my first time in a morgue. Yet today, I felt I couldn't breathe; the stank of death lay heavy in my lungs.

Lying facedown on a bed of metal with his feet protruding from the end of the table was my father, frozen stiff and body blue. The bullet hole went through his back to his heart. Reality sank, and this was the truth.

My father, Dr. Michael Harris, was never coming back. He was the last of the long lineage of Harris, who came from Sweden by way of England. Our ancestors were among the few early settlers who arrived through Ellis Island, searching for a better life. Some stayed in New York, and others settled and plowed the fields in Kansas. My father, who defied his family, chose to marry an Asian immigrant, believing genius saw no color. That was his saving grace among his many sins.

For reasons unknown, all the Harris descendants died at a young age. I was the last of the direct line, female and half-Asian, forced to deal with his funeral rights and not giving him what he always wanted — world recognition and envy. I could argue that notoriety was a form of fame. The memes made about him had millions of views, reposts, and hashtags.

"Poisoned and shot in the heart. Time of death was twelve-twenty." The mortician read from his chart.

"Poison?" I flipped the cloth off my father's corpse, studied the discoloration and marks. "Didn't he have cancer?"

He looked at his chart again and flipped through the other sheets. Then, he cleared his throat. "Yes. Colon cancer, poisoning, and a bullet wound."

"What kind of poison?"

"Belladonna. Nightshade. A genius doctor should know." The man sneered.

With gloved hands, I inspected the bullet hole and reviewed the results.

I closed my eyes and turned to the wall. Tears rolled down my cheeks. I said I wouldn't cry.

"And those belong to Dr. Harris." The coroner pointed to a box on the table of my father's things: my father's ring, a gold Rolex, a pair of cufflinks with his Alpha Epsilon Delta symbols, his leather wallet, and a bullet.

I stared at his wallet, torn between curiosity and hatred. There were two possibilities. One, whatever was in it, would show nothing. A man like Michael kept his life under wraps. If he were like me, he would not leave any evidence.

Two — it could show a side of him that I wished I knew. I resented him for decades. My therapists believed I was this way because of my parents.

Why did my parents hate me? Why did Michael abuse those women? Why did he forget his doctor's oath, and experimented on those children? Why did he apologize before dying when he could have been a better dad earlier?

I flipped it open. Some cards, cash, and ID.

The mortician snatched the wallet and box, and we did a little tug of war until I finally let go.

"This is evidence. If you want Dr. Harris's things, you can call the detective." He handed me a business card. The police investigation is not done."

A penny dropped out of the wallet and landed on my boot. I stepped on it and, when the moritician turned, pocketed it.

My father hated carrying coins. He believed that with his success, he deserved more than owning the smallest denomination. I remembered taking his pennies and filling those Ming pot urns my mother kept in the library. The pots reminded us that even in death, we would be together.

"Here are my flight details. The airport is expecting to receive the coffin at noon tomorrow." I handed over the documents. "I'll talk to Detective Ko and return for that box." I glanced at my father's corpse one last time and left.

———

It was an Asian belief that the number four meant death. Its pronunciation sounded like that unlucky word, and I would forever be linked to that number.

Twenty-four years ago, I was abducted. The pedophile who took me died. The boy who tried to save me died.

Fourteen years ago, a producer called Miyako died in my arms.

Four years ago, a patient, Ellen Han, and her unborn baby died under my care, and four days ago, both my father, Sophie Han, Gina Chen, an unknown driver, a security guard, and an ordinary woman, including several agents, were killed.

The list grew. Eli Randall was my first and last best friend. When coming to Seoul, I never imagined I would lose him. Park Ji Woon and Eli were both manipulative.

They lured me to Seoul. I was bait for Michael Harris. Both were searching for the grave of the unmarked children and the billions of dollars and gold he stole.

The smell of pine cones and Christmas wreaths tickled my nose. Eli was standing by the door with a silly mistletoe. He kissed everyone at the party with it and was determined to lock lips with me.

"No!" I laughed, shaking my head, scooting under his arms. Eli was faster, cornering me against the arches of my door.

"Come on, Aly! It's bad luck. Kiss me." He grinned drunkenly, hooked his arm around my waist, and pressed his lips on mine. I was drunk and didn't think too much about him trailing his lips down my neck. "You smell so good," he murmured between kisses.

He said something else, but I was watching the man standing by the tree across the road. The Christmas lights in bulbs of rainbow and red reflected on him.

"Eli! It's him." I pushed him away. "It's him!" I pulled Eli in and slammed the door.

"Who?"

At the windows, with my heart pounding in my ears. The man in the black hoodie and face mask stared back. He wasn't afraid we were watching him. When the cops came with their lights revolving, he was gone.

"People die," my father's voice echoed.

"Yes, they do," I replied.

Because I am the harbinger, I was Icarus, and the sun was death.

Alice

49

Ji Woon was drunk at a pop-up bar in the parking lot somewhere in Gangnam. He slumped over the table with two young women flanking his sides. It grated on me that they were flirting and taking turns to pull him up, cajoling him to leave with them.

I marched over and slammed my hand on the table. "He's taken."

The tipsy woman hesitated. They had the nerve to give me a look of disgust at my messy hair and tired face before dropping paper napkins with their numbers on the table and leaving.

"Alice, you came!" Ji Woon smiled, opening his bleary eyes. I crumpled the napkins and tossed them in a bin.

"Why didn't you say it was a tent? It took me thirty minutes to find this place." I pulled a stool to him. The plastic chair knocked his wheelchair.

"Sorry," my anger fizzled, and I sat down.

"I should have told you it was a *Pojang Macha*." Ji Woon slapped his forehead with his hand. His too-bright eyes riveted onto my lips. Each second he lingered, my cheeks grew hotter.

"You weren't replying to my texts. I was worried," I said.

"Worried about me?" He laughed.

He reached over and held my hands. His touch alone sent prickling sensations throughout my body.

"I thought you left again without saying bye." He sounded like a boy who thought he had lost his favorite toy.

"You were the one who left," I said.

The owner came over, and with my basic Korean, I ordered a grilled mackerel, a *guksu* soup, and another *soju* glass.

He laced his fingers through mine. "Do we keep our promises now?"

I turned to him, "Are you?"

I snatched the glass from him. "You shouldn't be drinking. Your wound hasn't healed."

He narrowed his eyes and stared at his cast. Guilt flushed through me. His injuries were due to me.

The empty glass clinked against mine on the table. He picked the bones from the mackerel before taking a piece to chew slowly.

"What's wrong?" I asked.

"I put him on house arrest."

"Who?"

"Chairman Park. Ex. He's ex now. I'm the temporary Chairman."

"Yes. Congrats. You pulled it off."

We didn't talk about it. All of Sophie's shares went to Ji Woon. Her lawyers had announced that the majority of what Sophie owned went to Ji Woon, with a tidy sum for Gina Chen, who, being dead, had no will, and not being a Korean citizen, the inheritance was donated to various charity organizations instead.

"I'm an unfilial son."

"Jerk, yes, but unfilial, well, that depends on how you look at it. On the bright side, he's not in jail," he smirked. Ji Woon glanced at me, and his lips lifted into a smile.

"His doctor says he's working himself to death. His heart can't take it. This is our last chance," he said.

"That Chairman has a temper." I clinked his empty glass and downed a shot. "And I should know. I beat him into a pulp."

Ji Woon laughed. "I wish I had seen that. Finally, someone taught him a lesson."

"Yeah. If he knew it was me, you might forget about introducing us."

"I don't care. I'm leaving it all. You are mine now." He squeezed my hand.

"I won't be so sure."

"Wait." He grinned. "Are you still thinking of running?"

"Ji Woon."

"I'm a selfish bastard. I'm used to being first. First to get the girl. First to admit I made a mistake. First to leave this world. First to admit I love you."

"I can't. I told you. I need to get back."

"I know. We will do this together. Just stay here with me a little longer. I'll wrap things up."

The soup burnt the roof of my mouth. It wasn't possible. I could barely hold onto myself. Each minute, each hour I lived in the cesspool of their thoughts and memories, my guilt reeked. I had gone far too deep to get out. The crimes they committed, the lives taken in their selfish pursuits. If he knew.

The nightmares of my past, my fears, and the horrors of rejection. I needed my meds and the normalcy of my life back in San Francisco. I had to stop the triggers that made Merle and the remaining ones come out and play.

The past week, Bailey gave help, but his hypnotherapy was limited to what I could do for myself and others right now.

"I'll clear your name. The police, media, and everyone won't hound you again. You'll leave Seoul a free person."

"It's too late, Ji Woon. Even with your power and influence, it isn't going to stop them."

The snow was falling lightly on our faces as we headed out of the tent. He caught my arms and smoothly dropped me onto his lap.

"You want me. He pressed his moist, cold lips on mine and opened them for air.

It was easy to fall into his trap. We kissed frantically, and our hands couldn't get enough. I tried to pull back, but he held my shoulders.

His voice dropped as his chest shook with his ragged breath.

"Tell me the truth. Tell me you don't love me, and I'll let you go."

Park Ji Woon was my first love, and I fell in love with him each time we met. Again and again. The red strings of fate are winding tighter and tighter.

He had a calculating, selfish, and cruel side that no one knew. Surprisingly, that side of him was what drew me in. He had demons, and so did I. He understood my pain, and that was what brought us together. With him, I didn't have to hide.

"It's not love. It's lust. I don't love you."

He laughed at the cruelty of my words.

His fingers intertwined with mine, draining the blood out of them. White knuckled and turned purple.

I refused to bend to his will. This was one of his traits, but I could be as stubborn as he was.

"Liar," he whispered. He dropped his hand and rubbed his five o'clock chin. "Why are you doing this? We were fine this morning." He lifted me off his lap and scowled.

I forgot he was still in pain and under meds. Ji Woon always puts on a good show.

The night was drawing in, and the sky was dark blue-black. At nine p.m. in winter, the air was freezing as the vapor from the boiling pots of soup rose in waves.

The image of my father's cold, lifeless body on the table at the morgue brushed my thoughts again. "He blocked that bullet."

"I would do that for you, too." Ji Woon muttered, knowing as always what I was saying without saying.

"I know. You saved me from Eli." I sighed. "I owe you."

"Owe?"

He looked away. "Are we counting debts now? Yes, you owe me. For my life, you owe me one night, and I'll consider it paid," he muttered.

We were two headstrong individuals who wanted others to see things from our perspectives, because they never did. Our problem was neither black nor white. Between the lines of good and evil were always shades of grey.

50

Ji Woon's apartment was a pair of twin buildings joined at the hip with a sky bridge and large triangular glass and metal windows. Lights from units lit like prisms in the night air, with green stairwells running up the sides of towers.

It took an eight-minute walk to get here after leaving the *Pojang Macha* tent. We didn't speak. Frost lined in sheets as his wheelchair rolled in silence. My hands held his handlebars tightly, bumping and sliding over the icy path. We entered the fancy modern apartment lobby with ceilings twenty feet tall.

San Francisco didn't have buildings like this. The rich in Silicon Valley showed their wealth in *Arcteryx* jackets on golf courses and over coffee, chatting about which next unicorn start-up they'd invest their billions in. In Seoul, the *chaebol* spent lavishly on luxury items and flaunted them with foreign trips abroad, bodyguards, and reveled in the respect of men and women in suits who bowed deeply when they and their entourage of executives entered their headquarters.

We were worlds apart. Ji Woon was the new Chairman of Park Entertainment, with a fifty-billion market cap. He became one of the most powerful men in South Korea, thanks to Sophie Han's shares, which were secretly assigned to Ji Woon in a will that only her lawyer knew. Therefore, the fake stock certificates I tore meant nothing in my vengeance.

I was the American neuroscientist whose road to fame was being kidnapped and hunted down, and for being the only daughter of a notorious doctor — child killer, mad-scientist surgeon, rapist, and Ponzi-schemes conman.

The elevator blinked, passing each level to the twenty-fourth floor, one below the penthouse with spectacular city views. He didn't speak, and I was too stubborn to ask. We got to his door, which had a digital key lock. I entered three times and got three buzzes.

"What's the pin?" I grumbled.

"The day we met." He reached over and typed it — month, date, and year. The door clicked open, and I rolled him down a dark, narrow hallway, with the floor lights automatically turning on like an airport runway. The living room was at the end, expanding out like a fan, with the open kitchen on the right and the full view of the city in front and to the left. The stars had fallen with the city vibrantly white, glittering diamonds and rainbow streams ebbing like the tide.

I strode to the window and studied the snow falling in powdered flurries. The surface of the glass was chilly, and as cold crept up my arms and chest, it became distinctly warmer. My breath misted as misery settled in my heart.

He was beside me, silent and waiting. This was our first fight. And maybe it was the thought I was leaving, and him realizing he couldn't hold me back. Tears rolled down my cheeks.

I was never coming back.

His arms wrapped around my waist. His head on my chest. "Don't go, Alice. Please. I'm sorry. I'm so sorry. I should have tried harder. It's my fault. All of it. From the beginning to now. Please, I don't want you to go."

I closed my eyes. It won't matter. Here we were again, like those years back. Thinking the world would end if we didn't spend this night. To seize each breath, each word, each moment together. The surge of desire struck me to the core. I wanted more than anything to be with him. Our fights seemed inconsequential and petty.

I leaned on his shoulder and closed my eyes. He pulled me onto his lap. The sound of his strong heart beating in rhythm to mine. Sweet melody, aching and deep. My pent-up frustration and anxiety melted away with his warmth. The world receded, and his love hugged my fragile soul.

His mouth dropped and brushed my nape, nuzzling until he reached my right shoulder and pushed my sweater aside, revealing my heart-shaped scar. I gasped as he kissed and nibbled gently at first, and then, sucking, leaving his mark over my heart. Then, he searched for my face, pressing his lips onto mine.

I opened my lips and let him in. His wandering hands slid to my hips, and with his hungry lips and tongue, he dipped his head down. Then, he stood up, leaning against one wall and pushing me to the corner of a window with his warm torso plastered against mine as he continued his bodily attack.

We kissed like there was no tomorrow. We struggled off our coats and stumbled down the hallway to his room, frantically pulling off the rest of our clothes and then limping afterward as I jumped into his bed. Nothing could stop us. I craved a memory of him branded onto my skin and heart.

Tomorrow.

Tomorrow could wait.

Tonight, we would make love to our hearts' content. Forget the sorrows. Forget the deaths. Forget Fate, which chose to keep us apart, or those people who wanted to tear us down and watch us drown.

I pushed him down, got on him, and rode with urgency as my body absorbed his grunts and thrusts, determined to fill every inch of myself with him and score his thoughts with my body - each cell, each molecule, and to the tiniest atom. He would remember me.

The sounds of our bodies slapping together. Our voices were apart and as one. Waves and waves of emotions hammered the shore, brushing through our skin, building into a tsunami, where my screams and his groans cut through his apartment and beyond.

He retook my lips and kissed them with greed. His dilated eyes held mine without pretense — whispers of endless love and prom- ises. We wrapped together, rolling back and forth, he chuckling and I giggling at the euphoria of our touch. Skin-to-skin sparks a-flying.

He pulled me on his lap, lifted my hips, and thrust up.

"You're mine!" He grunted and plunged in further as I rode him hard. "*Nan Naekkoya!*" Together, we moved in a hurried dance. Desperate and drunk with mindlessness. Taking as much as giving and arriving in sync. Pouring our essence, mixing our scents as one. White river flowing, loving, and feeling.

Later, he ran his fingers through my wet, tangled hair. Our bodies were slick with sweat, and I brushed my fingers across his lips. "Alice *naekkoya*," he smiled. "I should have asked you when we were in SF," he stared straight into my eyes. "Will you be my girlfriend? And, I won't take no."

I smiled, with tears welling, and nodded. Pipe dreams were sweet for a reason. It was false hope, but his smile was worth a billion lies.

"We will get through this together." He kissed me deeply.

I wanted to believe he was strong enough to push back the tide of naysayers. Brave and determined to fuck the world and anyone who tried to tear us apart. However, words were empty, and actions mattered. Until the day he had proven I would be alone. Always and forever alone.

Ji Woon

51

The smell of noodles and spicy broth hung like a cloud in the hallway. The smoke alarm was going to shriek any second. Ji Woon sprinted to the kitchen, turned off the stove, and switched on the range hood. The hood groaned and sucked the fumes with glee.

«*Naekkoya…*» Ji Woon took the pot off the stove and tossed it in the sink. "Your *ramyeon's* dried up." He pulled another clean pot from a bottom drawer and grabbed two more packets of noodles from the pantry. "I'll make you a new one."

He tapped his lips as he studied the contents of his freezer. "Are you allergic to seafood? Hmm, you had prawns the other day." He grabbed the tray of fresh prawns. "What about scallops?"

She didn't reply.

Ji Woon turned to where he had spotted Alice earlier after rushing past. She was standing listlessly by the window. Sun rays lit one side of her, highlighting the sharp hunch of her shoulders. Her gaze slowly shifted to the picture frames on his living room wall — new pictures of crested waves, powdery sand, and the amazing cloudless sky.

One picture of himself with his parents, Myung-Dae, and Sophie, was taken in front of their villa, and the other picture was of him and his father cliff fishing. Since December, he has been busy in and out of Seoul and has not noticed the wall. His brother must have snuck into his apartment and put the new ones up.

Alice rubbed her eyes with the back of her hand. Their eyes met, and his heart lurched at her sorrow. "Come here," he gestured to her. "Naeko, come." Last week had been crazy, and Ji Woon was ready to sleep for a month. "Come here, dearest."

The shadow of the room shaded her face when she walked over. Ji Woon blinked, and a man materialized in her place.

He blinked again, and the man stayed. Seconds of disbelief thawed as his mind processed this change. Michael was imposing — a giant, taller than him by a head with twice the shoulder width and thick arms —Michael, who was still admired at sixty for his chiseled looks, bullish influence, and intelligence.

Anger came in a burst of momentum. Ji Woon charged at the man, slamming his nemesis against the wall, and his hands grabbed onto the older man's neck and tightened.

The man struggled and gasped. For more than a decade, Ji Woon imagined killing him.

Ji Woon's heart sang victoriously. The devil in his nightmares. The reason why he'd stayed alive. Finally.

He shook the older man. Alice was messed up because of this sick asshole. Michael was a terrible father to Alice, just like his father was. If Alice had a normal childhood, Uncle James, Aunt Ellen, and Sophie were still alive, and Miyako hadn't met this monster, Ji Woon might not be dead inside.

He tried to wrap his fingers around the thick man's throat.

"I'm sorry…" Michael croaked. "I'm sorry."

Ji Woon flinched. These were not words he expected the devil to say.

"Sorry?" He squeezed harder. His thumbs dug into soft skin and cartilage, pressing on Michael's windpipe. Up close, the old man's weathered cheeks and trenched lines on his forehead showed his age. The man was taking on a shade of grey.

Ji Woon jeered, amused at how easy it was to take a life.

There was a pop, a breaking, and the man's arms sagged to his sides. His skin was papery, thin, and growing cold. The marks of Ji Woon's fingers formed petals on his neck.

"You took Miyako and my aunt!" His eyes burned like lava. Hate spewed in clumps hotter than coal.

He waited for the fight. The fight never came.

Silence. The big man lay limp in his arms.

A thought flashed in Ji Woon's head. Light in the mist, a clearing of air.

"Where's Alice?" Ji Woon scanned around his apartment in a panic. "Alice?" Seconds ago, she was here with him. He shook the big man. "What did you do to her?"

„Ji Woon…" Michael whispered. His last breath left his lips as his eyes closed.

"No…no…" Ji Woon stumbled back onto his couch in horror. He watched as the man morphed, turning back into his lover. Her head drooped, her shoulders sagged, and her legs gave way, pooling on the ground in hair and limbs.

He gathered her into his arms, checking her nose for breath and neck for a pulse. Her chest heaved suddenly, gasping. He pulled her carefully to his sofa, and her cold, cream thighs dangled over the edge. The marks on her neck faded, but it didn't stop him from seeing them vividly in his memory.

"I'm sorry…so sorry…so sorry…so sorry," he choked back his tears. "Alice…naeko…" he sobbed.

Time stretched into a never-ending spiral of guilt. Each second, each moment, each time, her breath staggered. His heart collapsed a notch further.

"Slowly, breathe in, breathe out, breathe in," he advised, watching her chest move. Seconds flew, and her eyelids flickered. Then, her eyes opened in the shades of brown and dappled with specks of green. Into the forest, he fell, watching her light on him.

„Ji Woon…" Her voice is smooth and warm, like coffee.

He stared at her throat, which no longer had bruises, no fingerprints, and no signs that he had killed him.

"You became your father."

He swallowed hard. Tears cut through his skin, searing down his jaw. "Alice, I…" He closed his eyes as his shoulders shook. "I wasn't thinking. I swear I won't hurt you. I didn't see you."

Her hand was on his head, combing through his hair. "You saw me change?"

He nodded and sniffled.

"You let him go?" she asked.

He nodded. "I did something so terrible…I…killed a man." His shoulders shook as he choked on his sobs.

"He was already dead," she sighed. "You can't kill someone who is dead."

"No. I did it to you." He covered his face with his hands as she patted him.

"I should have seen through it. You even felt like him."

"I know." She stood up. Her legs wobbled as she walked by him.

"Where are you going?" He pushed himself up from the sofa.

The hall echoed his steps with his brace. He watched her fold her clothes from last night and pack her toiletries.

"What are you doing?" His voice was rough.

"I can't be here, Ji Woon."

"No. It's over. He's gone. You said he left."

She shook her head. "No. There is more in me. The remaining ones. They will shock you, and you'll react again."

"I won't. Alice. It was just Michael."

"Michael," she scoffed. "I didn't want you to see me change." She rubbed her face.

He reached over to grab her, and she backed away again. "Don't touch me! Don't! I'm... I'm." Her voice dropped as her face crumpled into despair. She pushed him off, "You'll think I'm a monster, too."

He held her tight, "I don't! Alice, I see you. I will only see you! I'll get better at this. I swear."

She hammered his chest. Her cries were raw, a deluge of emotion, raw and deep. "If you love me, you'd let me go. Ji Woon, I need to go home."

"What if you don't come back?"

"I won't come back," she said.

"I can't let you go to San Francisco alone."

She pushed him off. He watched her pale legs disappear into her jeans, and her long sweater dropped over her head, wrapping around her curves.

He grabbed her wrist, "Give me two days! A little longer. We'll go together."

She slapped him off. "I can't be in Seoul. You saw what happened."

"It's an excuse, isn't it?" His voice cracked.

"I can't make you happy." She dragged her suitcase to the door.

"Happy? How can I be happy without you?"

"All of you are liars. My father, Eli, and you."

"Don't lump me with them." He grabbed her bag.

"Go save the world, Park Ji Woon."

"Why can't you wait a few more days?" He asked.

She grabbed the knob and turned it, "I can't." Her shoulders shook as she cried.

He took her lips and kissed her deeply. His fingers wound in her hair; their bodies molded as he searched for her tongue, savoring her like a beggar starving. He tried to show it all.

She responded to his hunger, filling up his broken soul.

They were euphoric, soaring high above the clouds, basking in the sun's warmth. And then, she pulled away, breaking that spell. Sliding from his touch, and like the passing of a warm breeze, her sweet scent lingered after the door clicked.

Merle

52

SAN FRANCISCO FLIGHT

Merle played with the syringe in her pocket and glanced at the FBI agent sleeping. She smiled as she recalled the shock on the agent's face when she stabbed Alice's sleeping drug into her thigh. Merle didn't need another set of eyes watching her. The merging of their minds frustrated Merle that her secrets were no longer hers alone.

The soft rumbling of the plane and the feeling of her gut sitting on her uterus were good distractions from the many thoughts and emotions running through her. Merle wished she could be like Alice - that cold-hearted robot. For Merle, everything was twice as much, senses heightened, ready to explode.

Daddy and Nicky were murdered by that asshole Eli/Cyrus. Cyrus promised not to touch Nick. The Belladonna poison she gave Daddy wouldn't have killed him. So, why did Daddy jump in front of the gun? It was Alice's fault. Merle swallowed back her tears. Daddy won't like to see her cry.

Again and again, the scene played out - the sound of the gun, the feel of the bullet passing through Daddy's body, and his last breath.

She frowned as she drank her plastic cup of red wine and stared out the porthole into the cloudy night sky. Briefly, she wondered what it was like to be free. Alice complained about sharing part of her mind. Merle had to share her body, too. And now, even her most private thoughts, Alice knew. Who had the upper hand? She sneered at her reflection.

Happiness wasn't something she knew she'd get. Without Daddy, Merle saw no meaning. Daddy said winning mattered, and she always hated Alice for that.

She glanced at the FBI girl by her side. What's her name again?

Her new guard was snoring. Merle could slit her throat, and no one would know. Her head was spinning with ideas. Her new rule was her old rule. Go psycho. Make Alice cry — screw Alice — ten times more.

At the back of the plane, the flight attendants were chatting loudly and gossiping about some celebrity cheating with someone else and some politician grafting and getting away with it.

Stupid fuckers. The rich always ruled. Instead of envy, they should try harder. Losing was for losers.

Merle hid things well. She was her father's best cleaner. Adding Cyrus to the mix screwed things up. Daddy shouldn't have trusted him. She grabbed another cup of wine from those bitches and decided to walk the aisle. She stepped on something skin-colored, rubbery, and squishy in the semi-darkness. She was about to reach for it when she spotted a pair of high-quality starlight black gloves on an empty seat.

"Are these yours?" She pointed at the cool gloves and wondered which designer brand they were from. The man sitting by the window seat looked up. His cap covered his hair and eyes, revealing only his smooth jaw and sensual lips.

Merle scanned his build. Strong shoulders, lean with nice biceps from the way his shirt clung. She watched as he flexed his sexy lower arm when he reached to grab the gloves. She slipped into the empty seat beside him. On impulse, she went over and brushed his lips.

He snatched her fingers, squeezing them till her blood wouldn't flow. Sparks shot through her, and instantly, her body was wet with desire.

"Who are you?" He squeezed tighter as she tried to pull away.

"Are you bored?" She pouted.

He tossed her hand aside.

She leaned back in her seat and stared at him through his shades. She always loved a challenge. He expected her to leave. He thought he scared her. He's doing the opposite. A naughty smile crept up her face.

His beautiful lips arched into a frown.

"Have you tried the mile-high club?" she asked, and before he could answer, she reached under his blanket and found him hard and ready.

He didn't stop her when she rubbed him. Grinning, she dropped her head under his blanket and took him. Minutes later, he arched his back as his muscled thighs tightened.

Merle smiled with her mouth full, relishing how Alice was reeling as she watched. A nice girl always swallowed, and she did just that.

—||—

Alice

53

They found Eli's body decomposed. The teeth matched, so this time, Eli Randall didn't escape. The news came from FBI Agent Odeh, who dropped by and delivered it succinctly as if he were talking about the weather, which was nice and foggy today. There wasn't an apology for lying to me and the world about Eli's death weeks earlier. With all eyes on them, they needed to close the case fast.

I broke down. Eli was the closest to family I had. Despite the bad, we had many happy times. I wanted to believe he meant what he promised back then.

"Aly," Eli laughed and flung his arm over my shoulder. "Forget Jason. Okay, let's make a pack. If you're still single by forty, I'll marry you. You'll be my second. It's always been my dream to have a harem. Count yourself lucky, I'm taking you in."

"Hey. I'm no one's leftovers," I hugged him. His hand was patting my head.

"Yeah. Bitches ain't my taste, but you're my one and only BFF." He kissed between my eyes.

I touched his favorite spot. Tears streaked down my cheeks.

The agents gave me a pitiful look.

Agent Odeh was one of the good guys. He wouldn't have lied, according to Agent Christy. Eli Randall, aka Cyrus Matel, was dead. The DNA proved it, too, and science won in the end.

Eli was finally dead.

54

Two weeks later

Twilight came under the dying light. The miniature red maple swayed with a light breeze, and a bamboo pipe bounced on the flat water basin, making a hollow sound. Large boulders were like mountains along a river bed of blue-grey gravel. Evergreen bushes with light pink and orange flowers added color to the landscape. Twin Sakura trees with branches intertwined stood on the back left side along the black bamboo fence stretching between my yard and the wall.

My father's urn sat on my bookshelf with my mother's. Their twin reflection on the window placed them in the center of my oasis. Until now, I had not decided what to do with them.

The bamboo pipe knocked again, and my heart skipped a beat. The fresh morning mist filled my lungs as I took another deep breath, holding on as I counted, and then exhaled, repeating this exercise. These days, I need this.

In the last ten days, Merle went on a path of destruction. Unlike the rest, she grew stronger, finding ways to circumvent my methods, popping up here and there, and throwing tantrums, making my life hell. The last straw came with her bomb scare, and I was forced to take time off and go for counseling. To make things worse, ever since I returned, Zareen had been putting pressure on me to collaborate with my father's open research as a basis for my thesis. She stubbornly believed being his daughter would add prestige to our school and validity to my work. Without Eli to bridge the gap, Zareen's insensitivity pushed me over the edge, and I lashed out. My boss was pissed, and I was seriously considering quitting.

At home, I didn't have to worry about the reproachful looks of others when Merle appeared. With my locks and alarms in place, I could be anyone I wanted, and I knew I wouldn't be a danger to anyone.

FBI Agent Christy was my constant shadow, and with her team watching, I was a prisoner in my own home. We didn't talk about Merle or my other personalities. The elephant in the room made breaking the awkwardness between the new agent and me hard, and maybe I didn't want to talk.

Today, I was finally alone at home. Agent Christy was at a meeting and will be gone for three hours.

A sudden movement caught my attention, and I blinked. My pulse raced as I scanned the greenery. In the shadowy corner of the alcove by the pine tree, a collection of dark spots beneath the foliage seemed to merge, forming a black blob, growing more substantial into the shape of a person crouching on the ground.

I held my breath.

The thing stood up - a man in a black hoodie took his first step. His hood dropped, revealing Eli's face. "Aly, did you miss me? I missed you a lot." He grinned as I watched him in shock.

"You're dead," I whispered.

"Am I?" he snickered.

"Impossible. I saw pics and the reports. They found your body."

Eli smiled and didn't say a word.

I took a step back. My breath halted as my mind coalesced. I swiveled and dashed into my house, slamming the sliding door shut and locking it as Eli came straight for it. He shook the door hard as I sprinted across my family room, past the kitchen, into the foyer, and up the three flights of stairs. Behind me, I heard the crash of the sliding door breaking and then his shoes slapping on the hardwood floor as he gave chase.

I flung open my door and slammed it shut. The reinforced steel door was meant to keep the voices in. The pin code door pinged as the locks fell in place. I dove into my bed and waited.

Any moment now, the door would shake. Any moment now, Eli would try to get in. Any moment now, he'd be calling my name. Ever since his betrayal, I hated that name more. Eli always liked calling me 'Aly,' and I gave in.

I slipped off my bed and rushed into my walk-in closet with a katana in my hand. Pushing a large luggage bag in front of me, I crouched and waited. Covering my ears and cowering, praying he won't come.

The whole house moved. The closet mirror swayed, and then it dropped with a crack.

The man in the black hoodie was staring in the mirror back at me. Rubber-faced with no eyes, nose, or mouth.

I choked. Tears were streaming down my cheeks.

My bedroom floor caved in. I was falling endlessly as the wind swept my hair to my face. Wet cheeks smothering with heat, searing my breath with smoke. I stumbled out of the closet with sea legs — a constant high-pitched burst in my ears.

My hand shook as I tried to tap on speed dial. The phone rang twice, and then it picked up.

"I need you," I said and hung up.

55

The hill behind my house was sprinkled green after days of winter rain. Wind whipped hair over my face. Through the tall grass and bushes, I searched for a path out. On the other side of the hill were rows of houses, some shops, and a bus stop that would take me to the BART train station.

Temperatures dropped as I climbed higher, using the sandy footpath, aiming for the line of trees at the top of the hill, then looped down again to the other side.

"You killed my baby!" She sobbed.

I spun around.

"Dead? She can't be dead!"

I turned to the other side, my heart hammering in my chest.

"Stop. Don't take her. Please, no. You can't take her."

"Okaasan?" I called out, breathing fast.

Instinct made me touch my face. My features are mine, not hers.

"My baby...my baby!" She cried.

I covered my ears. "Okaasan, stop!"

"I want her! Give her back!" she cried, sobbing and muttering. "Give her back!"

"Stop! Stooppp!" I shouted to the sky.

"Baby, my darling, baby," she cooed.

I shook my head repeatedly, pulling my hair with my hands. "Go away...go away!"

"Open your eyes!" she screamed.

Her ghostly cries came from everywhere. The wind took them, and like a whip, it struck me hard.

"It's your fault!" she screeched. "You killed her. You killed my baby girl!"

The fog rose high and blanketed my sight in ash white. I stumbled, not knowing which way was forward and which was back. Her cries taunted me. I saw her angry, dead stares filled with hate. Some days, I woke up burning with guilt, knowing I had taken from my mother her one happiness.

I was a thief, a cold-blooded killer.

I ran mindlessly. The ghost of my mother clung to my back relentlessly. My arms flay out, thrashing the air till I spot a speck of color. The more I pushed ahead, the clouds gave way to things — wood fences, cement pavement, shrubs, and houses laid in a row. Following a high wall of thick green ivy, I found an opening — a gate into a community pool.

"You can't have her! She's mine!" My mother fought him, grabbing that white box of bones in his hands.

Daddy pushed her, and she fell.

Her hands were gripping Daddy's pants, begging. "Please, Michael, give her back! My Alice. My baby! Give her back!"

My emotions expanded like a colossal swell, encompassing everything I'd experienced. Almost thirty years of broken selves, pieces of others, and never-ending nightmares pulled together into one massive tsunami.

My mind snapped, and I crashed. Saltwater tears poured down my cheeks.

I stumbled to the pool's deep end, dragging my feet forward to the voices calling my name. My knees gave way, and I dropped at the water's edge.

I looked down with blurry eyes.

From my reflection, I saw myself switching from my mother to Merle, to the many faces rotting inside, and then settling on Miyako.

Miyako.

Of course. The pool would remind me of her — the catalyst that started the chain of terrible tragedies.

My mother was wailing again, begging for her baby.

Once more, I changed. My hair wound tight into black curls, and my skin darkened to his coffee brown. My flesh and bones stretched to his flat chest and elongated to Eli's muscular legs.

On his face, his usual cheery smile was replaced with a cold accusation.

"Eli." I sobbed. Happy-go-lucky Eli, as I chose to remember. Not the psychopath who shot and stabbed innocent people.

I let him fall and watched as he disappeared. He was my only friend and my family, and I loved him.

I touched the pool. Rings of water spread from my finger outwards. Eli's features were wavering, adding sorrow to his unflinching gaze. The tree couldn't take the weight. It was either him or me, or both of us. To save me, he died.

It should have been me. I wouldn't have died because I couldn't, even if I didn't want to.

His sacrifice was for nothing.

I was nothing.

I hammered my chest with my fists, and they laughed. I hated them. I hated how lonely I felt despite them being here. Without me, things would be better. I peeled off my clothes.

In the pool's reflection, Eli was turning away. Ripples spread further the farther he went.

"Eli! Wait!" I kicked off my boots. "Eli!"

"Alice!" Someone was calling. "Alice!" Someone familiar.

I looked up. Was it the wind? I watched as Eli grew smaller and smaller.

"No! Eli, I'm coming too!" I shouted and jumped. The frigid winter water drove spikes into my flesh. A numbness spread over my body.

"Okaasan?" The young me saw her sitting by the window with a dagger in her palm. My mother squeezed the blade, and her blood pooled in her palm. "Okaasan? Why do you have a knife?" My child-like voice shook as I reached for her.

"Let her be," a voice said.

I turned to Miyako by my side. Strung around her waist was an entrails belt. The smell of rot made me sick. My stomach lurched.

Mother dropped her knife, and Miyako picked it up and handed it blade-point back to her.

"Do it here." Miyako pointed with a claw-like nail to her sliced abdomen. "It's messy, but it'd be quick."

My mother grabbed the hilt and plunged it into herself.

"No!" I screamed.

"Again!" Miyako shouted. Her eyes were red as fire.

"No!" I gurgled as my mother stabbed herself. Blood burst from her thin, chapped lips. Death came fleeting like cherry blossoms in Spring. The last memory of my mother was shredded, and then the void intensified with Miyako dying next.

More water entered my open mouth and flooded my lungs. Tight hands wrapped in a death grip pulled me down. This time, the water won't let me go. This time, I wanted to stay. I was tired of fighting Merle and them. Tired of their endless voices and objections.

I opened my mind — flung the door, and let everyone in—faces — old and young, female and male. One by one, they came through, taking over and dying for me.

The water was lit in hues of pink, orange, and red.

I died and lived and then died and then lived. Letting them vanish forever into the depths of nothingness.

With them went my guilt and regrets as I became weaker, losing more of myself, growing smaller and smaller with every passing second.

A black hoodie appeared. Red flaming hair, all else I remembered him naught.

Somewhere inside, Merle fought against the tide.

This was the end.

Peace was close. I heard my mother's heartbeat and reached for her hand.

 Ji Woon

56

The fog against the overcast sky was like a dream. The light from his phone beamed through the thick mist, and then, Ji Woon heard a woman crying.

"Give her back! Give her back!" Her voice, in a wrenching screech, tore through the silence.

"Who's that?" He called out.

Everything was gray, with low-hanging clouds. The winter evening was getting darker than the night.

Her whimpering and soft cries followed the sounds. "Alice?"

He sprinted down a row of deserted townhouses painted in pastel shades, looming over him like blown-out birthday candles. "Alice?" The voices were growing fainter as his heart sped up.

Not a single soul lurked on the street. Stuck in a terrible nightmare, mired in endless corners. "Alice?" His pulse raced. His head swiveled from side to side. Was his mind playing tricks?

Then, he heard her sobbing. The voice of the one he loved the most. It tugged at him, pulling at his heartstrings and his feet. He didn't know where it was, but it didn't matter. Anywhere with her was home.

"Eli…Eli. Please." The voice was different now, growing lower, more masculine. He steeled himself for the inevitable. This was what he had to accept and why he came to help.

"Where are you?" he shouted, following the cries.

"I'm sorry…," she sobbed, echoing in the trees. The leaves rustled, whispering as if in cahoots, hiding her.

"Alice!" He rushed along a wall of thick vines and spotted a rusty gate leading to an abandoned pool. "Are you here?" He pushed through the unlocked gate and spotted her in the clearing.

Standing, facing him, across the water, was his beautiful Alice. Pale as fresh snow with dark, wavy hair cascading down her chest, barely covering her nipples. Moonlight rays peeked through the clouds and lit her full breasts, exposing her stomach's smooth swell and down to the light V-sprinkle between her legs. Venus in the flesh.

Her eyes were full of tears as she stared at the water. It was her face that tugged him the most, then and now. Right from the very start, back when he met teenage Alice with jaded eyes. Her guilt, mixed with broken innocence, was a mirror to his own, reflecting his pain, path, and life.

Ji Woon stiffened as he watched her bend down, her gaze fixed on the dirty pool. Brown leaves and bits of dirt and dust, as well as dead bugs, were lying flat on stale, yellowed water.

A horrible thought crossed his mind. She wouldn't.

"Alice!" he shouted.

She didn't look up, staring at the water's surface as if there was something there.

"No!"

She lifted her eyes only, watching him and yet unseeing.

He stretched his hand out. "Don't…"

She jumped.

He dropped his phone and sprinted. With arms straight out, he plunged into the water, pushing through the debris, diving deep for her.

She sank with her eyes closed. Her mouth opened in a soundless cry as water engulfed her lungs.

He grabbed her waist.

She didn't struggle and lay limp against his chest as he pulled up with strong strokes to the surface.

His lungs thirsted for air. Desperation got them up. After pushing her out of the pool, he lay her down and tilted her head back to open her airway. Placing one hand over the other between her breasts, he counted as he pumped — rotating between pressing her chest and blowing air into her mouth. "Breathe! Alice! Breathe!"

He refused to let fear take him. He took another deep breath, pinched her nose, and blew. Again and again, giving her as much of his air as he could. "Damn it! Open your eyes and breathe!"

He pumped her chest hard, pushing out the water in her lungs. He could be breaking her ribs, but he didn't stop. "Alice! Come on!" He begged. "Come back to me. Breathe!"

Her body flopped against his strength. He placed his head above her heart and listened.

Nothing. Not a murmur. She was just a thing, a doll with no soul.

"Bring her back! Merle! I know you can hear me! Alright, I forgive you! I forgive you for Miyako and Aunt Ellen! Save Alice! Save yourself!"

He pumped even more. His arms were getting tired, but he kept a steady count, switching back and forth between pumping and giving air. "Come on! Merle! You can fight this. Come on! Save yourself! Save her!"

He stuck his fingers into her mouth and pushed her tongue aside to widen her throat for him. Then, he sealed his mouth against her lips and blew hard. Just as he was about to pump her chest again, she jerked up.

Water spurted from her mouth. Her arms flopped, and her body spasmed.

Ji Woon dropped to the ground, panting as he watched her turn to the side and puke the rest of the dirty water out.

Coughing and wheezing, she let him help her up. Her hazel eyes rounded in shock. "Ji Woon. I know where they are."

He angrily dried her with her sweater, squeezing the water out and hurriedly putting on the rest of her dry clothes and coat.

"Fuck them." Winter was forty degrees Fahrenheit. Her skin was ice cold, and after he dressed her, hugged her tight, and rubbed her arms, he cursed in fury into her wet hair. "Try that again, Alice, and I will kill myself."

57

Rain pelted like rocks on their heads as they stumbled into the cornfields. The boy tore off his jacket and bundled the shivering girl. Not far from them, the building groaned and creaked, and through the fire, he saw the man get up as the wooden beams collapsed.

"Come!" He grabbed her tiny hand and pulled her with him as they ran through the prickly stalks. "Hurry! Run!" The corn scratched and pinched their bodies, but the two children pushed on. Buckets of water from the heavens blinded their sight, and the girl shook. Her tiny legs tripped, and he pulled her up, lifting her body onto his back.

The man was coming. The monster was going to eat them alive. Chew on their limbs and torture their bodies with terrible pain. Their breaths misted in cotton ball clouds as they forged into the night. And just when he thought they were reaching the end of the maze, his next step landed right into deep, rushing water. The girl screamed, gulping water and flaying.

On instinct, the boy flung the girl back onto solid ground with both hands. The currents was the strength of hundreds of horses.

Lightning lit the sky, and in that split second, he caught the fear in her eyes before the water took him away. Swept by strong currents, he went up and down with the river, choking.

The water switched to an endless flow of doctors and nurses rushing past, pushing, slamming him on both sides. Machines were screaming, and the smell of blood choked his breath. Cries. There were cries of a woman, followed by a child begging. He turned around, panic clogging in his chest as he watched her bloody, bloated stomach heave. Her teeth grit, her face determined, and yet pale as frosted glass. Sweat trailed down the sides of her face, and tears sprang from her eyes, telling her this was her last.

"No!" He shouted, sprinting past the myriad white coats and nurses holding syringes. "No!" He screamed. "Eomma!"

———————

"Ji Woon. Wake up. It's okay." Alice touched his arm and shook him gently. He clung to her like she was his life preserver, dropping his head on her shoulder, relishing in her scent and warmth.

"It's a nightmare. It isn't real." Her voice, though barely a whisper, was clear as a bell in the fog.

He nodded because he didn't want her to worry. This wasn't the first time he'd experienced these dreams. From the moment they met, Alice chased away his shadows.

She pulled out from his arms, and he watched her walk on the cold hardwood floor to a long table by a wall with a fridge, microwave, and a hot water pot with a stack of instant coffee in a basket. Her studio bedroom was on the highest floor of her townhouse and had a locked door and a pin code inside instead of out.

He read about Alice locking herself from Bailey's reports. Her life was a string of locked doors and barricades.

"Here." She handed over a piping mug of latte. It wasn't his taste, but he drank it anyway. They stared out her large windows into the morning darkness.

A misty glow wavered among the tops of trees and hills, and in between the slanting, stacked rows of houses, tendrils of fog reached for them with longing. The mountains of green forests, in the distance, stood steadfast despite the changing of time. A feeling of rooting grew from the base of his feet, stretching his ankles, calves, and limbs to his thighs and onwards.

"Do you want to talk about it?" she asked softly into her mug.

He turned to her. "Do you?"

She chuckled. "I asked first. Dr. Park Ji Woon, how does it feel to be the patient today? What were you dreaming?"

He took a good mouthful of his latte. The sweetness lingered in the gaping space of his heart. From the corner of his eye, he felt her smile again. Saving Alice yesterday almost tore him to shreds. He wasn't sure if he would take any more of the abuse. Still, knowing he saved her, the sun would shine again tomorrow.

"So?" She nudged his shoulder. He picked up a throw-over from her couch and wrapped it around her bare arms. Yesterday, after his daring rescue, they staggered back to her home, showered together, made love, showered again, and made love once more in her Californian bed before finally succumbing to sleep.

"It's an old dream," he said.

"Tell me." She yawned. He took the mugs and put them by the windowsill. Then, he pulled her back to her bed, climbed into the covers, and snuggled. The cool air drifted in from the cracks of the window and sent a chill down his back.

"I wish this would last forever," he whispered.

"Me too," she replied sweetly. This was the Alice only he knew — vulnerable, beautiful, and brave. His Alice smiled as he pulled her closer, feeling her sleepy breath against his chest. They deserved this — happiness and peace for both him and her.

"Tell me a little now and a little more next time, and then more another time," she said as her eyes slowly drooped while he stroked her hair.

"I always thought there was something wrong with me. I was never good enough until I met you. You saw me at my weakest and told me to be myself, and then you left," he said.

He peered at his lover and tucked her hair away from her face. He read that she hardly slept with anyone. This was progress. In his heart, he wished. This was their last stop. Forever and always.

"I gave the Chairman position to my step-mother. You called, and I gave up my plans, *Naekkoya*. And, I told Bailey I'm taking a year off." He shook her gently. "Alice? Whatever you're going through, I'll be here. I'll help you through it. I'll show you I can live that simple life, too. You can be a doctor, a surgeon, whatever you want, my dearest. I'll support you." He kissed her.

Waiting for her to call him those past weeks was torture. Although he kept busy with inheritance issues, reassigning the Chairman's rights, closing the Michael Harris case with the police and FBI, catching up with his therapy sessions, and referring his clients to his juniors, he still found a lot of time to think of her. Bailey was disappointed that Ji Woon was leaving Salinger, but being a romantic himself, he cheered him on. Everyone was expecting *janchi guksu* noodles.

She opened her eyes suddenly. "I know." She raised her hand and touched his cheek. "You're right, I didn't want to die. But, can you love me too?"

Heat crept up his neck at the intensity of her sultry gaze.

"Merle." He tried to pull away, but Merle latched on, wrapping her arms around his waist and climbing on him, her thighs clamping his hips. Her long black hair cascaded down her bare shoulders and breasts. Her hot body, smooth and warm against his naked torso.

"She's watching, Ji Woon. You have to take me too." His body hardened. The memory of almost losing Alice made him curse. He pushed Merle into the bed, and his lips attacked Alice's heart scar and then her breasts. He plunged into her with desperation until her moans and his grunts echoed loudly in her fortified room.

An hour later. Alice walked out of the shower smiling, drying her hair with a towel. "Ji Woon."

"Yes?" He lay spread out, letting the cold air from the morning fog outside drift in and dry his hot, sweaty back.

Earlier, when Merle spotted his birthmark on his tailbone, she showed him a sex video online that Nick had taken years ago. It was the day he was drugged and left behind in an alley of a club. He remembered feeling violated and angry and tried hunting down his attackers with no success.

"It was you!" Merle chuckled. "You were her fucking one-nighter!"

He stared at the video. Once again, Fate had the last laugh.

He snaked his arm around Alice's waist and pulled her to him. She brushed his wet cheeks with her cool fingers and kissed him lovingly.

"Guess what?" Alice smiled.

"What?" he replied.

"The graves. I remember where they are." She breathed out heavily. "Will you come with me?"

He laced his fingers with hers. "Yes."

Alice

58

KANSAS

Our car stopped by the roadside of a forested area.

"We're here," Ji Woon said. Behind us were four more vehicles — FBI, local Kansas police, a forensics van, and an ambulance.

All around us were forests surrounding our one-lane road. Above the sky was a bright blue, cloudless, and endless.

"We'll have to hike in," I said. My heart was pounding as I pictured where we were going. Memories of the graves and the hoodie person were coming back.

Ji Woon grabbed his backpack from the back passenger seat and opened my door. We were dressed in hiking gear and thick winter jackets, though Spring was already here.

He went ahead, hacking the undergrowth with a small ax while I stopped where the tall pine trees loomed over my head, feet frozen stiff. Suddenly, something snapped, and I backed away fast, dashing, stumbling, and crashing into Agent Christy, Agent Odeh, and the law enforcers behind.

"Whoa." Agent Christy made a grab, but I slipped by her. Ji Woon caught up with me after a while.

"We can go slow. Take your time," he said. I sobbed on Ji Woon's chest. "No one's going to hurt you. Eli is dead." He brushed my hair, then tucked it under my beanie. "And you have me."

A cool breeze caressed my cheek and dried my tears. Slowly, I breathed and imagined taking those nightmares and tossing them.

Ji Woon squeezed my hand. "We're here to end this. You'll always be the bravest girl I know."

"Okay." He was right. I was ready for my new life.

Minutes later, "Turn left." I pointed. Flanked by Ji Woon and Agent Odeh by my sides, I couldn't flee even if I wanted to.

With Ji Woon's hand in mine and his body heat, muscles flexing, my legs moved on.

The cold airlifted almost like magic, and then cornfields suddenly surrounded us. Giant stalks reaching ten feet high and yellow husks drooping down. A dreaded unease crept over my skin — stinging prickles adding to the unreasonable panic.

Ji Woon stiffened by my side. Ahead, we saw a trickling stream cutting through our path.

Then, I saw it.

Flashes of lightning. A torrential downpour soaked my dress — a loud splash followed by my screams. A dark head who wasn't Peter, bobbing in the rushing waters.

I blinked, and that memory vanished. I turned to Ji Woon, who looked ghostly pale. "You okay?" It was my turn to ask, and he only nodded.

Orange rays of the morning sun cut through the woods and lit on pale white stones between tree trunks. We moved through the silent, dreamlike forest as one, stepping between the fir trees, and then stopped as our breath caught in our throats.

Headstones were placed, three by four, in the grove of the heavy snow-laden trees. Behind each headstone was a large mound of dirt. Twelve neatly packed earth, cleared of undergrowth as if someone had been watching over them. Surrounding each standing pile were snow-drop flowers planted about an inch apart. The dainty white flowers with their bell-shaped petals were my favorite. Growing up, I planted many around our farmhouse and had them in vases in my room.

Only my father knew what they meant to me — my constant hope and the symbol of overcoming the challenges in my life. A reminder that, although delicate like the flower, I was meant for great things if I set my mind to it.

Like the breath of a ghost, my heart squeezed. A date was engraved into each headstone in black, but the first one shook me to the core.

June 14, 1990

My birthday.

I ran my fingers over the black engravings on the cold lime-stone. The forensic team dug the mound and pulled out a faded white-flowered plastic box about the length of two shoe boxes. Under the first box was another plastic case with about a hundred gold bars. The agents and police were excited to see the gold. As for me, I was fixated on the floral box.

Ji Woon tucked my hair behind my ear and pulled me close. "Are you ready?" he asked.

My breathing grew shallow as I watched one of them pry the box open. In it was a baby skeleton wrapped in a hospital infant cloth. In her hands was a pink rattle with yellow flowers and a card written in my father's hand.

Alice
What matters is not your name.
All that matters is who you could have been.

I covered my mouth as my shoulders shook from crying. Ji Woon blocked my face with his chest.

Her bones. Her life was cut short before it began. Right from the moment I opened my infant's eyes, I missed her. I shared her name — my twin, my second heartbeat. I remembered the warmth of her tiny hand in mine till we were wrenched apart.

I was too young to comprehend the grief, lost in a world where I couldn't speak. I searched for her, pining and confused, not understanding how she could not be with me when she was with me for nine months. The anger and rejection I felt from my mother, who didn't see me, made me resent my sister. My mother always knew I wasn't my twin.

She was right. It wasn't her delusions that pushed her over. It was my father and I pacifying her loss by pretending everything was fine, which she hated most.

"Who's this?" Christy asked.

Ji Woon's hand ran over my back as I steeled my shoulders. "That's the real Alice," I replied.

Their mouths gaped in unfiltered shock. "If that's Alice, then who are you?" The agent asked.

I kept my eyes steady on the date carved in stone and studied the photograph of my mother carrying my sister's limped fetus in her arms. Mother's face was gaunt and distant. Her soul wrenched from her body, leaving a puppet in its place. Two years of postpartum depression kept my mother away. *Sobo*, my grandmother, brought me up with powdered milk and love.

We picked up the photographs of a small toddler peeking out curiously from behind Grandma, wondering who that woman was. My mother, Junko, reached out and gently touched my cheek. My father and grandma breathed a sigh of relief. Those same gentle fingers suddenly turned into claws, pinching my jaw.

"You're not Alice!" My mother swatted me aside. "Where's my baby? You took her! I hate you! Hate you! Bring her back!"

Ji Woon and the police were waiting. To heal my past, I first had to cauterize the wound. "I was born four seconds later." I swallowed hard.

"I'm Merle. Alice died at birth, and when I was three, my mother tried to kill herself. I became Alice. I…" Ji Woon squeezed my shoulder, and I stopped.

He was right. They didn't have to know more. I turned away as a wave of exhaustion hit. Ji Woon's fingers threaded with mine, and he hugged me tight, warm, breathing, and alive.

Agent Christy cleared her throat and pointed. "What about the rest of those dates on those tombstones? Do they mean anything?"

The second tombstone was Merle's. There were no bones in this box. It was the day my name, Merle, ceased to exist, and I became the new Alice.

In the box were kids' drawings of our family — my parents, myself, and Alice. I picked up an old stuffed squirrel that I, Merle, used to call Peanut, and another baby rattle with snowdrop flowers painted on it.

The next tombstone was dated:

December 4, 1996

"What about Nineteen-ninety-six?" Agent Christy glanced at us.

Ji Woon's hands pinched hard. I felt his racing heart against my back. "What's wrong?" I turned to him.

Sweat rolled down his temples. His breath caught as he pointed to that date. "I know that date," he murmured.

"You do?" Agent Odeh studied the headstone.

"That's when I got lost..."

"A big one!" One man shouted, digging the third hole. They were pulling out another plastic box and another packed with gold. The agents swarmed over to them gleefully. They were heavier and larger boxes, containing at least three hundred gold pieces, than the previous ones. Their grinning faces were like pirates with treasure.

"Nineteen-ninety-six. That was the day I was kidnapped," I said. The heart wound on my right burned. That was also the day my personality, Merle, appeared.

I froze when the forensics guy cracked open the box and pulled out a youth-sized dark green hoodie. At the tip of the hoodie was the symbol of a golden dagger with three lightning bolts.

I saw it again.

Lightning struck across the sky. Three times in golden light. A man in a dark hoodie, the hero who saved me. A slight figure with pale hands.

I shuddered.

"That's US Army special forces," Ji Woon ran his fingers over the embroidery. "Every year for Christmas, my Uncle sends me a larger size."

Next, the forensics guy picked up a faded blue girl's dress, cut from collar to edge. Splattered with white, yellowed flowers, stiff with decades-old brown bloodstains.

The world tilted, and a hollow sound rang in my ears. Over and over again, it echoed, booming as it emitted an endless cry. My lungs squeezed for air. I bent over and screamed, holding my hands to my ears as an imaginary fire consumed my body.

Red. Fire. Blood. Eyes. Him.

Terror. Pain. Hate. Guilt.

His cruel laughter. Stabbing my soul, draining out every drop of hope.

The smoke was thick, and ash layered my tongue.

I choked.

My breath was fire, and my rage burned deep.

The dragon rose. Tearing up through rotten wood and abandoned things.

My Merle was scared. She was crying alone. She didn't want to die.

I lunged in the air with my saber. Striking as lightning flashed behind my back.

Somewhere else, Ji Woon was calling my name. Somewhere safe where I had no right to belong. A cold thing dropped over my face. Something soft, something black. A piece of cloth. The smell of Ji Woon.

I caught a glimpse of his worried eyes and his loving face. Ji Woon hovered. Between dreams and reality, I reached for him. The image of him was flittering in and out as I chased like flickering fireflies zipping by.

Smoke. Fog. I was sinking fast and deep. They were catching up — the others who wanted me.

„Ji Woon…"

A man in a red checkered shirt covered in blood.

Skeleton fingers, glinting silver needles, clawing and gasping.

Two small heroes were fighting back -- one with mighty hands and a dark cloak, and the other with flowing hair, wielding a long, brave sword.

Apart from that, they were weak. United, they were strong.

I ran and ran through the forest of claws and sharp fangs. When I got to the road, I heaved and heaved, bending to the side, and puked.

59

Ji Woon was talking to the FBI and police. When he saw that I was awake, he returned to the car.

"Feeling better?" He popped his head in from the driver's side. "Here." He opened a bottle of water and offered it.

I took a good drink and felt the tension ease from my shoulders. He gave me a tissue, and I dabbed my crusted eyes. "How long was I asleep?"

"About two hours? The paramedics came by and checked you. They said you are fine." He rubbed his fingers on my chin, and I stared blankly down. Tears welled in my eyes.

Worry stretched across his brows as he stared at my shaking head. "Are you right? Alice?" His voice was soft.

I nodded my head. "It's just her," My lips trembled. "M..."

"It's okay." He pulled me into his arms and kissed my head. "You saved her. You did what you got to do."

I pressed my cold palms on my eyes. A migraine crept from behind my head and latched on from the back to both sides of my temple.

"Headache?" He stroked my hair gently.

"Yes." I heaved out loudly. "Can we go home?"

"Okay, take this first." He pulled out a tube of ibuprofen from the dashboard compartment and handed me the water again. "I'll tell Odeh." He rushed over to the officers and then sprinted back to our car. "They'll bring the evidence back to the Kansas FBI."

"What else did they find?" I asked.

He snapped on his seat belt. "More gold, a dagger, a bunch of sparklers, a vial of Solacoynin, and more bodies. One of the graves had two bodies, buried twice." He turned away.

"It's them," I sighed.

"Who?"

"Cyrus and Nadia."

"You think those are them?" he asked.

"Yes." Eli was right. Michael Harris's secret project worked. Transferring the cognitive brain to another body.

Frankenstein's best work. Impossible, improbable, and yet possible. No wonder my father was unrepentant in showing it off. Even now, some parts of his report seem more fiction than science. Stories were meant for movies, not real life.

These bodies would be tested with DNA and matched to the details of each child he worked on. If I weren't blinded by my revenge, I wouldn't have posted their private information online. The missing pieces were the parts he worked on for me. Things I didn't want to think about now.

Father was a doctor, but he wasn't one to save lives. He believed he could save humanity. Change them. A god amongst men. A man who'd go down in history.

"And the rest are probably the other sick kids or...his failed experiments," he said.

"Maybe," he replied.

I could see that Ji Woon was trying not to smile.

I sat up. "What?"

He grinned. His happiness was rubbing off.

"What is it?" I pulled his hand.

He breathed out loudly. "It's Noah! He's alive!" He slapped his hand on the steering wheel. He was laughing with eyes beaming like stars. "Noah's alive!"

"Really?" I sat up. "How?"

"Yes! There was an address on one of the photographs — a children's hospital in Kansas. The FBI called in. Noah was adopted at eight months old. He lives with his family in New York. His adoptive parents agreed to a DNA test."

"How old is he?" I asked.

"Four." He smiled. "His name is Elliot Wang."

I hugged him. Finally, a silver light. From now onwards, the tunnel wasn't all grey.

Ji Woon nodded with his eyes shining. "When I saw the graves, I expected the worst. Sergeant James, my *Samchon*, when he told me I would be Noah's *Hyung*, it was one of my best days." He glanced at me and smiled. "I planned to see Noah during school breaks, play catch ball, teach him Korean, and buy him Christmas gifts." He gripped my shoulder. "Alice, I wanted to show him I could be the best brother, cousin, man he can count on."

"Well, you can now," I smiled back. My heart warmed. Redemption. "You'll be the best."

It had been four years since Ellen died. Time flew with supersonic wings. I wondered how it would look back twenty, thirty years from now. When our sparks fluttered, what would we remember? What would I be? Would I still be extraordinary? And what happened to old Ji Woon when I still lived?

I stared at Ji Woon's happy face. I listened to him talk about his plans with Elliot. His happiness seeped into mine.

A small black cloud detached and lifted from the abyss. Up, up it went, turning from shades of grey and finally into a puff of white, filling my heart with joy.

It was hard to comprehend Michael Harris's mind. Those bodies were buried one by one by the person with the black hoodie. I saw them in my new memories of being in the lab, the secret surgical room, and watching my father work.

"Eli fooled the FBI. He was one of their secret informants, and he changed records, switched evidence, bribed witnesses and families, and gave the agents the wrong leads. The FBI is reinvestigating what they got."

"Why did they trust him?" I asked.

"He was closest to Michael."

"I don't believe he killed Nick." Merle blurted and sobbed.

"I'm sorry," Ji Woon glanced at me and Merle and patted our shoulder.

"Michael wasn't lying about the cadavers. The Kansas FBI found the records with Eli's signature. Those child patients who died were the ones on whom Michael performed his brain augmentation surgery. He had the families' signed consent on the risks, and those families are tight-lipped and lawyered up about their adopted children after the deaths of their own."

"So what happened to Noah?"

"The Kansas City hospital was too quick to pronounce Noah brain-dead. The director of the children's hospital said Michael brought in a baby in a coma, hooked to a machine, the day Aunt Ellen died."

He looked through the sunroof of his car and breathed out.

"They said Michael operated on Noah and revived him. They had to incubate Noah. Eight months later, Noah recovered. By then, my Uncle died from that bombing in Afghanistan, and his parents were in a car crash after."

He sucked in hard. "Years later, when I exhumed the bodies of my aunt and baby. When I found the baby had been switched, I dreamt of millions of ways to get back at Michael. For ten years, Odeh and I planned our attack."

I struggled to speak. "You must have hated me a lot."

"Not you. It took me a month to get over that you are his daughter, but when I saw you again, I knew I couldn't tear you down, too." He touched my face tenderly as if I would break. "I'm sorry I used you."

"I lied to you, too," I said. "But what about Merle?"

He closed his eyes and let out a big breath. "She saved you."

"Ji Woon. You don't have to force yourself," I said.

"Alice, *Naekkoya*. Haven't I shown you enough?"

Our car suddenly screeched and slid across the narrow one-car lane.

Ji Woon cursed as the tires lifted and landed on the icy road. Fields of endless white as far as the sky met the land. Spring might be coming in some parts, but this place was still locked in the past.

My childhood days were buried in the memory of empty spaces. My mother kept herself busy in her space, and my father was with his hospital team, celebrating the season with festive cheer.

I was forgotten. Mother and I were the things Michael Harris kept because he owned us and took us out to shine when he wanted.

The map flickered on my screen, and there was a buzz and a flash, and my phone turned black. "Do you have a charger? My phone died." I searched the glove compartment and the sides.

Ji Woon shrugged. "You can use mine," He patted his pocket. "Ah! It's in the trunk."

The air in the car was instantly stifling. "I need air." I pressed down my window further, letting the wintry chill from outside come in.

Ji Woon did not protest. His mind seemed lost, locked into the vortex at the end of the never-ending road. Being used to the California sunshine, basking in golden rays ninety percent of the year, I forgot life took a break here.

"I think this is the way back," I said. Around us, the pallid afternoon sky grew suddenly dark. Clouds gathered as lightning flashed in the distance.

He turned to me slowly, worry cramping his brows. "This place looks familiar." His voice dropped.

My heart raced as our car crept closer. We were pulled forward. Marionettes to the puppet master's string.

"Slow down." I raised my hand forward, "Here," I said, pulling out a copy of a yellowed, dusty police folder.

The police reports were among my father's possessions in his apartment, which he leased in San Francisco across from the hospital where my mother died. From the whispers of the nurses and doctors, I learned Michael Harris visited often. They kept it a secret from me because they knew we were estranged. Michael Harris came by a year before she passed, and I did not know.

Dr. Bailey hid those painful memories of that day I was taken when I was fifteen, and I was thankful. I didn't regret asking him to rewrite that day. If he had not, I couldn't imagine how I would have survived till now. However, after drowning in Seoul, I caught glimpses of Merle's memories of what she saw that day. Adding to the details of what I read in the police reports, those were enough to lock every muscle of my body into blocks of ice.

I wanted to believe I was stronger after those years of therapy and witnessing countless vestiges of horror and death. I was neither that little girl nor a coward anymore.

Fate was cruel, and my life was a path of shattered glass. Still, I walked through it, bloody steps at a time, jaws gritting in anger, determined. I was invincible because I had come so far with Ji Woon by my side. The dark no longer scared me. I was ready to move on.

"Stop here," I tapped the headboard.

Ji Woon stepped on the brake, and the car pulled to a halt.

I did my square breathing for a minute, and he waited calmly. Seeing would change things. The reins were tattering. Freedom was close.

"It's around here," I exhaled and gestured.

"We don't have to go," Ji Woon said.

"This was where the bastard took me."

60

The barn was no more. On this side of reality, twenty-four years turned the burnt rubble into a pile of sticks and black dirt. Surrounding the area was a sheet of ice and frozen undergrowth covered in winter white, except for that rectangular spot where the red barn used to be.

It was meant to stay dead. Dead like the man who snatched me from the playground was struck down by the heavens for the terrible crimes he committed. His soul was forever lost in this barren, cold wasteland as a reminder to others who didn't fear the wrath of the gods.

The old police report sketched a rough location of where it was. There were inroads and farms along the way, yet Ji Woon seemed to know where to turn.

We arrived at the spot. The fence that once gated the barn from the one-lane highway was rusty and broken on both sides—abandoned to nature, as was everything that was once a thriving farm a very long time ago. The cornfields that hid the boy and me were gone, and the irrigation canals around the land were dried up. Further up in the clump of forests ahead, across the stream that fed the canals, were the graves, almost as a reminder that death was not far behind.

We strayed everywhere first before coming back to where the barn was. It was easier to avoid the painful truth than to take another step forward. I wasn't the only one hesitating. Ji Woon was behaving strangely. His stance was stiff, and his eyes were shifty as he looked around.

"What's wrong?" I asked.

"Is this the spot where the barn was?" he pointed to the black dirt. He knew what had happened because we read the reports together.

I nodded, stood where the two large doors would have been, and closed my eyes. Like magic, charred beams and rusted metal roof pieces rose together with the barn's side panels. Red paint enveloped the entire barn, as I had seen it when I was six. The wintry sky of white and frost covering grass and weeds turned wet and dark. A storm gathered rapidly and blanketed the sky. Flashes of lightning sizzled, striking from the heavens, fifty times louder than an electrical line.

I screamed and crouched, covering my head with my trembling hands. "Get down! Ji Woon! Hurry!"

Ji Woon ducked with me, using his body as a shield. His hand was warm on my right shoulder, where the heart-shaped scar was burning and pulsating, sending waves of panic throughout my body.

It was *Deja vu*. A memory I didn't recall till now — the spark from one of the lightning strikes on the barn roof sizzled onto my shoulder, running a current down my torso to the ground. He was there too — the boy who threw himself over me when another spark struck his back.

"What's this?" Ji Woon's voice trembled as he lifted his head in horror at the light show above us.

I was projecting again, hypnotizing us. I was making Ji Woon see what I saw.

His arms tightly wound mine. Squeezing my shoulders each time the lightning struck. "Alice, what the hell is happening?"

"You see this too?" I pointed at the sizzling silver passing through the beams like wriggling laser worms. I chuckled hysterically. "Do you see them?"

Thunder boomed, and the ground reverberated into our bones. Then, there was the hammering of rain. The lightning struck through the metal gaps in the roof. Fire burst from shaky tinder wood beams and blossomed from the haystacks.

"Alice! Run!" Ji Woon grabbed my hand and dragged me to the swinging barn doors. Sheets of rain came sloshing in, pounding on our bodies as we fought to get out. On the back walls, flames hungrily gnawed on the rotten wood panels.

A girl screamed. We snapped around and saw a little girl in a blue-flowered dress struggling with a gangly man.

A boy in a green hoodie dashed past us, leaping onto the tall man's back and grabbing his red hair as he rode him. The man buckled, and the boy held on like a cowboy on his bull. The girl snatched a rebar from the ground, then, gripping the spear, she charged forward. The rod slipped through the man like meat on a stick. Blood streamed down the rebar and pooled onto the ground. Fire exploded in popping heat, and the beams fell. Both kids stumbled out of the open doors as the rest of the barn crashed and burned.

The barn vanished. Once again, we stood on the barren land covered in ice and snow. The wind whipped at our hair and nipped our ears. Our eyes adjusted, and in the whiteness of space, we saw her squatting in the dirt patch, crying. A collar and silver chain tied to her neck jingled as she moved.

I pulled Ji Woon along, side-stepping on large, jagged pieces of ice to get to her.

The girl in her tattered blue dress lifted her head. Her face was bruised, her lips chipped, and her body covered with scratches and dried blood. She didn't move when we got closer, staring curiously at us, not speaking.

"He's dead," I told her and pointed at her chain and the rebar. "We can help."

Her eyes lit with sudden fear. She shifted back and stopped when I showed her my palms facing up and then pointed at Ji Woon.

"He won't hurt you," I said.

Ji Woon found a broken piece of metal under some hay and returned it to us. "He's a friend." I gestured him closer. "We just want to get it off. Do you understand? Nod if you want it off, shake your head if you don't."

The girl nodded her head. She watched Ji Woon warily as he approached her slowly and flinched when he caught the chain.

He stuck the piece of metal between a chain link and pried it open. The chain fell with a loud clang. Relief passed through our faces.

"Can I hold you?" I asked.

She nodded again and froze when I picked her up.

"No one is going to hurt you again." I nuzzled her hair.

Finally, she smiled. And then, she raised her thin arms out for Ji Woon.

I handed her over, watching his tears running down his cheeks as mine did. Tiny, cold hands, barely the size of my palm, rubbed our wet faces. We leaned in, and together, our foreheads touched as frost fled from our breaths.

"You can leave now," I said.

She slid to the ground and ran to the open doors where the boy in a green hoodie was waiting by the light. His hoodie slid off, revealing dark brown hair and a smiling, young Ji Woon's face. They turned to us briefly, then stepped out and disappeared together.

"Why didn't I remember you?" Ji Woon cupped my face and kissed me.

"You hurt your head." I kissed him back. Snowflakes drifted down and brushed our eyelids. I blinked, and the remnants of that night faded away.

"Sergeant James found me in a canal stuck on a floating tree. When I woke up two days later, my father was there. No one told me about the kidnapping."

"I kept insisting a boy saved me. The police asked for a face and a name. I must have panicked and told them of another boy I met. They searched for two weeks. They never found you because you weren't blonde or blue-eyed. Bailey took my nightmares away. Twisted my memories so I could forget."

He pulled me tighter.

"I'm sorry, Ji Woon. I didn't mean to forget you." I scrunched my nose to hold back my tears.

"It's okay. I forgot you, too." He stroked my head. "So, Peter wasn't real."

"He was real to me," I said.

Ji Woon plucked my tears. "Peter. I wish I had met him once. He saved our lives," said Ji Woon.

We held our breaths. The last missing piece finally clicked.

Wax melting and reforming, no filters, no more lies. Every memory, every moment, every action taken by each one of my personalities — cruel, selfish acts — this was all of them. And now, they were gone — dead by my hand or their death as a sacrifice so I could live.

Merle was right. I was a hypocrite, a thief, and undeserving. I wanted the good things and fled from the bad. But each and every one of my personalities was me, and I was them. I fought to be the primary, and so I was to blame.

Something green caught my eye. At my feet, a bud of a snowdrop flower pushed through black dirt. My heart rekindled. From the ashes, I clung to that hope. Maybe there was another way, a different path to where I wanted to go.

Park Ji Woon wound his arm around my waist and pulled me close. His love was as bright as the sun above us. Despite my constant rejections and his devious plots, he kept this promise. He came back.

My past could hinder our future. Evidence might crop up later, which we might have to hide. Sometimes, our relationship would be tested — whether by his family, my dreams to become an ER doctor, or my plans to live in the US and not in Seoul. Ambitious, stubborn, prideful, and wanting control, those characters made us who we were. We were similar — birds of a feather, two broken souls, and many secrets.

Yes, secrets could haunt us. I had many, and so did he. Was there forgiveness? "Ji Woon," I started to speak.

He watched me with open, unwavering eyes. My heart grew at the sight of his unrelenting love.

"You said you wanted to start over. I'm afraid I can't. This baggage," I gestured to myself. "I can't make you take this. What they did, I'm messed up."

He ran his fingers through my tangled hair.

"I thought I could escape this, that I'd be okay. I remember what they did, like it was I who did them," my voice came as a sob.

Ji Woon placed his finger on my lips. "You are not them. You are Alice. My Alice, *Naekkeoya,* and I've done many things I'm not proud of. You might not forgive me if you knew. I'll spend the rest of my life making up. But we will be a family and never let our children feel alone. We'll give them the best and love them."

He kissed my eyes and then my lips. His breath lingered over mine. Heart to heart, body to body, and his soul with mine.

Ji Woon was right. The present and our future were what mattered. I could make myself forget, and so could he. Dissociation was what I did best. If there was anyone who had gone through enough pain, it was I.

Happiness. I deserved happiness, and so did he. He didn't need to know. The past was over.

It wasn't just one person. There were others.

I killed Sophie Han because she hurt me. And it felt good.

— || The End || —

ACKNOWLEDGEMENTS

This book has been a long time coming, half a decade if you think of all the revisions and giving up that went with the pain of sweat and tears. Squeezing blood from a stone is an apt Asian saying. Method writing is real, and in the case of this book, I'd gone through enough personas with my family and friends in this arduous, thought-provoking, soul-searching process.

Firstly, I want to share my love with my family, especially with my husband, whom I say has the "eye" – foresight for all things good and beautiful, including myself :). His belief that I should chase my dreams and no-nonsense constantly challenges me. I give hugs and kisses to my kiddos, who want to cook and never complain about helping around the house. And to Ma and everyone else in my family, your support also means a lot to me.

I am severely grateful to those who kept believing in me and the beta readers who had to go through my many revisions after my husband, who was the toughest of all critics, suggested I cut my book into two. It was for the better, and I hope that time will tell how your comments have set into my story. If it wasn't obvious how much I appreciate your support on my never-ending quest to put a mark on this earth, I did and still do.

So, let's give a round of applause to Joe, Nicolas, Debbie, Kelly, and Carolyn for their years of faith. And with my baby steps, falling and tripping, thank you to the ARC team of friends and fans who stepped up in the weeks just before my book launches to read and review my book — Michelle, Janice, Mindy, Joel, Jason, and Shuang — owing you guys and gals coffee and more. The initial dev editors and plot helpers, Ann, Annie, Anita, and others, thank you!

Shout out to the guys from South Korea, 감사합니다 Gamsahabnida – Choi Sung Kyoung, for the Super AWESOME book cover and Han Se Hwan for translations.

And last but not least, the behind-the-scenes guy who came only months ago and made my publishing company and book possible with his constant right-hand support, positivity, and detail. Jim Fung, Thank You for your assistance with marketing, research, and editing. The experiences we both gained through this process will help us grow and reach for the stars. Because, unlike Icarus, who dreamt of the sun, we see the Universe beyond.